VIMY RIDGE

ALPHABET COMPANY
BOOK 1

VIMY RIDGE ALPHABET COMPANY BOOK 1

First Edition published 2021

VIMY RIDGE

ALPHABET COMPANY
BOOK 1

BY
WHISKEY-JACK PETERS

CONTENTS

"Really enjoyed this story. Tells an important tale."

Sgt. M. Richards (Ret'd)

1 Commando, Australian Defence Force

ACKNOWLEDGEMENTS

I would like to thank Darío for his layout and design, Giusy for assisting me with Book cover details, Joshua for his proofreading skills, and Katie for helping me with the technical steps needed to get this book completed. Without you this story wouldn't have been possible to create in the format that you see now.

The researchers for this first story were myself, Sue Baker Wilson in New Zealand and also Sgt. R.D. Mandryk (Ret'd) Canadian Forces. I appreciated your help very much. Thank you.

Honourable mentions go out to Cpl. Mike Moran (Ret'd) Engineers - ADF, and Richard at the Warriors Path Academy in Queensland, Australia. [www.thewarriorspathacademy.com] Thank you for being my friends and inspiring me to continue on with my many writing projects. Without your energy to inspire me, I would have fallen on several occasions and not been motivated enough to continue. As others will confirm, writing is a very isolating hobby and that can play on your spirit; so my thanks to you for sticking with me on this journey. I'm very grateful.

CHAPTER ONE

There are some moments in a man's life that he will remember forever, that remain untouched in his memory, even after everything else has slowly faded away. Rarely, if ever, does the man know how precious the moment he is living through is. Johnny Hoagland certainly had no idea as he was finishing his meal, lying back against the barn's wall.

"Did you like it?" Christina asked him. An impish smile appeared on Johnny's face.

"Very much so. The foods good, too," he replied. It took Christina a moment, but when she realized he was speaking about the other thing they had just finished, she blushed and rearranged her clothes. But then, she realized she didn't care to project an image that wasn't true, since they were alone.

"Of course you did," she raised her head defiantly. "It must be the best you've had. You wouldn't risk my father's wrath if it weren't."

Johnny hugged her fiercely. "You know it is." He held her for a moment more before lying against the wall again. They looked out the small barn's open windows, taking in the thick trees in the distance, the overcast sky, the sound of the animals. The farm that belonged to Christina's family was in a remote area, away from the town, and Johnny could hear the animals clearly. He could see the colorful birds on the trees and knew that if he walked a few meters deeper into the forest, he'd see the wombats or even a few wallabies.

But he didn't have much more time to spare. He took a deep breath and stood quickly, then patted the dust off.

"We need to gather the sheep back in the main barn, right?" he asked. Christina nodded and stood as well. "I'll get started on that, and you get the tools from the shed. Your father wants me to help with the new chicken coop," he said. She hurried off, and he took a long stick to better manage the animals, and left the empty barn they usually enjoyed each other's company in.

With stick in hand, he started calling to the sheep and forcing them around the large fence. The sheep needed their time outside the barn, but the outer fence that surrounded Mr. Digby's farm was too large to manage the animals easily, and that's why Mr. Digby wanted to build a smaller one. Johnny saw Christina leave the tools by the still-unbuilt new coop and take a stick of her own, and then approach him. As they ran around under the sun, even though the air was getting colder by the day, they worked up quite the sweat.

"Do you think the new fence my father asked you to prepare will be ready soon?" Christina asked, thick beads of sweat dripping from her forehead. "I'd love to not have to run around so much, ya know? More time for... us," she added, and even through her breathlessness and shouting at the sheep, she managed to wink at him.

"I could have the holes done by tomorrow," Johnny said. "I've done up to there," he pointed at a spot in the distance, "and Mr. Digby said he wanted it up to there," he pointed farther away. "But I can take my time and finish it next weekend. I'll be down at the mines for the rest of the week, so I thought it'd be an easy excuse to come by again next week, ya know?"

Christina nodded enthusiastically. There was a very interesting glint in her eye and Johnny was about to comment on it, when he hit a sheep too hard, distracted as he was, and the sheep decided to hit back. It raised its back feet in a lightning-quick motion and made contact with Johnny's midsection. He was on his back before he had realized what was going on.

Christina's thunderous laughter filled the valley. She was laughing too hard, holding onto her belly, and the sound scared the sheep into the barn quicker than their sticks and shouts had. It took her a good minute to finally calm down and approach Johnny to help him up.

"Are you alright?" she asked, drying her eyes from her tears. Johnny took her extended hand and stood, groaning.

"Good enough," he grumbled, more hurt by her laughter than the sheep's feet. "If you're done having fun at my expense, let's go get started on the coop."

The work was hard, but Johnny worked harder. Working in the mine was both harder and more dangerous work, so doing things around Mr. Digby's farm was light enough to be considered 'fun'. Besides, he got to spend time with Christina.

Johnny had to form the structure's frames. Mr. Digby would buy the chicken wire next time he was at the town, so the structure and the holes should be ready before then. The roofing and the paneling would probably be done over the next weekend, by Johnny himself. Plotting out frames and hammering nails required some concentration, so he worked silently, with Christina helping by holding the beams steady or giving him nails.

After a long hour, they were done, and Johnny decided they deserved another short break. They returned to the smaller barn, now rarely used by the animals and mostly by themselves, and laid back down against the wooden walls. There was some food left in the basket, and Johnny started munching on it.

"When d'you think this whole thing will blow over?" Christina muttered.

"What, the Great War?" Johnny asked. She nodded. "Dunno." He paused. "I was thinking of joining, ya know."

Christina turned fully towards him and raised her arms like a boxer. "I'll kill you myself if you want to die so badly," she told him, her brow furrowed and her voice serious. Johnny laughed it off, but Christina kept the same look. "Me and my mum are cooking you good meals," she said, "and I think you're enjoying our little..." she let her voice trail off, a sly smile breaking her frown. But then she got serious again. "So, don't go thinking these things, alright?"

Johnny smiled and stood, stretching. "I wish we could spend more time together, ya know. We only seem to find the time when I'm here, helping your father do the chores he doesn't like doing."

"He also gives you chores when he wants to go fishing," Christina added, smiling up to him. Then she shook her head. "I think the only reason he hasn't gone to the War is he's too old and they won't take him. You boys and your wars." She sighed, but then made the conscious effort to push the dark thoughts of the German's 'Great War' from her head—she truly hoped it was *the war to end all wars*, as they said. She looked at the empty basket, and then back up to Johnny.

"You're finished with that, right?" Johnny nodded. Christina then pushed it away with her foot and laid back. "Ready for another go, then?" she said, and winked, pulling up her dress. She didn't need to say anything else before Johnny was on her.

"Let's hurry back now, my mother will come out looking for me if we take too much time," Christina said, after tidying up. Johnny was up and had the basket already packed before she had finished. "Now, that's a gentleman," she said, smiling. They closed a few of the barn's windows before they left, and Johnny picked up and stored the tools. They left, walking by the side of the barn.

They walked in silence for a moment, before Johnny spoke again. "You know, working the mines during winter isn't that much safer than going to war," he said. Christina looked ready to say something, but he continued quickly.

"I'm not saying I'll go join, ya know? But when it's cold—and you know how cold Bendigo gets during winter—the dynamite freezes up. The newspapers wrote about that guy yesterday, a gold miner, what's his name—Henry Tucker, that's it. He had a gold mining claim a few miles from Bendigo. He was using a modified kettle to thaw his dynamite, right? Well, either the dynamite was unstable, or the kettle's hot metal touched something leaking from the sticks, no one can know now, but the thing is he got himself killed trying to thaw it. Bad luck for him. They found him the next day, in pieces. And it's still May. Imagine how July's going to be."

Christina was silent for a few steps as she thought it over. "Ya know, mining's dangerous alright. But if you're not stupid, it's not as dangerous as being a soldier, is it?" she looked at Johnny who remained silent. "Guessed so," she said, satisfied with her argument. "No more of that war talk for now, alright? Let's see if mum wants help with the dinner. You must be hungry after all that..." she let her voice trail suggestively, "*work* you did back there."

Two boys rushed from the house, Christina's twin brothers, coming up to the couple. "Johnny, are you staying for dinner?" the older one said. Johnny smiled down, but Christina spoke before he could.

"Sure he will, Stephen. He's done all that work back by the barn, he deserves a nice, hot dinner."

"He better make sure he cleans up before he comes in my kitchen," an angry voice came from deeper in the house. The two boys ran back in, laughing all the way. "Stephen, get the plates from the cupboard," the voice continued, which Johnny knew belonged to Mrs. Digby, their mother. "Philip," she called to the other boy, "stop salivating in front of the stove, or your brother will push you in. Go help your brother, and make sure you don't break anything, or I'll break your fingers."

Johnny cleaned his boots by the entrance and entered. As they walked deeper in, they saw the large wood oven that was making their dinner. The smells made him salivate, even though he had eaten a couple of small meals already. He had really exerted himself back then with Christina, as he only got to see her about two days a week, and he tried to make every second count. Christina joined her mother, while Johnny went to wash up. He felt sweaty and dirty, but he'd take care of the second now, as the first would have to wait until he got home.

When he returned to the kitchen, he saw Mrs. Digby serving a steaming hot dinner, the two boys and Christina sitting at the table. He joined them, and graciously received a plate of baked vegetables with a little bit of chicken, probably from their own coop. He thought he had seen less chickens than usual.

"That father of yours," Mrs. Digby was saying, "he's late again. These little two devils have been pestering me for hours, hungry.

Though you two," he eyed Christina and Johnny, "seem hungrier still. I'm sure all that *work* has left you exhausted," she remarked. Johnny detected a not-so-subtle trace of irony in her voice. She paused for a moment, to let her disapproval sink in, then continued. "I wonder if he has forgotten what time it is. At least he's out there fishing for us. The only way I'll excuse him being late *again*," she put emphasis on the word, "is if he brings back a few good fish."

Christina laughed, knowing her father was in trouble, but the little boys' mind was caught on another word.

"Can we smoke the fish, mum?" Philip asked.

"No, I want salted fish," Stephen interjected.

"You both eat your vegetables, or there's no fish for you," Mrs. Digby shouted, covering their little voices with her own. Both quieted down to Christina's and Johnny's mirth, and all ate in relative silence.

Johnny was walking to his house, quietly thinking to himself about how to get to Christina's house earlier on Sunday, when he heard a familiar voice from the river. He looked up from the road to see a few men fly fishing in small boats. The river was calm and the evening sun was illuminating them clearly. Christina's father, Mr. Digby, was holding onto his line, pulling hard.

It seemed to Johnny that the fish on the other side was equally determined. It was pulling back, holding onto its own life. But Johnny had to give it to the man, he looked right in his element. He stood on the boat, his feet placed just the right width apart, and his face had such a determined look that Johnny couldn't help but feel impressed. The man was oblivious to the world, and even though his friends were shouting jokes to him, he had eyes only for the end of the line. Mr. Digby was fighting with the fish just like Johnny had seen men fighting each other, focused and intent.

Even though the man was old, he certainly knew how to fish. He might not be suitable for a soldier, but that didn't matter in the end. He was providing for his family as best as he could, and that was one of the reasons Johnny was so eager to help in the farm. Yes, spending time with his beloved Christina certainly was a major reason for that, but he had respect for the man. And then, Mr. Digby pulled out the fish, emerging the victor. As he saw its size, Johnny knew that the Digby family would eat well.

His musings took him to the river itself, afterwards. It was a river that hadn't been exhausted yet, and Johnny wanted to try his own luck. Maybe there would be gold to find, there, among the fishes. They didn't need it, so why should it remain there, with them? And looking for gold in the river certainly beat going down the mines. He wished he could have the chance to find out if there was indeed a nugget or two in there.

The sun had set and it was after nine in the Saturday evening when he arrived home. As he pushed back the fence, Luna, their family dog, ran up to him. She was wagging her tail so hard that Johnny feared she would twist it. He knelt by her for a moment, playing with her ears and patting her head. She was the family member most happy to see him, every day. He sighed, stood, and entered the house.

"Is that you, Johnny?" a voice came from deeper in. It was Cathy, his mother, and there was a slurring in her speech that he knew all too well.

"Yes mum, I'm back," he called. He hesitantly entered the living room to see her laying on the chair.

"You're finally back from being that man's slave," she told him, making an effort to get up but failing. "If you work, you should be paid for it, ya know."

Johnny was not in the mood to go over that argument again. "I don't mind helping Christina's father every now and then. He's a good man, and he's too old for some of the work that farm needs."

"Come here, help your mother up," she told him, her voice changing. He approached her and lowered himself so she could grab onto him, but she pulled back in disgust. "You stink," she shouted and turned her face away. "And you're so dirty. Your shoes are muddy and your hands full of dirt. It's not fair that he makes you work so hard, and yet he doesn't pay you a fair wage," she repeated.

Johnny sighed. "I'll go get washed, then." He turned again, and headed for the bathroom, before his mother stopped him again.

"Find your brothers first," she shouted. "Your father has left for that pub again," she added, and he barely heard her mutter as he was leaving. "We can barely put a hot meal on the table for you three, and he's drinking away our precious money."

She kept talking, but Johnny knew that it was half the booze talking. He knew that she had been alone in that house for quite some time, drinking and thinking too much about things. It must have been several hours for her to be this intoxicated. "Sleep it off," he told her, "and I'll find Richard and Mark, alright?" She grumbled something in reply, and he left.

He wouldn't have to search too much, at least for Mark, as he knew where he was. He had a secret place, somewhere to go when their mother was into her drinking again. Johnny would never tell her that, of course, and he always made a show of going around the house and making noise. He didn't really need to do the same this time, as he heard her deep snores before he had even left the hallway.

It took him less than five minutes to go to Mark's hiding place. He was in the chicken coop they kept behind the house, that their mother would have never thought to check. Johnny couldn't fathom finding solace in such a place. Though it did keep Cathy off his brother, so Johnny understood why it was slowly becoming Mark's favorite place.

Mark was taking a nap with his dog Bosco on his chest when Johnny found him among the sleeping chickens. "Hey Mark," he called in a whisper, "you alright there, mate?"

The boy woke with a start, throwing off the dog, but then relaxed when he realized it was his brother. "Hey Johnny. Did mum send you?" He patted the dog, which was thankfully silent, and she calmed down. She was a beautiful kelpie, black and tan, that he had for the last six years since she was a puppy.

"Yeah. She's sleeping now, though, so no need to worry."

"She was shouting before," he said, as he carefully navigated around the chickens, "fighting with me. When dad's not home, she fights with Richard. And when Richard's not home..." his voice trailed off, as he finally exited the coop, Bosco coming behind him, wagging her tail. Johnny patted her neck as she licked his hand.

"What happened this time?" Johnny asked. There was a gnawing feeling in his stomach, a worry that was slowly getting bigger.

"Dad was about to go to the pub, right?" Mark said. "So, mum started shouting about money and him leaving us alone. Though I think she meant herself, ya know? And then dad said that he had worked for that money, so he could spend it on beer if he wanted and left. Richard had already left by that time."

"But you didn't," Johnny said.

"No, couldn't make it in time. I didn't want her to find my secret place, so I waited for a bit before I ran off. She was on the bottle like she was thirsty for it all day," Mark said.

"Is she drinking more recently, you recon?" Johnny asked, the worry finally poking through.

"Think so, yeah," Mark said. "She's always wondering what dad is doing in that pub all night, without her, without us, and plotting about what she would do if she caught him."

"Alright, thanks mate," Johnny told his brother, patting his head playfully. "You have any idea where Richard is?"

"No, none. Must have his own secret place, ya know?"

"He must have," Johnny agreed. Besides, he had his own secret place, too, he thought. With Christina, he didn't have to put up with all this. Maybe that was another reason he so eagerly helped her father.

CHAPTER TWO

"Have you heard the story of the Wang miners?" Johnny lightly said to Richard as they were going to the Hoagland family mine. Richard had returned late into the night and had gone straight to sleep, only to be woken by Johnny in the morning to go to the mine.

"No, mate," Richard said, absent-minded. He looked tired, so Johnny thought to distract him from whatever thoughts were going around his big head.

"You see, the Wang miners were a family of six boys and a girl, right? They worked with their father in a mine, working hard even though the littlest was eleven. You know how hard the Chinese work," Johnny paused, watching if his brother was listening.

"And father keeps saying how you're lazy when a Chinese man would do twice the work for half-pay," Richard added, eyeing his brother, his tone mocking.

"That's right," Johnny said, satisfied his brother's mind was off whatever thing he was thinking earlier, even to just insult him. "So, they were working hard, ya know? And when you work hard, you strike gold. In this case, they found a vein, and nuggets as large as your fist. But they weren't the only ones working the mine. You remember what happened with Mr. Brown, a couple of months back?"

"He found gold and talked too much, right?" Richard asked, now invested in the story. Johnny nodded. "And he was later found with a bloody pick through his neck," Richard said, his tone sad. "They never found who did it, because they never do."

"And that's why father says, *always keep your mouth shut*," Johnny agreed. "But the Wangs didn't say anything. They knew the rules,

18

and kept their head down, told no soul, and worked hard. Thing is, someone saw them hauling the ore. And they didn't like the Chinese getting more than the rest, even though they weren't paid nearly as much, nor would they get the bonus an Australian would get if he had found the gold instead of them."

"What happened?" Richard asked. He seemed to be waiting for each of his brother's words, thirsty to see what followed.

"What always happens," Johnny said, with a tone of finality. "Everyone, even the little girl, was found dead next morning. No one knew who did it, but who looks too deeply into the deaths of the Chinese, ya know?" he shook his head. "But the story doesn't end there, no." He paused then, his brother anxiously waiting for a long moment.

"There was another family that took over the Wangs, friends of the mine's owner. They found the ore vein 'by accident' and worked it. But then, the littlest of the family fell down a shaft, ya know? There was more grieving than when the Wangs died, and they carried on. And then, another of the kids died, a little boy. A shaft collapsed on him, cracking his skull. This time, his big sister was nearby, and she swore she heard those Chinese songs the miners sing at the pubs sometimes.

"Then, she was dead, dynamite exploding in her hands when she was lighting the wick. And the rest of the family followed. One after the other. The vein the Wangs had found was left alone for a week, no one mining it, fearing what they called the 'Chinese ghosts.' But that wasn't enough." Johnny added a dramatic pause. "The men who mistreated any of the other Chinese were soon found similarly gone." Richard's eyes were wide like plates.

"But a little girl that hanged out with the mine's owner's son said she heard whispers in Chinese, and then in English. The Wangs, she said, asking for the vein to be mined by another of their own. So, the owner put one of the other Chinese families to it, and the deaths stopped. You still hear from time to time that someone who abused a Chinese miner died in a collapse, from a faulty dynamite, or something like that, though. They say that the Wangs have taken upon themselves to protect the Chinese miners."

"Or at least someone has," Richard muttered. Johnny was about to say another of the stories he had learned, but he saw a man coming towards them.

Johnny instantly recognized him, he was Asrar Ansari, an Indian who had come to Australia some time ago, and had set up a hardware store, with some help from the government. They were a huge help for the people living far from the bigger cities, and Mr. Ansari was well-liked, especially by Mick, Richard's and Johnny's father.

"Hello, Mr. Ansari," Johnny waved, and the man quickened his pace. As he approached, Johnny realized he had a worried look on his face.

"Hello Johnny, Richard," Mr. Ansari greeted the boys. "Is your father home? I need his help."

"No sir," Richard spoke first. "He's up to the mine."

"What's wrong?" asked Johnny.

"I was taking supplies to the Wilson mine in my wagon, but my wife was not feeling very well. One moment she was talking, and the next she was slurring her words, then slumped back, unconscious. I turned the horse around and as we were making our way to the town, in my haste, I hit a pothole, and the rear wheel cracked." He hanged his head in despair.

"I need to take my wife to the doctor. Mr. Hoagland's address is the only one I know nearby, so I came to him. I don't know what to do," he added, emotions coloring his voice.

"Richard," Johnny said urgently, turning to his brother. "Run to the town. Have the doctor come to our house, alright? Then find father from the mine. I'll fetch father's tools, I think I can help if the wheel isn't completely broken," he added, turning to Mr. Ansari. He shook his head.

"No, just cracked. I'm down this road, then left, by the clearing," the Indian man said, pointing.

"I'll meet you there," Johnny said. Richard bolted towards the town just as Johnny turned back and ran the way they had come. He didn't waste time, just grabbed his father's tool bag from the shed, filled a canteen with cold water, and half-ran towards the place Mr. Ansari had described. He caught up to the man and they soon met his horse and wagon.

Johnny took a quick look at the man's wife, who was slumped back and breathing raggedly, and then pulled the water canteen from his bag.

"Give her a little water, and try to see to her, while I do what I can on the wheel," Johnny told the man. Mr. Ansari took the canteen, thanking Johnny profusely. Then, Johnny knelt by the wheel and got his tools out. He prodded a few places and realized it was fixable, so he went to work. It took him a good few minutes, but soon they were up on the wagon's seat, going towards the Hoagland home.

Richard was alternating between running and walking fast, to avoid exhausting himself, when he finally reached the doctor's office. He went through the doors and the waiting room quickly, to find the doctor's secretary.

"Mr. Ansari's wife," Richard started, breathing hard. "She's unconscious, out by our house. Their wagon's cracked a wheel," he said between gasps of air. "Father's at the mine. Johnny went to get the tools, to fix it up and get them at our house. Can the doctor come?"

The secretary hurried to the doctor, and the tall man returned, his face serious. "You're Mr. Hoagland's kid, right?" he asked, and Richard nodded vigorously. "I know where you live. Let's go, my wagon's loaded. Come around the office, it's out back."

Richard walked after the doctor, glad that they would take the wagon instead of walking there. The doctor sat on the seat and Richard jumped on the back, careful not to disrupt any medical equipment or supplies. The horse started moving, pulling the wagon back the way Richard had just come. The wagon ate the ground quickly, and soon enough, they arrived where Richard knew he had to get off.

"You know the way, right?" Richard asked, and the doctor nodded. "I need to get my father, I'll meet you back at our house," he said, and jumped off, before sprinting away. He hurried to the family claim, the mine his father and his uncle got from their own father, to find Mick taking a break.

"Where have you boys been? It's almost midday," Mick Hoagland shouted as he saw his son coming up. "The Chinese work more, for half the money, ya—" he was about to add, but Richard interrupted him.

"We met Mr. Ansari, his wife's unconscious and the wagon's wheel was cracked. I got the doctor, he's heading for the house. Johnny must have fixed the cracked wheel, we didn't see the wagon as we came with the doctor."

"Mr. Ansari, the man who runs the hardware store, right?" Mick asked, and Richard nodded. "He lives just three miles from us, and he's a good man," he said, getting up. "Without him, we'd have to go down to the city to get hammers and nails, or to get new pickaxes. If he needs our help, we give it. You did well," he added, and patted Richard on the head. "Let's get back to the house."

"Besides, the Ansaris are one of the few families we know," Mick said, on the way. "We've barely been here a year, and they've been kind with us."

When Johnny saw the doctor's wagon pull up by their house, he was relieved. Mr. Ansari's wife hadn't recovered, and Johnny couldn't think of what to do. He had been pacing around the yard, running out to the entrance every now and then, only to see no one coming and return to his pacing. He had heard the horse before he saw it, and when the utility wagon finally appeared behind the fence, he ran up to it.

"Hello Doctor," Johnny said, as he guided his horse towards Mr. Ansari's wagon. "This way, did my brother fill you in?"

"He did, mate. Take me to Mr. Ansari."

The moment Mr. Ansari saw the doctor, he jumped up from the back of his wagon. "Doctor, you're here! Please, hurry, my wife—"

The doctor jumped off his wagon and was right next to Mr. Ansari in seconds. He took a look at the woman, and Johnny thought he detected a hint of fear in the man's eyes.

"We need to get her to my office," the doctor said. His voice was serious, and Mr. Ansari detected the same fear that Johnny had.

"Will she get better?" he asked, barely controlled emotions leaking into his tone.

"I'll need to examine her more thoroughly, mate," the doctor replied. He didn't answer Mr. Ansari's question, Johnny noticed.

"What is it?"

"How long ago did she collapse?" the doctor asked, avoiding the question again.

"About half an hour, maybe more?"

"There's a chance it's a minor stroke," the doctor said. "As she's still alive, I believe she'll recover. Let's take her back to my office, as quickly as possible. You did well, Johnny, to send your brother to get me," he told Johnny, before going back to his wagon. "Help me with this."

Asrar stared after them for a long moment, stunned. He had caught the implication in the doctor's words, that his wife could have died. It took him some seconds to gather his wits.

Johnny hurried to the doctor, glad to be of help. The man had retrieved a stretcher, and Johnny grabbed the other end and helped him place it on Mr. Ansari's wagon. Then, with Mr. Ansari's help, they carefully lifted the woman off the wagon and onto the stretcher. It took a bit of time to maneuver the light load, but they placed her slowly on the wooden bottom of the wagon, and then the doctor pushed a small pillow under her head.

"We need to go," the doctor said and sat on the driver's seat. Mr.

Ansari pulled a crate and sat on it, looking at his wife, his eyebrows frowned and renewed concern on his face.

"Mr. Ansari," Johnny called, and the man took a long moment before he lifted his eyes from his wife.

"What is it, mate?"

"Your wagon," Johnny said, then paused. "It needs some fixing up. I can finish working on it here and take it back to your store. That way you can have one less thing on your mind, ya know."

"That's very kind of you, mate," the man muttered. "Thank you. Your father raised a good man."

"Thank you, sir," Johnny replied, and waved his goodbye as he watched the wagon pull out of the yard. He watched them leave, to make sure they were rolling alright, and then turned his attention back to the wagon. He grabbed his father's tools and got to work, and his father joined him, adding his own expertise.

As Johnny was rolling into Mr. Ansari's store, he saw a young man, one of Mr. Ansari's sons, look up. It was Faiz-ul, who was a year older than Johnny, at twenty-two.

"Hey Johnny," Faiz-ul, said. "Why are you in my father's wagon?" He stood and approached Johnny, eyebrows furrowed in a way strikingly similar to his father.

"Mate, your mother collapsed, and the wagon's wheel was damaged, but I fixed it and had my brother call the doctor. I brought the wagon back, and your father took the doctor's wagon to his office."

"What's wrong, why did she collapse?" Faiz-ul asked. Johnny jumped down from the driver's seat and put a hand on the man's shoulder.

"The doctor said he didn't know for sure. But he did say he can help her," Johnny said, trying to console him.

"Thank you, mate," Faiz-ul told him, and grabbed his shoulder, holding it tight for a moment. "I appreciate it."

"And I appreciate your family supporting mine," Johnny said.

"I need to get to my father," the man said, and turned to the office in the back. "I'll lock up immediately."

"Let me help you," Johnny said, and hurried around the shop, closing windows, and locking locks. They had closed the shop quickly, and where hurrying down the simple roads towards the doctor's office.

Just as they arrived, they caught the doctor's secretary locking up the front door. Faiz-ul hurried to the woman and asked her if she knew where his father was.

"Mr. Ansari is with your mother. The doctor took her to the hospital," she replied.

"Do you know how she is?" the man asked, desperation bleeding into his voice, but the secretary shook her head.

"Sorry, my boy. They didn't stop for long here."

"Thank you, miss," he muttered and went back to Johnny. "I need to tell my brother and sisters," he told him.

"I'll come with you, if you want me to," Johnny said, smiling. The other man smiled back.

"I appreciate it." They half-ran to the Ansari home, and Faiz-ul pushed the door open. His two sisters and his brother crowded around as he got inside, Johnny following behind.

"Is everything alright?" Praveen, his brother, asked, immediately sensing the two men's mood and seeing their serious looks. His twin, Shireen, took a couple of steps closer to her brother, concern clear on her face. Veda, the youngest of the kids, barely having entered puberty, grabbed her sister's hand.

"Everything's going to be alright. Mother's in the hospital. I'll go see her."

All the siblings started speaking at once, then.

"Mother is? What's wrong? Did she fall off?" Praveen said.

"What happened? Why is Johnny with you? Did he have something to do with it?" Shireen asked.

"Where is mummy? Daddy?" Veda said, tears in her eyes already.

"It's going to be alright," Faiz-ul repeated, though his own voice was strained. "Johnny helped father with the wagon, and his brother got the doctor. They helped us much today," he replied to Shireen, who left her sister's hand to hug Johnny's feet.

"Thanks Johnny," the girl said and Johnny patted her head.

"Your mother's going to be alright," Johnny said, hoping the repeated attempts at calming them would help. He was disappointed to see that they didn't. Veda started crying in earnest, and Shireen looked painfully sad. Praveen put an arm around his sister's shoulders, though Johnny was sure he spotted a tear run down his cheeks, too. Faiz-ul took Veda's hand, and pulled her inside.

"We need to get mother a change of clothes," he said, "and lock up. Get ready!"

Johnny was about to go further in to help when the young man turned and looked at him with a sad smile. "Thank you for your help, Johnny. I really appreciate it, mate. I can't ask for more, though. Go on, get back to your mine. I'll deal with it." Johnny smiled back and nodded.

"Mate, if you need anything, don't hesitate to ask, alright?"

"Sure will, thank you!" Faiz-ul said, and got inside, his brother and sisters crowding around him and asking him questions, in a mix of English and their own native language. Johnny could hear the fear in their voices, even if he did not understand their words.

Johnny knocked on the Ansari store door to get Faiz-ul's attention. The man looked up from storing the shelves and smiled when he saw Johnny.

"Hey mate," Johnny said, entering. "How did things go yesterday? How's your mother?"

Faiz-ul sighed. "The doctor said she had a minor stroke. She's better today than she was yesterday. She spoke to me, recognized me, even asked me how my siblings were feeling. But she couldn't get up, ya know."

"How's your father taking it?"

"He's with her now. He can't get away from her for long. I think he needs to be there more than she needs him there."

"So, you're working the store by yourself?" Johnny asked and Faiz-ul nodded. "How long, do you think?"

"Mother used to do so much around here. And the doctor said she'll need many months to recover fully. She'll be in the hospital for the next month, at least. I'll be working here for the entire day, every day, for now, I think." Faiz-ul sounded sad, but Johnny could see the man's determination.

"That's good that you want to support your family, mate. If we can help you with anything, tell us, alright?"

"Thanks, I appreciate it," Faiz-ul nodded. Johnny smiled at the man, who seemed older to him now, and bought nails and a hammer, as his father had requested. He left quickly, to avoid his father's ire for being late.

Over the next few days, Johnny passed by the Ansari store a few times, some to buy supplies and some just to see how Faiz-ul was doing. He rarely saw his father around, and the young man was working harder than he had expected. Every time Johnny passed by, he saw Faiz-ul either restocking shelves, helping customers, hauling heavy-looking crates around, or getting orders down from the wagon and into the shop's storeroom. He never saw him lazing away or taking a break.

Johnny asked about his mother a few times, and he got the same reply each time, that she was getting better, but she couldn't leave the hospital yet. Every time he saw Mr. Ansari, the man looked drained and worried. Johnny thought that if Faiz-ul hadn't taken responsibility for the shop, Mr. Ansari would have closed it down for as long as his wife was in the hospital, at least. That could very well mean a significant lack of income, with the added cost of hospitalization.

After a few days, though, he was finally seeing Mr. Ansari light up again. The dark circles under his eyes slowly vanished, and he was more cheerful in his greetings.

"She's making great progress, ya know," Mr. Ansari had replied one day to Johnny's inquiries. "She's doing better than the doctor hoped. She's completely normal again, in her head. She speaks clearly and doesn't confuse Faiz-ul with Praveen anymore. Only thing left is for her body to heal enough so that she can get back on her feet."

Faiz-ul kept on working like a bull, though. Every time Johnny saw him, he was on his feet, doing something. His father often rested in the back of the shop or worked the less demanding posts, like keeping an eye on the storefront or doing the paperwork. Faiz-ul was doing all the hauling, all the stocking, all the driving around and delivering orders.

One day, Johnny realized he felt bad for the man. It was as if he had forgotten to relax. Too much work is not good for anyone, he knew. It made life go by and filled you with regrets. That day, they had visited the shop with his father. Mr. Ansari was sitting behind the counter and Faiz-ul was stocking the shelves.

"The mine's going well enough," Johnny told his father quietly, "so do you think I can get Faiz-ul fishing this Sunday?"

Mick looked at the young man. "He's been working the shop every day since his mother's stroke, hasn't he?" Mick asked Johnny in the same tone, who nodded. Mick approached the counter. "Your son's a hard-working man, mate. You must be proud of him," he said, and Mr. Ansari sat straighter, his face beaming with pride. "Works like a Chinese, he does. If only Johnny worked as hard," Mick joked, and tried to grab his son's head to mess with him, but Johnny evaded him.

"It's been a while since you last got out, right?" Johnny asked Faiz-ul. "I want to take you out, remind you to relax."

"You're right, that's the proper thing, right? The Ansaris have been a great help to us, they have." Mick told Johnny. Then, he turned back to Asrar. "I'll need some dynamite, and my son wants to go fishing with your son." Faiz-ul approached the counter, as well.

"I can't, sorry," Faiz-ul said, shaking his head. "Can't leave the shop. And I don't have dynamite right now." Johnny was disappointed that Faiz-ul disagreed without even discussing it, so he was about to object, but Mr. Ansari stood quickly.

"You do need a break, ya know," Mr. Ansari said, standing next to his son. Faiz-ul looked more different than the rest of his siblings, more like his mother than like his father. Johnny also suspected that his hard-working nature was also inherited from his mother.

"But you're too tired, staying with mum all night every night," Faiz-ul replied. "I can't take a day off, it'll be too much on you."

"I've worked the shop alone, before. And if I need to make a delivery, I'll get Praveen. He's eighteen now, a man as well."

"But—" Faiz-ul started, but Mr. Ansari interrupted him, turning to Johnny.

"He'll come. This Sunday. Come pick him up, eh? And I'll put an order in for your dynamite."

"A couple of crates will do, thank you Mr. Ansari. And I'll be here Sunday morning, to take him fishing."

Faiz-ul threw a glare at his father but relented. "Ya know, I do need a break." He turned to Johnny. "We'll get you your dynamite to your door as soon as possible. Shouldn't take more than a few days. Thank you for your invitation, mate. And leave the cooking of the fish to me. I have something I want you to try."

Johnny nodded, smiling widely. When they left the store, he was more excited than he had been for days. He was looking forward to fishing with Faiz-ul, as well as for the man's ideas about cooking.

Johnny entered the Ansari shop early Sunday morning, and he saw three men inside. Mr. Ansari was instructing a determined-looking Praveen as the younger man was walking around the shop, restocking the shelves. Faiz-ul was helping and offering some advice, but mostly stayed back and observed his brother. To Johnny, it seemed that Praveen was also growing into a man, step by step. Their father must be proud.

After they exchanged their greetings, Faiz-ul stepped out of the store with Johnny.

"He took full responsibility, ya know," he said, gesturing towards his brother. "He stepped up and said that he'd care for the store by himself today."

"That's good for him, mate," Johnny said. "The more hands knowing the work, the better."

Faiz-ul took a small bag with him.

"What do you have there, mate?" Johnny asked.

"Fishing line," Faiz-ul said, "and a surprise. Let's go catch us some fish!"

"The mine feels like a second home," Johnny told Faiz-ul as they closed up on the area. "There's a river nearby, we'll be fishing there. This is where your father brings us our supplies," he said. They walked closer, and Faiz-ul examined the area.

"Looks interesting. Is that the entrance?" he asked.

"That's right. Do you want to look inside?"

"Yes, but after we fish. Morning's the best time for fishing, ya know?" Faiz-ul said, smiling. They hurried through the mine's main area and to the nearby river. They stood on the bank, and unfurled their lines.

Johnny soon realized that Faiz-ul was good at fishing. He was careful and diligent, and Johnny raced him to see who could catch four fish first. Faiz-ul won, but Johnny was just one behind. They grew hungry as time passed, and soon hunger made them pack up and get back to the mine.

There were already cooking utensils and a firepit on the surface of the mine, one that Johnny and his father used to cook or make tea. They sat by the fire and cleaned the fish while the fire was getting ready. After they had prepared the fish, Faiz-ul took them and put them in a pot. He added water from the river and cut in a few more things from his bag that Johnny didn't see clearly.

He stirred for a while, and as the water grew hot, an amazing smell started filling the air. Johnny was surprised at how good the food smelled. It was a strange spicy smell that made his mouth water. It was the best thing for the chilly evening.

"This is fish curry," Faiz-ul said as he served his friend and himself.

"I haven't had curry before," Johnny said, and he happily took a deep spoonful. His taste confirmed what his smell had inferred, the taste was spicy but rich, and there were some vegetables floating around. "It's really good!"

"Yes, it's my specialty," Faiz-ul proudly said. "With mum in the hospital, I improved my cooking. Even she says it's good."

After they ate and washed up, Johnny caught Faiz-ul staring at the mine entrance.

"Do you want to see how we work?" Johnny asked.

Faiz-ul nodded. "I know a thing or two about geology, and it's remarkably interesting. I've been wanting to explore a mine since we moved here."

Johnny stood quickly, excited to show his new friend the mine. "Come!" He took a lantern from a shelf and lit it, and then led Faiz-ul through the dark corridors. He had something in mind to show him, and he walked quickly, excited. Then, he turned a corner, and arrived at a small, new tunnel.

A few white gashes shone in the darkness, a quartz vein. Johnny smiled, and extended his hand like a showman. Faiz-ul, his mouth wide, approached it in awe.

"This is quartz," Johnny said. He caressed it, and Faiz-ul did the same, lightly touching the white ore. It felt rough to his hand, and he could see gashes from tools.

"How do you do it?" Faiz-ul asked, still taken over by awe.

"Hard rock mining is tough," Johnny said. "Look." He took a tool and got to work.

It took a good couple of hours for Faiz-ul to satisfy his curiosity, looking around the mine and trying various mining techniques. When they got back to the surface, it was getting darker.

"You can come again, if you'd like," Johnny said. "Next time, we'll do something easier than hard rock mining. We can prospect the rivers for gemstones or gold. We've been planning to do it for some time, and we'd love the assistance. Besides, it's easier than hauling around cargo back in the store," Johnny added, smiling. Faiz-ul smiled back.

"I don't know about that, mate. Most of the time, I just wait for customers, ya know," he said modestly, looking down. "I'd like to be of more help to my family, too. I'm seriously thinking about expanding, ya know. The store's great and all, but I'm very interested in geology. If you taught me, I might be able to get work somewhere, so even if the store didn't go well for a time, we'd have some income."

They sat around the fire again and attacked what little fish curry remained, hungry from the hard work they did down in the mine. Mining was demanding work, and even though they were hardworking men, it didn't mean they got tired less easily.

Johnny asked Faiz-ul about his mother, and they spoke at length, sharing stories and aspirations until they saw that they'd need to leave if they wanted to get back home before it got completely dark. Johnny led him to a point from which Faiz-ul knew his way back, and then turned to go to his own house.

When Faiz-ul got home, he found his father putting his siblings to bed. The man smiled, seeing the huge smile his son had on his face. They sat together in the living room, and his father brought them a beer each.

"How did it go?" Asrar asked.

"It was fun," Faiz-ul replied. He sipped at his beer. "We went fishing and I made him some fish curry. He hadn't tried it before," Faiz-ul smiled widely. "Then, he showed me a quartz vein, and how they mine. The mine is so big and labyrinthine, you can easily get lost if you don't know the way."

"Mick's family has been here for a year, but the mine has been worked by three generations. It belonged to Mick's father, and now even Johnny and his brothers work it," Asrar explained.

"Fishing was very fun," Faiz-ul continued, "and relaxing. I feel refreshed."

"It's good you took a day off. And I'm glad you enjoyed your time with Johnny. He's a good young man and his family has helped us a lot. Especially with your mother," Asrar said. "They're good men. If it weren't for them, the doctor would have seen her much later. And who knows what would have happened…"

Faiz-ul nodded. "There's something else. We talked about mining. How it's done, and what to look for. He showed me a few techniques. I've been interested in geology recently, I've even talked to a few other miners."

"It's good to have interests," his father said, interrupting him. "But don't forget to focus on the store. We've gotten a large loan to stock it and to get the building, the wagon, everything. This is a new business, just a year old. We need to pay off this debt before we start looking around for more."

"I know, but a mining operation might help speed that up, ya know," Faiz-ul said.

"It'll incur more debt, that's what it will do. Especially in the beginning." Asrar was serious. "Focus on the store. We can't afford fighting on two fronts."

"Yes, father," Faiz-ul replied, looking at the floor. He knew his father was right, but that didn't mean he'd stop dreaming. Or researching.

The very next morning, after his father had left for the hospital, he sent Praveen away to the store first, to open up. Faiz-ul hurried to the bookstore, and he caught the owner unlocking.

"Good morning Mr. Campbell," Faiz-ul greeted the man. "Do you mind if I order a book?"

"Good morning to you too, Faiz-ul. Of course you can, mate. What do you need?" The man entered the store and got out a small notebook. "I have a new shipment of those new detective novels coming up. Do you want something like that?"

"No, sir. I'd like a book on geology, specifically one on prospecting and gold mining. I want one with techniques and more practical knowledge."

"Do you have a title or a writer in mind?" Mr. Campbell said as he wrote down what Faiz-ul told him.

"No, I'd take your recommendation."

"Excellent, mate. It might take a while, but I'll let you know when it arrives, eh?"

Faiz-ul entered the Ansari store with a spring in his step. He found Praveen having just opened and went on to help him. Not only had he gained a friend the last few days, but a renewed interest in mining.

Mick heard the wagon wheels before Johnny. He let his lunch aside and hurried to the entrance of the Hoagland claim. He spotted Mr. Ansari's wagon coming from afar and called to Johnny to come and help. Johnny ran up to the entrance and arrived on the same time as Mr. Ansari did.

"Hello, Hoaglands!" Mr. Ansari greeted them loudly. "I have your dynamite."

Mick spoke with Mr. Ansari as Johnny went around the wagon, unloading the two crates. He grabbed them and carefully moved them off the wagon, then placed them inside their entrance. Mick and Mr. Ansari chatted, Johnny's father asking after the man's wife.

"She's getting better. She'll be out soon, though she'll need to rest for months. I'll have Faiz-ul helping at the store at least up to the summer, I think," Mr. Ansari said. "And, mate, I'd like to congratulate you," he told Mick, patting his shoulder. "Your son has a good heart. Thank you for taking my son out, he enjoyed his time, and his interest in mining and prospecting grew. You might have him asking you if you need another pair of hands, soon, even though I told him he should be focusing on the store," he said.

"He's welcome to come, with your permission," Mick said. "Only with your permission."

"Thank you again," Mr. Ansari said, and turned the wagon around.

"Thank you for coming out here, as always," Mick told him, waving. He patted Johnny's back and grabbed one of the crates. "Let's get them somewhere dry, eh?"

Johnny grabbed the other one and followed his father. They entered the mine and navigated the passages, going to a storeroom they had designated as dynamite storage. The dark passages that led to it had no oil lamps, to avoid their flammable fumes. When they arrived in front of the wooden door, Mick let his own crate down and pulled out a key. He placed it in the huge lock and turned, then pulled the door open. It was empty since they had run out of dynamite after they had ordered it, but there was a bale of hay.

The hay helped keep the sticks warm and dry, which was especially important in the coming winter. Mick pushed the bale open, and then placed the first crate, and then Johnny's crate, in the heart of it. He pulled the hay around, covering it completely, and pushed it as hard as he dared, to pack it close. Then, he pulled back to examine his work.

As he was looking at it, he felt a shiver run through his body.

It was getting very cold in the mine, and he would need to do something about that. He left the storage room and locked up again, putting the key back.

"I think we should get a cover for the dynamite, too," Mick told Johnny as they returned to the surface to finish with their break. "It might keep the sticks warmer."

"They will be frozen solid soon," Johnny agreed. "Do you think we should be looking into those thawing kettles?"

"We have a kettle, you think we can modify it?" Mick said.

"The new ones have a chamber where you can put the dynamite in, and you avoid having it too close to the fire," Johnny said. "I saw one in the Ansari store. It boils water and then the heat thaws the dynamite. It's safer than keeping it over a fire, that's for sure."

"I'll ask Asrar next time I'm down at his store. If it's a good price, I'll order one."

"The worst thing's the nighttime, ya know," Johnny said. "It gets about zero degrees out after the sun goes behind the mountains. And it's not even July yet."

They looked at the fire for a few moments longer, then Mick stood. "Let's get going, gold won't mine itself, ya know."

"What do you mean, I can't go?" Johnny asked, exasperated.

"You can't go to slave under that man—" Cathy started angrily but was interrupted by Mick.

"We decided," he said, much more calmly, "to go prospecting. We'll all go, your brothers too."

Johnny thought about it for a moment. He wanted to see Christina, his girlfriend, and not only see her with his eyes but…

"I heard that deeper in the bush, people found gold in the rivers," Mick continued. "We'll take Luna and Bosco out, and go camp next to the river for the weekend." Johnny was hesitant, but then saw his brothers' eyes shine. They'd all been talking about prospecting in the river. It was much easier work than mining, and there was a chance of getting a good haul, which would help pay the bills.

"If you've decided, then I can't say no, can I?" Johnny relented. "I've been wanting to go out there, anyway."

"Then it's settled," Mick smiled.

Over the evening and the next day, they prepared. They packed the tents, some food, the tools and equipment they'd need to survive in the bush for two days, and everyone was told to stay close and to not get lost in the woods. "Anyone who strays and is lost, will stay lost," their mother had said, waving her finger angrily.

On Saturday morning, they got up as early as they could get the kids up, shouldered the sacks, and started walking. Luna was running around their feet, glad to be out of the house. She barked at every bird happily, as if greeting a friend, and wagged her tail so hard that Johnny thought she'd sprain it. Bosco was running next to Mark, who was patting her head often, talking to her in a low voice.

The bags were heavy but the weather was getting colder, so they at least avoided sweating too much. Johnny tried to enjoy the trek, despite him missing Christina terribly. He would have to make it up to her over the next weekend, and he had just the way. He smiled to himself, earning the jest of his brothers.

The dawn's light filtered through the trees, giving an ethereal look to Bendigo's bush. They spotted wallabies and various birds, like cockatoos and parrots. Their noise gave the forest its life, and as they went through denser parts of the bush, Johnny spotted a couple of foxes, as well. The dogs chased after them for a bit, but then returned to their owners' extended hands.

It took them a few hours to reach a spot that Mick had heard of, marked by a huge tree towering over the rest right next to a riverbend. First, they set up their camp. Two tents, one for the boys and one for the parents. Then, they retrieved their tools. Each man got a pan, put on a cap, and went to the river.

Their mother stayed by the tent, picking up some wood. She made a fire pit with stones, then set the wood and started working on getting a fire up. She had matches with her but wanted to try the traditional way. She was working with thin little branches and some dried grass and leaves, and eventually got a small fire running. Then, she prepared a pot over it, boiling water, to prepare a stew.

Johnny picked a spot by the riverbend, placed his feet in the cold water, and started examining the river bottom. He packed his pan, then loosed pebbles and other larger pieces. He added water, used it to take away dirt and other useless sediments. He kept working, then when he saw he had nothing useful in his pan, he emptied it and packed it again.

It took a few repeats of that until he found shiny traces of something different. He cleaned them and put them in a pouch, then emptied the pan and packed it again. Prospecting was slow and tedious work, but he enjoyed it. He let his mind wonder, looking at the trees, and listening to the animal life. He could hear many birds and knew that their pretty songs would wake them up the next morning just as the sun would appear over the horizon.

He saw Mick, expertly shifting through the riverbed, finding shiny

41

traces himself. Johnny saw observed his technique, trying to mimic him and improve his own. His father was an expert prospector, and Johnny had a lot to learn from him.

Mark and Richard were making more noise. They had gone deeper into the river and were scooping up rocks and gravel. Johnny realized they were trying to reach bedrock, and then starting again. They were braver, since the river's rushing current was stronger there, and they had more work than Mick or Johnny did, who had remained near the shore.

Johnny kept an eye on his brothers, partly to make sure they were alright, and partly to see how they were doing. And he was glad to see them put shiny traces into their pouches. The family was doing well.

A splashing sound took his attention away from his brothers, and he saw Luna rushing to the edge of the water. She was having fun with Mick who had set his pan aside and was playing with the dog for a bit. Bosco was swimming in the deeper parts of the water, around Mark, who was often playfully splashing her with water, and she was barking back.

They worked for hours while the sun was out, then ate a quick lunch before continuing. The dogs were lying by the fire, warming up after their swim, and all men were working by the shore, each a few steps apart. Johnny was glad to see more shiny traces going in Hoagland pouches.

As the sun began to hide, the water in the river grew unbearably cold even for their ankles. They gathered around the fire, drying their clothes and getting blood back into their feet. As they were around the warm fire, Johnny let his eyes wander.

Cathy was smiling, a hand on Luna's head and another on Mick's hand. She was enjoying the warmth and talking to her husband about nothing in particular. Johnny caught parts of the conversation, her speaking about how long had it been since their last family outing, and how much she had missed seeing the stars with no housework waiting for her.

Johnny stared at the image for a long moment, feeling something was different. Then he realized what it was; his mother wasn't holding a bottle of liquor. Come to think of it, neither parent had drunk a sip of alcohol since last night. He didn't say anything, hoping to avoid breaking the spell.

Mark was hugging Bosco, both man and dog lying closer to the fire. He had dared the deeps the longest and was feeling the coldest. Johnny could still see shivers shaking his brother's body once in a while. Richard was sitting close to the fire as well, laying on his back and looking up.

Johnny laid back as well. The sky was dark, the sun hidden for enough time for the stars to come out. The black expanse was filled with stars, all shining brightly. The more Johnny stared, the more stars he could see. The main mass of the stars, with the cloudy colors around them, were making the sky look like a painting.

He was hearing the fire sizzle, quiet words from his parents, the light snoring coming from Richard, the low noises of insects and animals. The night had a strange feeling, almost magical. Then, Johnny heard a very strange sound. Laughter, but a woman's laugher. He realized it was his Cathy's laughter. How long had it been since his mother laughed? Had she ever truly laughed since they moved to Bendigo, or was bitter half-laughs the only thing he had heard from her?

He felt the lightheadedness of sleep coming, then. The cold was biting, and he could see his exhale misting. He stood slowly, and shook his brothers awake.

"Let's get in the tent, mate," he told Richard, before moving to get Mark up and into the tent. Then his parents stood too and hid in their own canvas tent. Johnny and Richard put Mark in the middle, and glad for each other's warmth, they slept peacefully.

Myriad of bird sounds woke them up the next day. As Johnny left the tent to relieve himself, he saw that the blades of grass were covered in frost. It was getting very cold, and he wasn't looking forward to putting his feet back in the water. Though, he knew that he would soon have to.

Johnny didn't have to wake anyone else from his family up, as the birds were doing a much better job of it than he ever could. Both of his parents were up by the time he had returned, and he could clearly hear Mark and Richard stirring and cursing at the birds.

After a quick breakfast, they were back at the river again. Luna and Bosco weren't in the mood for the cold waters this time and chased birds and a wild cat they had discovered deeper in the trees. A few more little shiny pieces went in their pouches, their hard work being rewarded. Then, lunch and a few more hours of prospecting, before they set about packing up. Johnny saw neither parent touching alcohol the whole time, and Cathy retained that wide smile through the two days. That single fact made him happier than the gold they found.

"Two ounces!" Mick told them, back at home. "We found two

whole ounces, boys. I sold it and settled a few debts." He was smiling widely, holding the certificate he had received from the tester. Mark and Richard rushed and examined the piece of paper, and Johnny was glad that they helped fill some holes. Maybe next time, they could invite Faiz-ul along. Then, he thought about inviting Christina along, and camping with her, away from her parents or the chores he had to do to see her. His mind wandered, going back to the last time he saw her, and he wasn't focused on the discussion anymore, and had a silly smile plastered on his face.

CHAPTER THREE

"Good morning," Mick shouted as he entered the Ansari store.

"I'll be right with you, mate," he heard Asrar call from deeper in. Mick stood by the counter, looking around the store as he waited. He saw Asrar and Praveen working in the back. Praveen was carefully and diligently moving crates and objects from the store into the Ansari utility wagon, while his father was giving him instructions and taking notes in a thin notebook.

Even though the boy was barely eighteen, he was focused and hard-working, just like his brother. Mick was glad for the Ansari family. Everyone was helping out, covering the void of their mother's temporary absence. The Ansari couple was always working, helping the community with their store and excellent services, and Mick tried to favor them instead of going back to the bigger cities for supplies, and he knew the rest of their neighbors did the same.

After a few minutes, Asrar was satisfied everything was going well and left his son to continue, returning to the front and sitting behind the counter.

"Good morning Mick," Asrar greeted him. "How can I help you today?"

"There's something I've been wanting to make," Mick started. "The mine's been getting bigger. I need to make a cart system, to move around ore and dirt more easily. How much would it cost to order metal strips? I have the tools to make them into tracks."

Asrar nodded and pulled a piece of paper from under the counter. He wrote down a few numbers. "That's the price for iron that's good enough to support a loaded track. It's per yard. Keep in mind that I'll be needing an order in advance, because I don't stock that much metal."

"Seems reasonable, mate," Mick muttered, looking at the piece of paper. "I'd need some metal to make the carts, too. Would that use the same kind of iron?"

"You could do it with a cheaper metal," Asrar said, noting down another price. "Depending on how large you plan to make it, I think twenty to thirty yards per cart would be a good estimate," he noted a few other numbers. "How many carts are you thinking of making?"

"At least two, but maybe more."

"Then, the eight or more wheels would cost you about this much," he wrote another amount at the end of the page.

Mick nodded. "That's a great offer, mate. Much appreciated."

"Anything else I can help you with, today?"

"Sure, one last thing. Do you have those heavy wool blankets for horses, for the winter?" Mick asked.

"Ya know, I think there's a couple in the back."

"I'd like to get one. I want to keep the dynamite warm. Frozen dynamite doesn't go off and warming it up is always a risk."

Asrar nodded and called Praveen, asking him to bring the horse blanket over. A few seconds later, the young man had returned, carrying the heavy blanket, which Mick took from his hands. He paid, and inquired about the man's wife before leaving.

On the way to the mine, horse blanket under his arm, Mick tried to calculate how much gold he'd need to sell to get the metal he needed for his project. He really hoped they'd make good progress in the vein they had found, over the next few days. Upgrading infrastructure was always his top priority.

"Do you think these are enough?" Johnny asked, pulling back his hammer and chisel. Mick looked up from the holes he had been making on the same rock face and examined what his son had made.

"We need a couple more," he said, and turned back to his work. They hit their chisels with their hammers against the wall, shaving off pieces of hard rock. They cut and cut, and the metallic sounds of the hammer hitting against the chisel's base, and the sharp sound of the chisel scraping against the rock, were the only things that they were hearing. Their ears were adjusted to the sounds, filtering them out.

"That should be enough, eh?" Mick said, pulling back. Johnny finished his own last hole with a couple of hits and pulled back too.

Each man picked up a few sticks of dynamite and shoved it as deep as they could into the gashes they had created, then took the fuse. Mick carefully measured the fuse so that they had at least five minutes to get out of the mine. Then, he checked everything again. He didn't want to waste expensive dynamite because of a bad calculation, nor did he want to get blown into pieces by a miscalculated fuse.

When he was satisfied that the work was good enough, he pulled out a match.

"Ready, mate?" he asked Johnny, who nodded. Then, he set fire to the fuse, and turned away. They calmly walked towards the mine's exit, since they had allowed themselves enough time to get out. After they reached the surface, they walked a few feet away from the entrance and got behind the firewood they had collected and stacked.

Johnny settled down, his back against the wall of the heavy wood, and Mick sat next to him, waiting patiently. A few minutes later, several explosions shook the ground, and they saw clouds of dust blowing out of the mine's entrance. A couple of more explosions followed, and more dust vomited out of the hole on the cliff face.

After Johnny and Mick were certain all the dynamite had blown up, they went to their small camp and sat down. They allowed the dust to settle for some time, resting by the fire and talking idly. When they judged it clear enough, they hurried down.

Mick quickly went through the rubble, pushing aside pieces of rock, until he saw something that made him exclaim loudly. Johnny hurried to him and saw him holding a large rock that had a white brush going through it. Quartz, which had an exciting potential for gold! Johnny yelled in glee, and Mick's smile stayed on his face as he surveyed the rest of the rocks.

He was glad to find several more pieces of quartz and knew that more were waiting inside the walls. Mick examined the walls of the shaft, marking a few more spots he wanted to break open to follow the quartz vein.

"This way, right?" Johnny pointed at a wall, and Mick nodded.

"The quartz goes that way and the vein should get fatter," he said, still smiling. "Alright, here's what we'll do, mate," he said as he walked to the exit. "We wait for the dust to settle fully, first. While we wait, let's get started on building our carts and supports for the shaft, eh?"

They hurried to the surface and went to another woodpile, one with timber that could be used to make everything they needed around the mine. They got to work, cutting and trimming timber into usable pieces. They made the support beams to be carried into the mine later, and then worked on creating the carts. They put a few hours in, had a break, then worked some more.

The next day, they started by making more holes for dynamites. For hours, their chisels scraped against the walls, creating the little holes for the sticks. When it was time to light them up, Mick did the same careful calculations, set the fuse, and they walked up to the surface. More explosions followed, and when they were sure it was safe, they worked on the carts for a few more hours.

When they surveyed the result of the explosions, they were glad to see more chunks that had the characteristic white of quartz. Mick's smile from the day before grew bigger and he was filled with excitement. They hurried up to the surface and kept working on the carts to the end of that day. Then, after the dust had settled, they set about the next phase of their work.

Since they still hadn't made the carts, they picked up the large buckets from storage and walked down into the mine. They filled it with pieces of stone that looked interesting, then moved up to the surface, where they had a stone crusher. They activated it and emptied their buckets inside. The machine ground down the ore, so they could extract the gold or other metals.

Many more pieces of rock remained after their explosion and moving buckets full of literal rock was awfully hard work. They took a few breaks, but in the end worked with few interruptions for days, moving up buckets of rock and grinding them down.

Johnny shoved another fence pole in the ground, then took a step back and sat down. He took a moment to gather his wits. The work at the mine had left him so exhausted that even though it was finally

Saturday and he was at Christina's house helping around, he couldn't feel excited. He was barely standing up.

Christina approached him, her eyes shining wildly. "Wanna take a break?" she told him. "Father's gone to the house for a snack, and I thought you might want a… snack of your own."

Johnny's eyes shone and he nodded. He tried to stand, though he ended up needing help from Christina. They hurried to the barn, where they took their break and took advantage of the fact they were alone to catch up. They had missed each other terribly over the last few days, especially since they hadn't met the previous weekend, and went at it like rabbits. Christina did most of the work, as Johnny was aching all over.

Later, Johnny was back outside, putting up the fence poles. Some time later Mr. Digby came by. In the few hours after Johnny had started, he had managed to make truly little progress, and the man noticed. And he knew that Johnny was no slacker.

He examined the young man for a long moment. "You look exhausted," he commented.

"I am, sir, we've been doing demanding work at the mine. We found a good fat quartz vein, and we've been expanding the mine."

As Johnny spoke, he saw Mr. Digby's face drop. He was probably planning to sneak away for the weekend and put the work on Johnny's shoulders. Then, he saw another emotion, an idea forming in the man's brain.

"Mate," the man said, approaching Johnny. "Christina and I were talking," he said, eyeing his daughter who had come from the barn, her clothes and hair tidy enough to hide what they had just been doing. "I know you're tired from working all week down at the mine, though I've been awfully glad for your help here, ya know. So, what would you say about me paying you for your work?"

The fog that was clouding Johnny's thoughts instantly left, excitement chasing away his tiredness. If the man truly planned to pay him, it'd mean a lot to both his family's feelings, as well as to the progress of their work at the mine. They could settle a few debts, as well.

"I would appreciate it, sir," Johnny said, smiling widely.

"A fair worker's wage," Mr. Digby said, "seven shillings for a good day's work," and they shook hands on it.

With renewed vigor, he spent the next few hours finishing up with the fence poles. When there was a neat semi-circle of poles in the ground, ready, he set about putting wire between them. There were not enough hours in the day, so he came back on Sunday to finish with the wires. Besides, he always liked spending more time with Christina.

A few hours into the morning, Christina brought him a lunch and he took a break, which they took advantage of properly, and then he returned to work. By the end of the day, he had progressed much, even though he could still feel his shoulders sore from carrying ore around.

As the sun was coming down, Johnny saw Mr. Digby coming from afar. The man was looking over Johnny's work appreciatively.

"This looks good. It won't need much now more, eh?" he said when he was in earshot. "You did some excellent work here, mate."

"Thanks," Johnny said, glad that the man appreciated it. If he was paying for it, Johnny wanted him as satisfied as possible. The fact that he took advantage of the time he worked on the man's farm to make love to his girlfriend as much as possible was also an incredible benefit, he thought, though he kept it to himself.

"Here," Mr. Digby said, pulling out an envelope. "For your work. You can leave when you're ready, don't let it get too dark." It felt like the envelope contained more than what Johnny was owed, probably backpay for a few of the previous days of work.

Johnny shook the man's hand, a huge smile on his face, and bid him goodbye as he returned to the house. He hurried to Christina, bid her goodbye properly, then left for his own house.

"So, he finally grew some dignity," Johnny heard his mother mutter, though she didn't say anything else. He had given the envelope to his father immediately, not even thinking about it.

Mick opened it and looked inside. "That's great, son. Congratulations on your hard work," he said. He patted his son's back. "Rest, now. We can pay the advance for the wheels and the metal to get started with the tracks, with this."

Johnny collapsed at a chair, barely awake. He needed to wash up before he went to sleep, though.

"As soon as we get the carts going, it'll be much easier to move the ore. No more heavy buckets," Mick told him to cheer him up. "Maybe this week, if we're lucky, mate. I'll go tomorrow, first thing."

"And I'm off to my bed, good night everyone," Johnny said, standing up. By the time he had reached his room, his thoughts of washing up were forgotten and he was asleep before he hit the bed.

Mick hurried through the streets then entered Asrar's shop.

"Good morning," he called and went straight for the counter, seeing Asrar look up. "I am ready to make my order," he said, smiling.

"That's good. How much would you need?"

Mick brought out his notes. "I'll need eight wheels, and..." he paused, then gave him the paper. "This much."

"I'll need two days," Asrar said. "I have a local source, so it'll take less time."

Mick left more excited than he had entered. He was looking forward to setting up the cart system and not hauling a single bucket of ore again.

CHAPTER FOUR

Two days later, Mick was knocking on the Ansari shop again.

"Mick, your metal's here," Asrar said when he saw him. "Do you want to check it over?" Mick greeted the man then followed him to the back of the store. He saw the long beams of metal and the small wheels, neatly packed on the store's back.

Mick approached it and hit a beam, hearing its sound. Then he examined all beams carefully. "That's good iron," he muttered. He then went back to Asrar. "Here," he gave him the envelope.

He returned to the beams, thinking about how to take them up to the mine, when Asrar pulled him out of his thoughts.

"Give me a hand, mate," he told him. Mick turned and saw Asrar putting some beams in his cart, along with Faiz-ul. "I'll get them to your claim. Do you want a ride up?"

Mick smiled widely and started moving pieces of metal himself, carefully placing them on the cart's floor.

"I have more deliveries later, so put your metal on top of these crates," Asrar instructed. Then, he and his son went about bringing more crates in the wagon, placing them in neat lines, tight together, so they wouldn't move around too much. Mick knew some of them had dynamite inside, and he didn't want to risk any unwanted explosions either.

"Let's go, mate," Asrar called, and Mick climbed up the wagon.

When they arrived at the mine, he saw his two sons already waiting for him. Johnny and Richard set to unload the wagon with the help of their father.

"Put them up inside," he told them, and grabbed a few beams himself. "Thank you for the ride, mate," he called back to Asrar as the man turned his wagon around and left, waving to the three Hoaglands. Mick left two of the beams outside the mine, then gestured at his sons. "Let's get inside."

As they entered, he felt a chill run through him. It was getting very cold down there. He guided his sons deeper and put the metal in a storeroom that he locked to avoid anyone sneaking in and taking it to a smeltery, then he took the new horse blanket to the dynamite crates. He unlocked the heavy door and placed the blanket over the bale of hay that enveloped the crates. He hoped it would be enough to keep the cold off them, so they wouldn't need to risk thawing them later.

Then, he returned to the surface. Johnny and Richard were already getting the tools ready.

"First, we make the tracks," he told them. He took them aside to a working area they had prepared for that and showed them the basic process. The work was hard and long, and only the first step of their designs, but they had only themselves to count on, no workers to do the heavy work for them. It took them a few days of non-stop work before they had a few tracks ready for installation.

When he was satisfied they had enough to start, Mick took the boys down into the mine. He took the buckets with them and armed them with picks and shovels.

"We need to make the ground as level as possible, to hold a track," Mick explained, and started cutting away at the rock. "Here, look." He kept hitting it, and the boys realized what the man was doing. They took their own picks and started chipping away at the floor, then moving pieces of rock and soil they removed into the bucket with their hands or shovels. They filled some parts with dirt and chipped away at jugging rocks that didn't interfere with them walking around but would catch at the underbelly of a cart.

"Good, now you keep at it." After Mick had shown them how to work to prepare for the tracks, he returned to the surface to work on more beams. The boys worked the mineshaft floor, filling in holes and removing other rocks, and Mick worked the beams so that he would have more ready as the boys progressed.

As the sun was setting that day, Mick felt a strong shiver, even though he was doing heavy manual labor. It was getting too cold. He left his hammer down and went to the side of the mine, pulling out a bale of hay. He pulled it up to the entrance, then called for Richard. As the boy went though the mine up to his father, he brought two buckets with him, with the more promising pieces of rock, and threw them in the crusher. Johnny, carrying two buckets of his own, went to the crusher, too.

"Richard, take this," Mick pointed at the hay, "and go check the dynamite crates." Richard nodded and hurried away, pulling the bale of hay with him.

After Johnny emptied his own buckets inside the crusher, he got a pan from the storage and waited by the crusher's output. With what little light was remaining, he wanted to shift through the dust, to see if he'd find any gold. They had found many promising chunks of stone over the last few hours, and a few days back as well, and he was curious to see if their gold mine was finding any gold. He emptied the crusher and took the dust back to his father, so they could examine it together.

Richard took the hale awkwardly through the narrow underground passages to the thawing shack. He left it against the wall as he unlocked the heavy door, pulling it open. Then, he pushed the hale inside the room. As he entered, pushing the hale against the wall inside the room, he noticed that the dynamite crates were covered with a heavy woolen blanket. He pulled it up and saw that there was a bale of hay already covering the crates.

He looked at the bale of hay against the wall, then looked back at the dynamite crates. *One is enough*, he thought to himself. He covered the crates up again. *They even have a blanket.* Leaving the hay against the wall, he closed the door, then headed back towards the surface.

The whole house was smelling of the tasty stew, as Cathy was preparing the table. She had bought lamb specifically to make them stew, and she knew that they enjoyed the warm food in the cold winter evenings, but they had still not returned. The food was ready, but no one was here to eat it. Mark had already eaten and was in his room. She put some away for Luna and Bosco, as she angrily washed some of the utensils she had used.

She worked all day, too, and they should respect the fact she had set out their dinner. They could tell the time, they had no excuse; when it was time to play or for Johnny to go and see Christina, they knew what time it was perfectly. Only when it was time to come home did they forget about it and about her own hard work.

It was after seven when the two boys and the man entered the house. Cathy was waiting for them, her face already set in a deep frown. All three entered, their heads lowered, obviously knowing that she would be angry. She was about to set off when Mick went a few steps forward.

"Look, dear," he told her. He extended a pouch, which she took in her hands and opened. She saw the fine golden dust inside that she had expected when he gave her the pouch, but not at the quantity she had expected. She tried to guess.

"Three, no, four ounces?"

"Five!" Mick said, smiling widely. "We shifted through the rock crusher today and found this."

"It's finally enough to change those bloody curtains, isn't it?" Cathy finally smiled, letting the frown fall from her face.

"And pay some bills," Mick added. "You can go and get your curtains soon, after I sell this and deposit the money."

Cathy stared at the man for a few more moments, then nodded, showing her happiness. "That's good, dear. And congratulations to you two, as well," she said, hugging her two sons. "I was hoping we could replace those curtains sometime soon," she said, then turned towards the table.

"There's lamb stew. I hope it's still warm," she added, then sat at the table, and Mick and their two sons quickly joined her. They fell on it ravenously and seemed to enjoy it. Cathy was glad that even though the stew was cold, they liked it so much that they didn't mind.

"I'll meet you up in the mine," Mick said to Johnny. Johnny would go to the mine, to prepare for the work on the carts, while Mick would go to the town to sell the gold. Richard and Mark said their goodbyes to their parents and oldest brother then set out for school. All four encountered the same thing, the potholes in the roads, in the one passing by the house, and even the larger ones that led to the city, which were filled with water that had frozen over.

Winter was slowly grabbing hold of Bendigo, and all four male members of the Hoagland family, independent one from the other, pulled their coats tightly around themselves, to keep the cold out and to maintain their body warmth. Their manner of walking was similar, all taking after Mick's quick and long strides, and they huffed against their hands in the same way too.

Mick entered the town and hurried to the gold buyer. He sold his five ounces, then hurried to the Ansari shop. He paid off his whole tab, glad to be able to finish with that, then put the rest of the money on credit, in the family account. His wife would later be able to buy the curtains she had been wanting for so long, and even a piece of clothing or two.

He set off to the Hoagland mine again and met Johnny there, then both set to working on the ore tracks. They went deeper in the mine and started assembling the tracks in place and would soon be able to use them efficiently. Mick couldn't wait to see the carts running on those tracks, carrying the ore they were working so hard to extract. It would make life so much easier.

"It's done," Mick told Cathy that evening. "I've paid up the hardware store account. The minecarts and tracks are paid for, as are the dynamites. There was even some money left over, which I put into the account. You can go tomorrow to get the curtains you've been wanting for so long," he held her close. "Get something for yourself, too. How long has it been since you had a new dress?" He smiled wide.

Cathy gave him a peck. "That's very good," she muttered while he held her. After a few moments, she left his arms and went to the kitchen. "In a few minutes, I'll have dinner ready."

"Ya know, I'm starving," Mick said, entering the kitchen. "We're on a good path, at the mine." He sat at the dinner table and tried to relax his stiff back and shoulders.

"We'll be improving our productivity greatly over the next few days. Johnny and the boys have been helping me tremendously. We've prepared tracks and the boys have been leveling the ground. We started assembling the tracks today, me and Johnny. And we started work on the carts themselves. We prepared the wood a few days ago, so now it's easy to assemble the cart. We got one ready today already!"

"I'm sure you can't wait to stop hauling the ore by bucket," Cathy said.

"That's right, luv! I am looking forward to testing out the system we've set in place. A cart is ready, and we're done with the first set of tracks for one cart. It'll make moving ore up so much easier. Wheels are a great invention," he added, and laughed. Cathy hadn't seen him this glad in a while, and his laugher was contagious.

The next day, Mick gave Cathy a goodbye kiss as he was preparing to leave. "Take care of your mother," he told Johnny. "Don't let her carry too much weight." He left quickly, eager to get to the mine. He was hoping he would make good progress that day.

After a good breakfast, Cathy finished some chores around the house and got ready to go out with Johnny. They walked to the town, their first stop being the fabric shop. Johnny looked over the fabrics silently while his mother picked a few then haggled with the shop owner. She didn't want to spend too much on the curtains because she had more plans for today. She finally settled the price with the owner on a nice pair of cream-colored curtains, ordered them to length, and said she'd return later when they'd be cut and ready.

"Let's go to the clothmaker's too," Cathy said.

Johnny groaned. "I don't think you need my help picking a dress. I can wait here."

"We aren't just going to buy me a dress," she told him, and started walking, making him follow her with more groans.

"What, then?" Johnny asked.

His mother didn't reply, and instead entered the store. She greeted the owner cheerfully.

"What can I get you today, luv?" the man said.

"I want three pairs of wool socks, for my boys," she said, smiling. "Two are boys, one is this handsome young man." It was getting too cold, and their old socks had too many holes in them.

The clothier picked the three pairs from a crate, as Cathy continued speaking.

"I'll need a pair of pants for my eldest son," she added. She heard Johnny gasp behind her, surprised, but she was glad to be able to buy him a new pair of pants, as she knew that he had been needing one for quite a while. She let him choose the color and cut, and then she chose a simple dress for her own, before settling the payment with the owner.

On the way to their house, they took the ready curtains as well. Johnny was walking behind her, holding most of their purchases, while she was quietly humming to herself.

While Cathy and Johnny were in town, Mick started working at the mine. He was worried about the cold and the first thing he went to do was check the dynamite. When Mick unlocked the door to the thawing room, he saw the bale of hay laying against the wall. Richard had never put the hay over the dynamite crates, he realized. It was freezing in the room, and he felt a dread settling inside the pit of his stomach. He approached the bundle, removed the blanket, and opened the crates.

The dynamite had frozen. He cursed loudly, the words echoing around him. That was why he had asked Richard to put more hay over the crates. If only the boy hadn't been so careless, they would stand a better chance of having usable dynamite. Though it truly was freezing inside the room, so even the added protection might not have helped in the end, he told himself. He didn't want to lay too much blame on his son, even though he knew that if a worker had done the same, he would have fired him immediately.

With no thawing kettle and no money to buy one, he would have to deal with the frozen dynamite another way. He needed the dynamite to work, as it was too much to replace, and a thawing kettle would cost too much right now, especially after the big purchase of the mining track equipment. He had to find another way to thaw the ice.

There were buckets up on the surface, and there was the creek nearby. He had other tools around the mine, though he couldn't create a thawing kettle out of the materials at hand. The contraption was too complicated to make with buckets and the iron strips that they had been using for the tracks. But then, he thought of another way.

Since he had the buckets and there was a source of water nearby, he could boil water in the buckets, then surround a crate of dynamite with buckets of boiling hot water. The heat coming off them, along with the steam, would certainly help, even completely thaw the ice. Having decided on his course of action, he grabbed one of the crates, locked the door behind him, and went to the surface.

As he walked through the dark corridors, he was thinking of how to minimize the danger. Fire close to dynamite was never a good idea, so he would make a barrier with something that wasn't flammable between the dynamite and the fire and put them a good distance apart.

A nagging thought wouldn't leave him alone, that if he had asked Cathy to not buy anything they didn't need immediately, like the curtains, or the pants he knew she planned to buy for Johnny, they would have the money to buy a thawing kettle. But he couldn't bear asking his wife to not buy the things she had been wanting for so long.

She had been asking for the curtains for months, and he knew that Johnny needed the pants. That was one of the reasons he had allowed Johnny to take the day off and go with her. And she needed a new dress. She had patched most of their clothes so many times that some had less than half of the original fabric remaining.

He shook his head to push the thoughts away. No, he would make do. There were many ways open to an inventive miner like himself, he would just have to discover them.

When he arrived at the surface, he left the crate and brought some old hay with him from the storeroom, a bale that had been decaying. He laid it out on the ground, packing as much as he could, and placed the crate on it. That way, the cold from the ground wouldn't seep into the crate, obstructing his efforts at thawing the dynamite.

As he was packing the hay, a strong wind picked up. It was cold out, but not as cold as in the mine. Here, there was the sun at least, dispelling some of the cold. Down in the mine, in the darkness under the surface, there was no sun to help with the freezing cold or the moisture. The wind threatened to take the hay away, but he put the crate on it in time, and it just picked at the dry pieces of hay that were scattered around.

With the crate in place, he propped it open, and then he went about gathering large stones or pieces of excavated rock that they had determined held no value. He laid them in a long line, and the line slowly became a wall. He built it up to three feet high, and he felt it would be enough to protect the crate from the fire. Then, he started working on the fire. He would have to build it big enough to boil a few buckets of water.

He made a firepit then stacked firewood on it. He picked thinner branches and dry hay and then used a match to light the fire. He knew it would take a few minutes to get going, so instead of sitting around and wasting his time, he propped a couple of larger pieces of wood over it and went to the stone crusher. The machine needed maintenance.

The stone crusher was very important to them and their livelihood, and he had to keep it maintained. He worked on it for a while, cleaning its parts and making sure everything moved smoothly. After about half an hour, he was satisfied with his progress. He looked back at the fire and saw that it was going well, so he grabbed a bucket and filled it down at the creek. On his way back, he grabbed a piece of firewood to add to the fire.

He placed the bucket to boil, and then took another empty bucket to the creek. Again, on his way back, he added another piece of wood to the fire. On his fifth trip back, he decided to take some pieces of gum tree wood, as he had many lying around. When he added them to the fire, though, they kicked off a lot of sparks. A few flew towards the crate over the wall, guided by the wind, and he grew distressed. That would be highly dangerous.

With growing worry, he grabbed two buckets of boiling water. With the hot and heavy items stressing his shoulders, he turned towards the crate. He took a couple of steps towards it, with intent to check it over for any strong sparks.

He never got to it, though. When he had taken his third step, the sparks that had landed on the crate set the dynamite on fire. The explosion that resulted was tremendous. The rock wall he had made was thrown apart, and the fire and blast that came with the explosion sent Mick flying. He looked like a ragdoll as he was thrown against the wall. However, while a doll would then fall harmlessly on the floor, Mick collided against the rocky outcroppings near the mine's entrance.

The hard rock was merciless. Mick's head smashed against the wall, his last thought that of regret. He was already dead when fell on the floor.

"Where is your father?" Cathy asked Johnny while they were setting the table, as if he knew. He could hear the anger in her voice. Johnny looked at the clock. It had already been dark out for a while.

"Maybe he's still at the mine, finishing up something," he said, though he didn't sound convinced. After a few minutes, he looked at the clock again. "It's pretty late," he muttered to himself. "I'll go check up on him." He picked a lantern and his coat and left to the sound of his mother's muttered curses about his father being late once again.

Johnny walked quickly through the cold night, using the activity to warm himself up. The nights were very cold without the aid of the sun to dispel it. He pulled his coat tighter around him and upped his pace.

When he arrived at the mine, he was greeted by a horrific scene. The first thing that he saw was the angry black residue of an explosion. He saw the embers of a fire dying down. Large rocks were scattered around, like a boy's discarded marbles after a game. And a dark mass was lying on the ground near the entrance of the mine.

He hurried to the dark mass. He was feeling a horrible sense of foreboding as he approached. Under the light of the lantern, his worst fears were confirmed.

His father was lying dead on the ground. A pool of blood was centered around his head. The rock wall had splashes of blood. His clothes were charred. Johnny fell to his knees next to it, extending a hand, as if to grab hold of him and bring him back.

He stared at the body, unable to believe what he was seeing. His father was dead. Why? What had happened? He didn't know how long he was staring at the lifeless body, at the face full of terror and regret. At some point, he closed the empty eyes of the corpse. Then, with a gargantuan effort, he stood. He had to find who did this to him. His father wasn't stupid. Someone must have done something wrong.

There were remains of wood around the scene. Some pieces were obviously firewood, long, irregular, thick branches. Others, though, weren't. He found the half-burned remains of a dynamite crate. Then, he found the buckets. Some of them were crushed against the wall, while others were relatively intact, only shoved away. There were still warm water puddles in them.

With an idea forming into his mind, he rushed in the mine, going to the thawing room. He unlocked it and went inside. The scene held more answers.

On the side of the wall was a bale of hay. There was one less crate under the hay and the horse blanket in the middle of the room. He checked the remaining dynamite quickly. Frozen stiff.

A scene replayed in his mind, with terrifying clarity. His father asking Richard to check the dynamite and to take a bale of hay down here. The bale of hay that was now laying against the wall. The strings were still tied around it. Richard hadn't even attempted to add the hay to the bundle.

Hay was good at insulating against the cold. It would be even better than the blanket, Johnny knew. Richard hadn't thought for himself, hadn't even obeyed their father. He had just carried the hay here, then abandoned it.

The scene was so clear that Johnny remembered exactly how he had been feeling. He had been tired, and he knew that Richard had been tired as well. Maybe that was why he didn't think for himself, he didn't use his initiative to cut the bale apart. If he had cut the bale and had spread it over the wool blanket, the added hay would insulate the crate from the freezing temperatures underground.

If Richard had done what their father had requested, Mick wouldn't have to thaw the dynamite. It would have been cold, but not frozen. If Richard hadn't been lazy, their father would be alive now.

Johnny's world became an angry blur. In his rage, he couldn't remember if he closed the crate, if he replaced the wool blanket, or if he locked the storage room's door. The only thing he clearly remembered doing was grabbing his lantern so hard his knuckles turned white and running home.

He stumbled in the dark a few times, but he didn't care. He pushed through their home's yard, and saw Richard finishing some work outside. His brother turned to look at the maniac Johnny was, and took a step back, incomprehension on his face.

"Johnny?" he asked. "Everything alright?"

Before he could get another word out, Johnny let out a blood-curdling scream of rage and threw himself on his brother. Tears were running down his face as he mounted him and started throwing punches uncontrollably. He was screaming incoherently, and Richard was screaming back, trying to get away. His brother was both stronger and larger, though, and he couldn't move.

Hearing the commotion and fearing the worst, Cathy rushed out of the house holding a shovel. When she saw the altercation lit up by the discarded lantern, she hurried to her sons, screaming at them to stop. Johnny had drawn blood from Richard, his fists red.

She realized that Johnny wasn't listening to her, wasn't listening to anything. She hit Johnny with the shovel she was carrying, pushing him off Richard. Then she discarded the tool and grabbed Richard. The boy was bleeding profusely from cuts on his face, and he seemed dazed. Johnny seemed unconscious when she spared him a quick look. What had happened to make Johnny go into such a rage?

As she helped Richard inside, she saw Mark, fearfully staring out the door. She gestured for him to help her, and they both laid Richard inside the house, on his back. She hurried to the kitchen, grabbed a towel and a bowl of water, and gave them to Mark.

"Go see about your brother," she told him, and then attended to Richard. The boy had taken considerable damage, and she knew it would take days for him to recover. He was dazed and not really replying to her questions, though he kept repeating he didn't know what he had done to Johnny.

After a few minutes of cleaning Richard's face and determining the amount of damage, she stood angrily. She grabbed her belt. The boy was in trouble, and even though he was twenty-one now, that didn't mean he got to do anything he wanted. Especially not beat his brother's face into a bloody mess.

She left the house, the belt in her hand. In the lantern's light, she saw that Johnny was sitting up and staring pathetically at the ground. His brother had cleaned his fists and face from the blood he had received from the fight. She grew angrier, and approached Johnny, ready to give him a particularly good lesson.

"Why did you do that, you—" she started, but Johnny's muttering interrupted her train of thought.

"He's dead," he said.

Cathy froze. "Who—" she started but Johnny interrupted her again.

"Dad. Mick. He's dead."

She took a couple of steps forward, then knelt next to him. Maybe she heard wrong.

"What?"

"I found his body."

"What?"

"When I got there, he was already dead. He probably died instantly."

"What?" she repeated dumbly.

"He's dead," Johnny shouted. "He's dead, and it's Richard's fault!"

That shook her enough to push her out of her stupor. "Tell me what happened," she told him.

"I found the remains of a fire and a dynamite crate. He was trying to thaw the dynamite. I went down in the mine and saw that Richard didn't do what dad had told him. He was supposed to put hay around the dynamite, but it was just lying there, against the wall. He was probably too tired to open the bale and put it over the blanket."

Cathy stared at her son for a long time, unable to do anything. Tears were running down her face. She could hear Mark crying softly next to her, staring at the bloody rag and the red water in the bowl. She didn't know how long she stayed there, but at some point, the cold was unbearable. She went back into the house, sobbing. Mark followed her quickly.

Johnny stayed longer on the ground, feeling the cold seeping into his bones, and the freezing air piercing his clothes. He didn't care, though.

It was Luna who pulled him out of his daze. The dog sniffed him and lapped at his tears, then nestled on his lap. But he could feel her shivering. The cold was too hard on her. Out of pity for her, he stood and took her inside the house.

Mick's funeral was a large affair. The man was known to the whole community, and many attended, even people who knew him as nothing more than a client. The Ansari family was there, even Mrs. Ansari, supported by her husband. Mick's brother, Jimmy Hoagland, came to speak to Cathy, and said a few words during the service.

Other people spoke as well, though Johnny couldn't pay much attention to anyone. Christina and her family attended, too, but Johnny kept his distance, and one of the reasons was his mother. She was in a very bad state and he didn't want her to lash out against the Digby family. Mick was interred in the cemetery, and everyone slowly walked back home.

"Hey Johnny?" a voice echoed through the mine. Johnny recognized it and left his pick on the ground. He dragged his feet to the surface and met Jimmy, his uncle.

"Hey," Johnny said. He walked past the man and grabbed two empty buckets. "How can I help you, uncle?"

"How's the mine going?" Jimmy asked. Johnny shrugged.

"As always," he muttered. "There's rock to be broken and carried to the crusher."

"What's that iron for?" Jimmy pointed at the half-finished iron beams.

Johnny paused before answering, as thinking about his father felt like picking at an open wound. "A project father started. He wanted to build a cart system."

"Why don't you finish it?"

Johnny shrugged again. "I might, at some point." He went

towards the entrance of the mine again, and Jimmy watched his nephew carry the empty buckets, his head down, and vanished inside the darkness of the mine.

He decided to follow him for a bit. "How's your mother?" he asked as they walked deeper in.

The man shrugged again, and Jimmy was growing more worried with each shrug. "As well as can be expected," Johnny said. "I saw her a couple of days ago, I spent last night here."

"Do you do that often?" Jimmy asked carefully but didn't receive an answer. He observed Johnny passing next to a locked door and saw his jaw grow tense and his shoulders straighten.

Then, they arrived at some broken rocks. Johnny left the buckets down, filled them up with rocks, and grabbed them. Jimmy took one from his nephew's hands and helped him move the ore up to the crusher. He wordlessly helped his nephew carry three more loads up before he spoke again.

"If you need anything, will you let me know?" Jimmy asked.

"Sure," muttered Johnny. It didn't seem to Jimmy like he had any interest in calling him up on it, though. *Everyone works through grief in their own way*, he thought to himself.

"Alright, mate," he said then. "I'll see you around, eh?"

The young man waved goodbye at him and returned to his work, as Jimmy walked away, more concerned than he was when he had arrived.

Johnny kept breaking stones and moving them to the crusher. He wasn't checking them for gold content, for quartz, for any indication they held something useful. He was just breaking stones and moving them to the crusher.

Every time he passed next to the dynamite storage room, Richard came to his mind. How his face had looked when he had beaten him. How guilty he had looked at the funeral. And Johnny grew angrier every time.

Maybe his father had been a little stupid by lighting a fire so close to the dynamite. But it was Richard's fault that he had had to do it at all. It was Richard's fault that the dynamite was frozen and unusable. Even now, he hadn't been able to thaw it safely. He had to break rocks by hand and move them to the crusher, again by hand because Mick wasn't here to help him finish the cart system.

It grew dark and cold, after a while. Johnny abandoned his tools somewhere and left, dragging his feet to his house. There were two reasons he was slumping and his feet were unwilling to keep walking; the first one, though of lesser importance, was that he was exhausted. The second reason, and the one that was the heaviest in his mind, was the image he knew he would see when he opened the door to his house. When he finally arrived, he saw it just like he did in his mind's eye.

Cathy was laying on the couch, a wine bottle in her hand. Johnny noticed another empty bottle by the foot of the couch. *Two already, huh?*

"It's late," she slurred as he entered. "Where were you last night?"

"I slept at the mine," Johnny said, going towards his room.

"I had made dinner," Cathy called after him. "You're the same as him," he heard her add, half to herself.

Johnny had no willpower to deal with her accusations. He went the long way around the house to avoid passing by Richard's door, and entered his own room, hiding under the covers. He was stinking, but the covers were dirty as well, exactly as he had left them a few days ago. The only difference with the mine's floor was that the bed was a little warmer.

His mother hadn't been attending to the house after Mick's death. What little income Johnny had brought from the mine had been going to the wine, and he wasn't sure if he wanted to keep bringing more money just for her to get drunk on. His sleep was fitful and was interrupted once by Cathy's loud argument with Richard, who had also returned late. Then, Johnny slept again to the morning.

The birds awakened him, and without speaking to anyone, he left for the mine. The dark corridors felt safer than his home now, and he dug through the hard walls using only his pickaxe. The dynamite was frozen because of Richard, he kept telling himself. He didn't know how long he dug before he felt the pangs of hunger and he hurried to the surface, to cook a quick lunch.

As he sat on a hard rock, waiting for the soup—that was more water than anything else—to boil, he spotted a figure coming from afar. He squinted against the light but couldn't make out who it was. Only when the figure was closer did he realize it was his brother.

"Johnny," Richard greeted him when he was closer. He was dressed to work.

"Go away," Johnny said. He didn't want him invading the last refuge he had. The young man took a few steps towards him.

"Listen. I want to help," he started, but his brother interrupted him.

"Go away! I don't care!"

Richard's eyes grew wetter, but Johnny wasn't moved. He didn't want him there. This was *his* place. He saw Richard turning his eyes away in guilt, and he thought that it was good that he was feeling guilt. Maybe next time he wouldn't be so lazy. Though there wouldn't be a next time, would there? They had only one father.

"I quit school," he muttered. "I want to help our family."

"Even if you find twenty ounces of gold, it still won't help the family. Mother will just buy more wine," Johnny said bitterly. "Mark will still go out with holes in his clothes."

"That's another reason," Richard added. "I can't stay at home anymore. You of all people should understand. You're running away from her, too."

Johnny shook his head, his eyes flashing with rage. He wouldn't let him get take advantage of his compassion.

"You won't come here," he told him. "Go work the creek when you don't want to stay in the house. Take Mark. Do whatever you want, but you won't come here."

"Alright," Richard muttered. He passed Johnny, took a pan, and hurried away.

Johnny spit after him, then stood, his appetite gone, and went back under the earth.

Over the next few days, Johnny saw Richard every morning, hurrying to the creek to work with his pan. He didn't know what he ate, though he probably took a few bites of half-prepared food from the house, just like Johnny did. During the weekends, he saw Mark coming with him, probably to hide from their mother.

The few days that Johnny went home, he saw his mother drunk. After dark, she would grab a bottle, and drink until she slept. During the day she would do a couple of things around the house, make sure her sons or herself wouldn't starve, but then, she would go back inside her bottle.

Johnny understood that completely, though. She and Mick had been married for decades. And they had uprooted themselves and come here a year back, for a better life. And yet, the only thing Mick had found was his death.

As soon as that thought hit him, he threw his pickaxe away. Mick had only found his death in the mines. There was nothing for Johnny here but the same fate. He didn't want to die in the dark, looking for gold dust to feed his family. Maybe the mine was cursed, or maybe his family was cursed, but he wanted to leave, to go as far away from it as possible.

Mark hurried to school. He was late once again, because his mother hadn't woken him, nor had she made him any breakfast. Or any lunch for that matter. He took some stale bread and ate it on the way.

He missed his father terribly and understood his mother's feelings. She was probably missing him even more. But she made the house a bad place to be. Mark couldn't stand the voice she had when she was drunk. It made him angry, disappointed, and sad.

And his brothers weren't doing any better either. Richard cried every day and Johnny wasn't helping him, wasn't telling him what he needed to hear. They were both stupid. Their father was gone. Didn't they have a duty now to the family? Instead of following their duty, they behaved like their mother. Drunk, but with sadness, not with wine—but drunk nonetheless.

Mark, with nothing else to do, had explored the area with Bosco, though he enjoyed his little secret space the most. And he hated school. The other kids picked on him, because he was still smaller, and they made him angry. He didn't like being angry.

When he arrived at the school, he saw Bob, a known bully. The boy was bigger than the rest and bullied everyone. He had his own little group of boys, and they all feared him. Mark went the long way around the school to avoid Bob, but the older boy saw him and called out. Mark didn't hear what the bully was saying, so he chose to ignore him and went straight for the school door.

But he found three boys standing between himself and the door. He felt angry. Why did they pick on him? Didn't they have anything better to do?

"Hey, it's Mark the Crybaby," Bob shouted when he was nearer. He was the one who had coined the nickname. Mark, the day after his father's funeral, had cried when another boy asked where he had gone the previous day.

"Please, let me enter," Mark said between clenched teeth.

"Please, let me enter," Bob repeated in a mocking voice, then mimicked a crying gesture, making loud whining noises like a little baby.

Mark's frustration grew. He was angry at his mother for not being a mother. Angry at his brothers for not being brothers. And now he was angry at Bob and his soldiers for not allowing him to enter the school.

"I don't want to hurt you," he muttered, and ignored Bob's mocking voice, instead trying to push through the boys blocking the entrance. They shoved him back, and he fell. He stood up, hands trembling. Not from sadness, but from rage. His vision was cloudy, and he felt his blood boiling.

"You can't hurt me, little crybaby," Bob said, towering over him. "You're nothing but a bug."

Mark let out a scream then, frustration boiling over. The pure rage contained in the scream made the other boys stumble a step back, but Bob stared him down. He was a tough boy, but Mark wasn't seeing Bob. He was seeing his mother and his brothers. His punch found Bob's cheek, and he stumbled. Mark saw the boy's face change from the proud mask of arrogance to a scary visage, like a monster. He screamed back and returned the punch.

The punch that he returned made Mark fall back, but it was followed by more. Punches and kicks found his stomach, back, and head. He felt pain piercing through him. He tried to kick back and heard a boy shout, then kicked some more.

Only the teachers finally managed to separate the boys, and they all were cradling the bloody markings of a serious fight. Mark had taken the worst of it and the teachers had him go back to his house with strong recommendations to see the doctor. Mark knew, though, that his mother would barely notice his bloody face. He dragged his feet back and when he entered, verified his mother was passed out on the couch, hangover or still drunk, and he retreated to his room, passing out on the bed.

CHAPTER FIVE

Johnny opened his eyes, staring at the wooden ceiling of his room. He stayed like that for a while, slowly returning to reality after a fitful dream. He had dreamed of working in the mine with his father when an earthquake hit, and they rushed up. Johnny had left the mine just in time before it collapsed, but he hadn't seen his father anywhere. He had searched frantically before he woke up feeling more tired that he had before he slept.

The day before, he had felt something change inside him. And now, as he laid on the bed, staring up, he couldn't even imagine going back to the mine. He wouldn't go. There was nothing for him there but death. And there was something else burning in his mind. Despite Christina's insistence, he was still thinking of the army. He felt he had a duty, and he felt he could help. He had skills rare in the wider world, from working in the mines the last year that he had been here with his family.

He slowly got up from the bed and tidied it up. He organized his room quickly, threw away what little garbage had gathered from his last few nightmarish days, and then got dressed. He took his small bag and left the house without checking in on his mother, who he spotted was sleeping on the couch, nor on his brothers, who had the doors to their rooms closed. He took the road to Bendigo.

"Will you fight now or wait for this?" a poster asked. It displayed an army of gray-dressed German soldiers, everyone looking the same, pointing their rifles at a distressed-looking young man. An older man was lying dead on the ground already, and a woman was clinging onto one of the soldiers' feet, crying and begging for her life. A barn was on fire in the background.

The poster was hanging on the wall behind a small table in one of Bendigo's streets. Two men were sitting on chairs, looking bored. They were dressed in their uniforms, brown and green, and Johnny saw that one of them was higher-ranked than the other one, at least judging from the amount of insignia on his shoulder and breast.

He approached the desk and the two soldiers looked up.

"Good morning, mate," the higher-ranked one spoke first. "Ready to fight for your country?"

"I've been ready for a while," Johnny muttered then nodded.

"Here," the soldier passed him a form. "Write down a few details, and you'll be fighting the Germans in no time."

Johnny took the form but noticed that the division he would applying for was the infantry.

"Is only the infantry looking for recruits?" he asked.

"You'll get accepted there the easiest, mate," the other soldier said. "You need to pass evaluations for the others."

"I thought the 175th tunneling company was looking for replacements to help in France," Johnny said. He opened his bag and got out a newspaper page, which had a full-page article on the creation of the Australian Tunneling companies. He laid it on the desk. "I want to join the 175th tunneling company," he said.

The two men exchanged a look, and then looked back at Johnny. "You think you have what it takes to be underground, near enemy forces, without seeing the sun for that long?" the officer said. "It's hard on the nerves, mate."

"I've been working in my father's gold mine. I know how to dig and how to move underground, and I don't have a problem with confined spaces," Johnny said. The two men exchanged a few quiet words, and then retrieved another form.

"We'll get you in the 175th tunneling company, then. They're already in France, so you'll be shipped out to basic training very soon."

Johnny smiled widely and took the form. As he wrote down his name and some other details, he looked up again. "When?"

"The next train is leaving on the first week of June. Wednesday. Get ready and say your goodbyes," the officer replied, and Johnny nodded. He wasn't planning on saying any goodbyes, though.

They gave him a list of a few things he should get, and he left quickly. After a few quick stops, he returned home. He would quietly settle a few debts with what little gold he had remaining, and he would get his affairs in order, then leave.

The one thing he wanted to do was write Christina a letter. He took a piece of paper and a pen and stared at the empty page for a while before putting any words down.

He didn't know how much time had passed before he had written the first word, but when he did, the words came haltingly and uncertainly. He didn't want to waste any paper or ink, so he paused and stared at the first few lines for a while. Finally, he finished the letter quickly. It read:

My dear Christina,

By the time this letter reaches you, I will be on my way to France. I couldn't stand working in the mine anymore.

I love you and I will miss you. You will be in my thoughts always. Take care of yourself, and your family.

Yours,

Johnny Hoagland

It was a simple letter, and he was a simple man. Or at least that's what he told himself as he wrote down Christina's address on the envelope to take it to the post office the day before he left. He felt the words weren't enough, but he couldn't find the right words inside him. He was filled with a mix of excitement and dread, finally going to fight the Germans, but on the other hand, leaving behind everything he loved.

Which, if he was honest to himself, was Christina. There was nothing for him in the mine, there was nothing for him in his own house. The distance that already existed between his mother and himself had grown with the death of his father, and his brothers were each in their own little worlds. And they were young. He had to provide for them, and this was the best way he could think of.

Going away was the best possible decision, he told himself once again. He had been thinking about it for so long, and he wanted to go. There was nothing for him here.

He mailed the letter in the evening before he left. He settled everything that he could settle, even drafted a simple will as the head of the house, after his father's death. He asked the post office lady, a woman who knew his mother, to tell his mother that he had gone to France if she saw her over the next few days.

Johnny doubted that his family would realize he was gone, though, for quite a while. His brothers would probably be the first to wonder, and they wouldn't ask their mother; she was too lost in the booze to reply, and they knew it. Johnny thought that they would realize what had happened when the first paycheque would arrive. He would ask the army to send back most of his pay. Depending on his circumstances, he would keep the least he could.

But as luck would have it, Johnny's letter left the post office on that very night. By the next day, it was in Christina's hands. She cried when she read it, but before she could think, she put it away and ran out the house. She arrived at Bendigo train station to see, in her relief, a line of scared-looking men ready to board. Among them, she spotted Johnny. She ran to him, pushing aside the ticket lady.

"What do you think you're doing?" she shouted, her voice raising over the noise of the station. Johnny stared at her dumbly. He didn't know how to react. "Did you really believe—" she started, then a hand grabbed her arm. She turned angrily to see an army officer looking at her sternly, though he had understanding in his eyes.

"You're getting in the way, lady." He looked at Johnny. "Take this elsewhere." Johnny nodded quickly and took Christina further down the platform, away from the people getting in and out the station. He opened his mouth to speak but Christina interrupted him.

"Did you really believe I'd let you leave like that?" she told him. Her eyes shone with her rage, and Johnny saw that she was trembling.

"I—" Johnny started, then Christina spoke over him.

"I know you can't *unenlist* now," she said. Her voice was still loud enough to carry, and Johnny could swear that everyone was staring at them. "But I won't let you go if you don't marry me now."

Johnny stared at her with surprise. He did want to marry her, but he had wanted to do it afterwards, when he was more certain of what his future would hold.

"There's no priest——" he muttered, but then she pointed at a man further back.

"There's one there," she said. Johnny turned to see a man in clerical clothes, probably a chaplain judging from the insignia on the robe. The man was staring back, a mix of enjoyment and apprehension on his face. Johnny realized they had the attention of the whole train station, with dozens of eyes on them.

"C'mon mate," one of the newly enlisted men from the train shouted. "Do the right thing!"

Another man joined him. "Get on with it!" he shouted. "There's Germans to kill!"

"Yeah, mate," a third one added. "Do it or she'll find someone better while you're away!"

Suddenly, everyone was shouting their piece of mind, and Johnny was overwhelmed. But he did want to marry Christina. As he remained frozen in place, Christina, smiling widely from what she perceived as encouragement by the others, marched towards the chaplain.

"I am Christina Digby, and that man isn't going to get on board unless he has married me. Can you marry us, father?"

The man nodded, a wide smile on his own face. He followed her back to where Johnny was standing, having regained some of his composure.

Johnny took Christina's hands, and amidst the shouts of the other enlisted and the various train passengers, married Christina on the Bendigo train station platform. He didn't even hear the words the chaplain spoke, he just spoke his agreement in a clear voice and kissed her at the end. Christina, now of the Hoagland family, kissed him back and they held each other tightly for a long moment before thanking the priest, who left them alone. Most of the passengers returned to their business, their interest quenched.

After they released each other from the hug, they stayed there, eyes and hands locked.

"That doesn't mean I want you to go," Christina said, her eyes filling with tears she had managed to hold back but were now overflowing.

"I know," was all Johnny could manage to say, choking a bit himself.

"Recruit Hoagland," they heard an officer shouting. Both turned to see that all the enlisted had boarded, and the train station was almost empty. "Get on board," the man ordered. "You'll write to your missus when you get to training."

Embarrassed, Johnny nodded, and turned back to Christina.

"I love you," was all he managed, and kissed her deeply to a few jeers from the train. Then, he held her tightly for a long moment, looked at her eyes again, and before he could think more on that, before he could regret it, he boarded the train. He got on it quickly and found a seat, then looked out the window to see Christina. She was obviously holding back more tears, and he felt his own eyes growing wetter.

Thankfully, the train left shortly after, and Johnny was left alone with his thoughts.

CHAPTER SIX

Johnny stared hard at the items before him. He didn't recognize the use of all of them, but he saw he had the materials to build half a tent, he saw uniforms, he saw many tools. Cleaning tools, sewing tools, even cooking tools. Everything was made to be carried in a backpack he was issued. The quartermaster had been strict when he gave Johnny the items, ordering the young man to take great care of them. He'd take them to war, and his life would depend on their condition.

He looked around quickly. Thirty men from all over Australia with equally apprehensive looks on their faces, and gear similar to his own before them. They were in a giant barn, which was recently remade into a training area. There were chairs nearby, and more desks.

Johnny felt somewhat disappointed as they were still in Australia, since he wanted to see France. They had taken them to what he guessed was a rich man's estate, which was probably either commandeered or donated to the army. They were stationed away from the enlisted training to join the infantry, and Johnny couldn't understand why. Wouldn't they all be soldiers in the end? Didn't he need to know how to use the gun, or how to march, or do other infantry things?

All recruits that wanted to join the tunneling company were with him, and he was surprised at how many they were. But then again, many families worked in mines like his own. His thoughts were interrupted when a man entered the barn, screaming even before he had passed through the doorframe.

"Recruits!" he screamed. "Stop wasting my time and gather your things! Gather around now!" Johnny was surprised at the volume of the man's voice. As he gathered his things, he wondered if the army promoted to officers judging by the aspirant officer's maximum voice volume. He was one of the first to pack his gear tightly, and he stood before the man. Judging from his insignia, he was a sergeant.

The sergeant's face was red from shouting, and he kept shouting at the recruits who were taking more time to pack. He approached them and shouted, right by their head. The poor men were probably close to losing hearing from that ear.

When they finally gathered together, the sergeant ordered them to put the bags on their backs and follow him. They moved out of the barn and walked through the estate into a large open area.

"Set up your tents, two men per tent," he screamed again, and stood there overseeing their preparations. He commented often and brutally, even disassembling a few tents and asking the men to reassemble them correctly. At the end, he never looked satisfied, but told them it would be enough. By the time they had assembled the tents, the sun was already setting, and the sergeant ordered the men to sleep.

As he said it, a smile spread over his face, though Johnny saw it lacked any warmth. "Sleep, because you will need all the rest you can get," he said, and Johnny could swear there was an evil note in the man's voice. He huddled in his tent, under the blankets, but sleep eluded him for quite some time, and he knew that the man lying next to him was going through the same thing.

He turned and tossed, and it was obvious to Johnny that the man sharing his tent wasn't used to sleeping on the ground. The cold weather was piercing through the blankets, and Johnny longed for the warmth of the fire. He felt like he wanted to hug a burning log, just to push the cold out of his body.

When Johnny finally felt like he was falling asleep, a loud voice brought him out.

"Get up, ladies," the sergeant called, holding a lamp. "It's four in the morning, get up!'

Johnny followed the other man out. They were both shivering from the cold. It was July, and being up the hills didn't help, either.

"Get washed, get shaved, and be here in an hour."

"Where will we get washed?" a man dared to ask.

"How will we heat the water?" another added.

"No fire, no heat," the sergeant said. "There's a creek there," he pointed. "And you have been issued buckets."

Johnny heard a few men muttering curses under their breaths, but none dared oppose the mad sergeant further.

"What are you waiting for, ladies? Do you want me to hold your hands?" the sergeant screamed, his face getting red again. The men rushed back in their tents to look for shaving razors, lights, and the bucket. Then, they all hurried down the hill towards where the sergeant had pointed them.

Johnny was dressed in multiple layers and he was still cold. He couldn't even begin to imagine how cold the creek's water would be, or how cold the air would feel against his bare skin. Bathing in such conditions sounded like a nightmare. And yet, he found the creek and set about disrobing, like all the rest.

Using the bucket, he washed his face, his teeth chattering. Then, he quickly washed the dirtiest parts of his body. He didn't dare immerse himself in the creek, and no one else did either. He even saw a few of the men only washing their faces and nothing else.

His hands were numb as he shaved, and he didn't even feel his skin getting nicked, only saw a point of blood on the blade. He didn't care, and the horrifyingly cold water of the creek stopped the bleeding immediately.

By five o'clock, they had gathered in three lines, facing east, under the directions of the mad sergeant.

"Ladies, I am your platoon sergeant, and you'll know me as Sgt. Milat," the man said. Then, he pointed at another man next to him. "This is your basic training platoon commander. His name is lieutenant John Kelly."

Lt. Kelly started speaking then, taking a step forward.

"Recruits, I will be in charge of your training," the man said. Johnny felt a smidgen of relief, as the man seemed more stable than the sergeant. "The 175th Tunneling Company has important and demanding work. We can't have weaklings messing that up, nor can we have children who break down after a few days underground making the work harder for the rest of our soldiers. This training will be hell. We will weed out the weaklings, we will build up your stamina, and we will teach you how to be useful to your country and to our allies."

Johnny felt more relief, though it was now mixed with apprehension. The man made sense, but logic wouldn't make the next few weeks any easier.

"After your training is done," Lt. Kelly continued, "you will join the 175th Tunneling Company in France, already working there underground. Any questions?"

No one raised their hand. Besides, it was too early to have questions. Most of the men looked half-asleep to Johnny, despite the cold bath and the sergeant's shouts.

"Good. Sgt. Milat?" Lt. Kelly said, and the sergeant went to the side. He took a deep breath and then started shouting.

"Let's start, ladies," Sg. Milat called and started running in place. "Let's pump some blood in those cold feet of yours." Then, he started running, and Johnny and the rest followed suit, the lieutenant following them from the side, observing and assessing them as they ran. Soon, Johnny was getting winded and was impressed when he saw that the officers were keeping pace excellently.

They ran for several miles cross-country as the sun's first light was breaking through the darkness of the night. The run was doing a great job at dispelling the cold that had crept inside Johnny's body from his bath, but his feet were in more pain with every mile.

"Halt!" Sgt. Milat shouted at some point, and Johnny was glad for the break. He put his hands on his knees as many others, and took deep breaths, feeling as if there was not enough air to quench his needs.

"Don't stand around," another shout came from the sergeant. "We take breaks like this," he added, and fell into a pushup position, arms supporting his body up in an angle with the ground. Some men groaned, but they complied quickly. After a couple of minutes, one of the men fell, his arms unable to support himself.

Sgt. Milat stood and approached him. When he was right above him, he lowered his face and screamed right on the recruit's own face. "Did I say you can take a nap? Give me twenty pushups right now." As the man hurried to comply, the sergeant stood up straight again and looked around angrily. He pointed at two other men.

"Your form is off. Give me ten," he called and observed them force themselves to do a full pushup, despite the tiredness that Johnny was sure they were feeling.

The sergeant gave two more guys pushups to do and then ordered everyone up. "Sleepy-time is over, ladies," he called and started running again. The recruits followed, and Johnny could hear many of them breathing hard. He was wondering how he would manage it when he realized they were running back. The lieutenant and the sergeant had turned them around, back towards the encampment.

Johnny forced the despair out of his mind and focused on the ground. The time it took them to arrive at the encampment felt like an eternity, but when they saw their tents, Johnny realized that the sun had yet to appear in the sky. It was significantly lighter, though. He guessed they had spent about two hours running in total.

The sergeant had them stand in three rows again. "Wash up. Take every chance to wash up you can get. Then, change into your fighting gear. Come to the quartermaster, today you'll be getting your rifles and you'll be starting your classes." Some men's faces lit up at that, though Johnny wasn't all that excited. He didn't really like guns.

The water at the creek wasn't any hotter, since the sun's rays had yet to touch it, but as their own bodies were significantly hotter after two hours of running, it was easier to wash up. They quickly complied with the sergeant's orders and changed into their gear, then hurried to the quartermaster. The lieutenant was waiting for them outside the building.

As they lined to get their guns, the lieutenant spoke to them seriously.

"You will be given the Lee Enfield .303. The gun you will each be given will be yours. From that moment onwards, you will be the only one responsible for the weapon. It should be at perfect condition, at all times. I don't care how far you think yourself from the fighting, your weapon is your life.

"It will be inspected, and you will be punished severely if something is amiss." He paused, observing the recruits getting their brown rifles. When everyone was holding one, some awkwardly and others with more certainty like Johnny, he gestured for them to follow him. "Come. First class will be held in a few minutes."

They entered in an auxiliary building of the estate to see long tables and Sgt. Milat holding a weapon like theirs. Johnny felt as if the sergeant's weapon was shining much more fiercely than their own, as if it was in pristine condition, having been received the day before. The sergeant pointed at a few items arrayed before him on the table.

"Get those out of your gear," he ordered, without any introduction. The recruits did so, arraying them carefully. Then, the sergeant showed them how they disassemble and reassemble the weapon, where they needed to clean it, what needed oiling, and many other details that Johnny tried his best to remember. Then, he had them all mimic him, walking between their tables. Every mistake was rewarded with five to twenty pushups, depending on its severity, and by the end of the class, they had learned the basics of maintaining the weapon, one way or another.

Then, he had them all ran with the weapon and their kit, and after a long hour of running, he had them go once more through the maintenance procedure. Johnny saw how much dust had gathered in it after just an hour and was horrified with the idea of the gun's state after a full day of activities.

"If I see even one mote of dust in it," the sergeant screamed at them, "you'll deeply regret it. Get cleaning!"

On the next morning, they repeated the previous day's run, but they did it with their guns as well. The run was harder because of the added weight, and he was still tired from the day before, as Johnny hadn't been able to sleep well on the ground in the incredible July cold. The freezing-cold water of the creek had woken him up barely enough to shave and get dressed.

They ran and ran, until they were exhausted, and then they ran some more. Johnny felt as if the sergeant had made them run more than yesterday, but he had no way to measure it, as the estate was still unknown to him. When they arrived at the camp again, they were barely standing up, and it was just a few minutes past seven in the morning. They still had a full day ahead of them, something that filled Johnny with dread.

After their wash, they set about cleaning their weapons as well as they could, without comfortable tables to lay on, and without guidance. After two hours of running, there was dust everywhere, and the lack of places to put things on made everything ten times more difficult, especially considering it was the first time they did it without observation. Right after Johnny had finished maintaining his gun, he heard the now familiar screaming of the sergeant.

"Gather round, ladies. Let me see your kits!"

The sergeant carefully examined their weapons and their tents. Johnny jumped at the volume behind the scream he directed at a recruit.

"What is this?" He was pointing at something. Johnny dared to take a couple of steps and crane his neck and saw that many did the same. The sergeant was pointing at a gun barrel, and its owner was trembling, too scared to answer. Johnny realized there was a cotton swab there, one of those they had been issued to clean the barrels, a long four-inch stick with a tiny bit of cotton on the end.

"If you were to fire the gun, do you know what would have happened?" the sergeant kept screaming. "Do you even begin to understand how important cleaning your gun is? Do you believe that when you are tunneling under the German's feet, they will happily allow you eight hours of sleep, time to shave and bathe, and then some time to clean your gun and the rest of your kit from the hellish dust in the rocky French ground?"

The recruit didn't speak, he had been left utterly dazed by the volume of the sergeant.

"I am speaking to you!" the man said, and the recruit was forced to shake his head vigorously. "That's right, they won't! You will be getting barely three hours of sleep, you will be digging all day, and you will be fighting for your life! And if you shot this gun, you'd suffer more damage than the enemy!"

The sergeant then turned to the rest of the recruits. "As punishment, you will all march for a bit," he said.

"How long is a 'bit?" Johnny heard a recruit ask another in a low voice, but the sergeant heard them and turned to face the two of them fully.

"A measly ten kilometers. Ready, start!"

The march was so hard that Johnny could feel his feet blistering more with each step. Their new boots weren't yet broken into, and each step brought pain along with it. The sergeant and the lieutenant seemed relaxed enough throughout the ordeal, pushing them to march in better formation, to keep their back straight, and a myriad of other things that Johnny could barely pay any attention to.

Then came more classes and more endurance training. When they were back to the camp, most of the day had passed. The recruits fell on the ground, exhausted, and some pulled off their boots. Johnny had been looking forward to removing his boots for some time, and when he finally did, he thought it would feel relieved. But as he pulled off the shoe, little pieces of skin followed. The blisters and the blood had fused his skin with their socks and the boots' leather, and it was excruciatingly painful to remove them.

The sergeant observed them, seeing them groan and gasp in pain.

"Soak them in water," he said after some time. Johnny, eager for a solution, turned his eyes to the sergeant, and saw that all the recruits, to the last one, focused completely on the man.

"Soak the boots in water and walk around in them without the laces done. It'll help loosen them up and get molded to your feet." Johnny could swear there was a hint of empathy in the man's voice, but it quickly vanished. "Get started, get washed, and rest. You won't have such luxuries in France." He left them and most of the soldiers hurried to their feet amidst groans and rushed to the creek. They spent some time doing exactly as the sergeant had suggested, before washing up and hiding in their tents to escape the brutal cold of the Australian winter.

As the sun hid behind the mountains, it grew unbearably cold. Johnny put on his woolen socks, even though his feet hurt and protested, and he laid back down. He huddled under the blanket and wished he had a burning log to hug.

The sergeant's shouts woke them up the next day and they started preparing for the day ahead. As Johnny removed his woolen socks that had proven so helpful during the night, he realized that the blood from his blisters had dried and fused with the socks again. As he removed them, the wounds opened. Judging from the groans he heard around the camp, he was not the only one in that condition.

They washed up, got dressed, and started running. During their run, Johnny's wounds rubbed against the boots, sending jabs of pain up his legs. He tried his best to ignore it and after a while it was a dull ache that stayed with him but at least it didn't make his eyes tear up.

After their run and their washing up, the sergeant took them to another support building. As Johnny followed the sergeant in, he saw chairs and other soldiers standing behind them. The sergeant had a few of them, along with Johnny, sit on the chairs, and the soldiers got working on their hair. When they were done, Johnny and the rest had a buzzcut so low that there was barely any hair on their head. Not that he minded; the only advantage hair had offered was a little bit of protection against the cold, but even that was lost when they were drenched in sweat.

The sergeant took them out again then. "I discovered something yesterday," he screamed at them. "You march like you haven't walked in your life before. I will need to teach you to walk, it seems." He had them march up and down the yard, shouting more instructions. After a while, they were drenched in sweat, little pieces of their recently cut hair along with the salty sweat making their eyes tear up, their feet hurting after their blisters had their own blisters, and the sergeant screaming for them to stop was like a divine choir of angels in their ears.

Johnny and the rest were taken to the barn. "Your clothes are an important part of your equipment," Lt. Kelly told them. "You'll be caring for them out in France, and you need to sew your nametags on them yourselves." The lieutenant showed them where they would sew on the tags. "The leather items are to be marked with ink." Again, he showed them where to mark. "If you think sewing is women's work," he said to a few jeers, "think again. There won't be your lovely wives or girlfriends or mums up in the trenches. You have to cook, you have to sew, you have to take care of your items, or you'll die a quick death."

When they marched back to their encampment, the sergeant went through their tents. "Your tents are messy," he screamed, pointing at a tent that Johnny could only describe as pristine. "This is unacceptable. Your kit must be squared away, everything perfectly ready to be grabbed at a moment's notice!" He walked over to one of the worst ones. "What is this?" he pointed. "Do you think this is a tent?" He pushed at a flap and the tent fell apart. He pulled the tent sides and started throwing stuff away. "Do you call this an organized tent?"

Then, he straightened up, and waved at one of his corporals. The man hurried to him. "Do you see that tent?" he pointed. The corporal nodded. "It's abhorrent to my eyes." The corporal hurried to it and mimicked the sergeant's dismantling it, to two recruits' groans. Sgt. Milat had a couple other soldiers dismantle more tents, before having the recruits line up.

"So, ladies, you have your orders. Today is sewing day. Go and prepare your things. We'll march some more in the evening." He left with quick steps, leaving the recruits to their sewing. Johnny was glad to be doing that instead of running around the estate, as he felt his feet were in a horrible condition. He had never gone through that before, and he feared that his feet would be ruined forever. The evening's march was no less tiring. At the end of that day, he tried to do more of what the sergeant had suggested, to make his boots easier on his feet. He hoped it would soon prove useful because he didn't know for how long he could take it.

As they were packing up to go to sleep, the sergeant appeared and started shouting about surprise inspections. Some recruits were already sleeping, and Johnny was tending to his feet. They all stood up quickly, and he heard other recruits throw quick kicks to the sleepers. Two tents were dismantled under Sgt. Milat's orders, and the poor recruits spent a good hour trying to put their things back together according to the order drilled into their heads by the sergeant.

By the end of the week, Johnny was stiff and sore everywhere on his body. His feet had thankfully been hardened enough to avoid bleeding every day, and he was slowly getting used to the hard earth, but he was still trying to adjust psychologically. He could see it in everyone's eyes. There was always a note of apprehension there, the same one he felt.

Here, there was no "tomorrow" or "next week", there was only "now." There was no sense in making plans when he didn't even know when he would have lunch. The sergeant was constantly pushing them, keeping them on their feet, never letting them have their guard down. It was a world completely divorced from the one he usually lived in, where he had a clearer idea of what the next day would hold.

They were expected to be ready to go at any moment. Sgt. Milat would appear and order them for a quick run as they were settling in to sleep, or he would tell them they could rest for a few hours, and then come only minutes later to make them do a march. There was no true rest at any point, and the stress was getting to them. They had even gone for runs in the middle of the night.

That day, Sgt. Milat woke them up even earlier than usual. "Get up, ladies," he shouted, walking among their tents. "Today's a special day."

Johnny got dressed quickly and was one of the first to line up in the dark, facing the sergeant. The rest of the recruits gathered, and the man started speaking.

"Today, you'll be making your obstacle course. The lieutenant will show you the log pile, and I will be showing you where to dig and where to put the logs. But we don't like slackers, as you well know," he added, and Johnny heard a few silent groans, "so if you take too much time to bring the logs, you'll be doing leg raises holding the logs, or some more running holding them up. I will personally make sure all of you are on time," he said finally, before turning to walk away. The recruits followed him through the estate.

They walked to a large area that had been cleared from trees. The sergeant pointed at deeper in the woods, where Johnny could see a path through the trees.

"The log pile is that way," he said, and Lt. Kelly motioned for the recruits to follow. They walked in a comfortable pace, and when they arrived at the stacks of logs, Johnny thought they had been walking for about fifteen minutes. Then, they walked back to the obstacle course area, ignoring the logical argument of some recruits to take a batch of logs with them.

When they arrived at the cleared area again, they found the sergeant and a couple of corporals sitting on a log, each holding a clipboard to measure their times.

"Did you enjoy your walk?" the sergeant said sarcastically. "You will have ten minutes to go each way. Twenty minutes in total to go and bring a log here." Some people started complaining, but a look from the sergeant silenced them immediately. "You know what happens if you don't. Go." And with that, they were off.

To fulfil the time limit, they would have to run, once empty-handed, and then carrying the log, Johnny realized. He prepared himself mentally for another tough day and started running. He tried to keep a good and quick pace, so that he would have to exert himself less when he would be returning while carrying the log.

He was one of the first to arrive at the log pile, having left more than half of the recruits behind. One corporal was there, but Johnny didn't have the time to examine what the man did. He grabbed a log and hurried back. When he arrived, he was about to set off again, when the sergeant stopped him.

"First you have to place it," he shouted to him and another recruit who had arrived first. "Take a shovel from there," he pointed at a log that had some shovels placed on it, and Johnny grabbed one quickly. "Then dig there," he told Johnny, "and you there," he told the other recruit, pointing. Johnny hurried to the spot the sergeant had indicated and started digging, pacing himself. He tried to do it quickly enough to appease the sergeant, but slow enough to get his breath back.

As he dug, he momentarily thought of home, of when he used to do work for Christina's father on the farm. He dispelled the thoughts to avoid getting too emotional and kept digging. The sergeant then showed him how to shove the log inside the ground, and then pile the ground back in. Then, Johnny was off again.

It took three trips before he grew too tired. Then, it took him one minute longer to return with the log. The sergeant had him stop immediately.

"Twenty leg raises," the man shouted, and Johnny put the log against his feet, and started to do the exercise. After five repetitions, his abdomen was killing him. He managed to complete all twenty without dropping the log, and he stood, trying to keep his hands on the side and his body erect even though he just wanted to lie down and rest for a few hours.

"Dig there," the sergeant told him and turned his attention to other recruits that had come late. "Thirty leg raises, it's your second time you're late," he told someone else, and Johnny heard the groans from afar.

The sun was shining brightly, doing little to dispel the cold, when they brought them their breakfast. Sgt. Millat gave them half an hour to eat, and then they resumed their work. Johnny was late twice more, and by the time he had finished the last set of punishment exercises, his stomach was about to spill forth its contents. He put more effort into running to avoid having to do the exercises again and vomiting on the ground, and probably getting punished even harder for that.

After many more trips—Johnny lost count—they called a break for lunch, which was again brought to them. Johnny had no idea how far away they were from the main buildings, but it was probably a few kilometers at least. Then, more wood hauling and more hole digging followed, until it was getting dark again. And then, finally, Johnny arrived at the wood pile to see less than ten logs waiting. He grabbed one and returned, having found a good rhythm by now, and started digging where he was directed. He saw Lt. Kelly coming and talking with the sergeant, telling him that there was no more wood.

"Great," the sergeant said and turned to the recruits. They gathered around him, a hopeful light in their eyes, waiting to hear the words they longed for. Instead, the sergeant smiled his evil smile.

"Now, the wire obstacles," he said. Most were too tired to groan and just obliged, getting the gloves and cutters offered by the corporals. They set to work, putting wire between logs, nailing supports, measuring distances. Johnny finished and joined them, focusing on handling wire, which was something he had some experience doing.

It was tiring work, and while it was certainly less tiring than hauling wood, it was exhausting to do after having hauled wood for most of the day. When the sergeant called for an hour-long break for dinner, Johnny was deeply pleased for the rest. They would have to jog back to the main building and return afterwards, but at least they would get a longer break.

The hour passed quicker than it should, and they returned to work. Johnny focused all his remaining energy on it, and at some point, they were finally done. It was after nine in the evening when they returned to their tents, but the day was far from done.

Johnny first hurried to wash himself. The creek's water would be still a little warmer than usual from the sun's light, and it would only get colder, since that light was vanishing. He knew that it was still too cold, and felt his skin prickle up as he splashed it against him. He washed the dust and sweat away, carefully washing only where he needed to. Then, he hurried back to his tent. Everything would be inspected in the morning, and he had no intention of doing pushups for having three motes of dust in his gun.

He disassembled his gun quickly and set about cleaning it. His eyes were heavy with exhaustion but seeing the weapon filthy with dust made him panic a little bit. If he missed even one nook, he'd be punished severely. He used his determination to work despite his sleepiness, brushing and cleaning furiously.

Out of the corner of his eyes, Johnny saw a similar scene playing out around him. He could see the other recruits dragging their feet, their movements sluggish, barely able to hold their eyes open, but forcing themselves out of pure willpower. Digging and setting up the obstacle course all day had been more exhausting than simply running around, and yet they were expected to have their kit and guns in pristine condition, everything orderly to perfection.

Johnny focused back on his work, cleaning the day's dirt from the barrel and the other little crannies of the wooden and metal gun. Then, he focused on his things. He had pulled off the pieces he had required for his river bath in a hurry earlier, and everything was in disarray. He threw a longing look to the woolen blankets, shivered from the cold, and started putting his things in order. Then, after he thought he was done, he imagined the sergeant over him and tried to see things as he would, which made him rearranged some of his things to better fit the officer's excessive demands.

It was midnight before he thought he could pass the inspection the next morning. He pulled the blankets around him quickly, stopping a shiver, and lied down to sleep. Even though he was terribly cold, exhaustion made sleep come easily.

Over the next days, they used the obstacle course to learn how to move like a foot soldier. Then, Sgt. Millat had them dig holes and short tunnels in various spots of the estate. Then, back at the obstacle course. It was clear to Johnny that the sergeant was observing them carefully, pushing them harder each day, so that they could reach their limits, and then go past them. He heard one of the other recruits call it "beasting", though Johnny hadn't heard the term.

Each day was more torturous, the inspections more careful and the punishments more severe. If someone had told Johnny what he would be going through, he wouldn't have thought himself able to do it, and yet, here he was. Jogging, digging, cleaning, keeping everything orderly, then doing it all over again under harsher conditions, under harsher threats, only to repeat the cycle again the next day.

The sergeant allowed them less sleep every day, barely four or five hours, and Johnny found himself falling asleep while eating a few times. But still he pushed through. On the end of every week, they would move their tents to another area, and the sergeant would time them as they unmade them and remade them. If someone was taking too long to pack up his tent, the sergeant would order him to stop, empty his bag, set up his tent, and then tear it down once more—and as many times as needed to reach his required time. If someone took too long to set it up later, the sergeant would dismantle it himself, and have the recruit redo it faster.

On the second week, it was time to use the weapons they had so meticulously cleaned over the previous days. Sgt. Millat had them clear up an area three hundred meters long. Then, they put up firing lines, which were raised mounds every hundred meters. They did the setting up as well as the firing in full combat gear, which was heavy and awkward to move in. Johnny persevered since he knew that war would be even less comfortable.

The thing Johnny liked the least was bayonet practice. Using parts of the obstacle course, they hung sandbags which they had to pierce while running through the whole course, in full gear, with helmets and everything. The sergeant insisted they screamed the whole way, and if someone was too quiet, he would do pushups in his battle gear, which was of course significantly more difficult than in their fatigues.

And during the night, a few hours after the sun had set so that the darkness was thick, the sergeant ordered them to get up and march. He took them through different paths every night, changing the course so that they wouldn't get used to it.

One night, Johnny saw one of the recruits suddenly vanish from sight. A couple of corporals rushed after him, following his shouts, to find him fallen in one of the trenches they had dug the previous day but hadn't refilled correctly. Johnny also rushed to the man, hoping to be of help, and saw that his leg was sticking out in a wrong corner. From his limited understanding of anatomy, Johnny thought the man had broken his femur. The entire group stopped their marching and the sergeant went through trench-digging procedures once more, even though they had already been taught how to dig, as punishment. They slept little that night.

Many of the recruits suffered injuries, usually from falls during the night marches, but also from many other activities. Nothing they did was safe. A few had to be taken off the training due to their injuries, and Johnny didn't know if the men were relieved or disappointed. Maybe both; they had invested time and effort in this, and to lose everything because of a fall felt silly and disheartening. So, Johnny, learning from their examples, redoubled his efforts in making sure he was careful where he stepped and managed to avoid any serious injuries.

Something he didn't expect was how hungry he was. Every time they ate, he was starving and would attack his food with the ferocity of a wild animal, and it would never be enough to completely satisfy him. Most of the time, he fell asleep hungry, he woke hungry, and he went through his day feeling his stomach grumbling. Every time he bathed, he saw that he was slowly losing weight, even if he was also building some muscle from all the training. Other recruits that had been slightly heavier than him had lost weight more obviously, the lines of their skulls more prominent behind their skin and muscles.

Everyone was looking worse for the wear, but Johnny kept telling himself that this was for a good cause. The soldier's salary was good, and they would be fighting against a horrible enemy. They were being useful in the greater scheme of things, and they were training to better themselves. No matter how many times he told himself that, though, his stomach kept grumbling.

"Good morning, Mrs. Hoagland," Christina said as she entered the living room. She found the woman lying on the couch, a bottle of booze empty next to her. She took it away, and then set about preparing a breakfast for the kids and herself. She knew that the woman would get up hours later, in search for more booze. At least Mrs. Hoagland wasn't opposed to Christina living here, since she was now a married woman. Not even her father had been opposed to it; after she told him Johnny had married her and he had gone off to war, he had softened up a lot. Christina only hoped it wasn't because he pitied her.

Richard came down early, like he had the days before. "Good morning," he muttered as he sat on the table. Christina stole a look at him and saw the usual despair in his eyes. It was hard being suddenly the head of the house with his father gone and his older brother off to the war.

Mark came down later. She had stayed up late tutoring him, so he looked tired, but he did make an effort to get up at a good hour. Richard ate quickly, then stood.

"Where are you going?" Mark asked in a small voice.

"To the mine," Richard muttered. "Found a creek bed that's dried up yesterday, I want to search through it."

"Take care," Mark said, and Christina echoed him. She put a small bundle on the table, which Richard took after throwing a tiny smile at her. She had packed him some food so that he had something to eat before dinner.

Christina saw that Mark stole a glance at his sleeping mother, then returned his eyes to his plate. Christina sat next to him, putting her hand on his.

"I miss dad," he muttered, low enough so that only she could hear him. She knew he wouldn't show this side to his mother or to Richard, as they had to be strong men, and not weak boys, even though both were barely old enough to qualify as boys. In Christina's eyes, even her beloved Johnny was just a boy, trying to take responsibility for things that shouldn't be his responsibility yet.

"I know," Christina replied. Then, she saw Mark looking at his mother again.

"She is so different now," he said. "After dad died, I think she died a little, too." Christina could do nothing but nod silently. Johnny had told her that their wedding had been rocky lately, but that didn't mean that Mrs. Hoagland didn't miss her husband.

"Everyone mourns their own way," she said after a long moment. "And you need to finish school. Are you ready for some studying before you go to school?" she tried to put a note of excitement in her voice even though she knew Mark didn't really like studying; was there a child who did? However, Mark smiled a little and nodded. Christina grew truly excited and got up to bring him his books.

When Richard arrived at the claim, he went the long way around to avoid stepping too near the entrance. He didn't even look at it. He didn't like doing that because his imagination often provided the details according to what Johnny had told him. He hurried to the dried creek and worked the pebbles away carefully, shoveling away what he had already searched through. He found no shiny dust that would indicate the presence of gold, but he had much more to look through.

As he searched, he suddenly remembered that Johnny had mentioned something about Faiz-ul going to look for gold with him. Maybe he could ask him to come.

When the sun was at its highest point, he paused to nibble through what Christina had so thoughtfully packed for him, then returned to looking through rocks until it was dark. When he couldn't see anymore, he hurried home.

The next day, he rushed to the hardware store just as they opened.

"Hey Faiz-ul," he muttered and approached the man. Faiz-ul returned his greeting. "I was thinking," Richard started, hesitated for a moment, and then resumed, "would you like to come with me at the river that passes through my fath—my family's claim?" he corrected himself. "There should be some gold if we panned together."

Faiz-ul stared at Richard for a few moments. "Why me?" he asked. Richard could detect that there were many emotions behind the man's voice, but he didn't know exactly what. He smiled a little, then.

"Johnny told me you were a great cook!" he said. That had the result he wanted, and Faiz-ul laughed a little, and Richard joined, the ice broken.

"Sure, then," Faiz-ul said then. "But you'll have to promise me to take me inside the mine someday. I want to learn more about geology and how to mine underground. Would you teach me?"

Richard felt apprehension fill him quickly, as well as other emotions he had been pressing down these last few days. Despair, terror, loneliness.

"I, uh, I don't know much about blasting," he muttered. "I haven't used explosives much..." He felt a shiver run through him and tried to suppress all the images that his imagination conjured.

Faiz-ul understood instantly and felt bad for asking. He knew how the boy's father had died.

"Then, you could teach me some basics, right? How to use a pickaxe, what to look for when digging, how to make supports," he suggested, offering a few examples. He saw Richard relax, but there was still tension on his shoulders.

"Sure, I could do that," Richard said. "At some later day, though. Is that all right?"

Faiz-ul nodded, then hurried deeper in the store. He told his father something and when his father nodded, Faiz-ul returned to the front. "I can come," he said and followed Richard out of the store and up towards the Hoagland claim.

CHAPTER SEVEN

Veda came out of her mother's room with a wide smile on her face, and her father noticed it. He looked at her and she gestured with her head at the empty plate she was holding in her hands.

"Mother ate everything," she said, her eyes twinkling with excitement.

"Finally, after so many days," her father said, his own face breaking into a wide smile like his daughter's. Veda hurried to the sink, stepped on the stool, placed the plate inside, and ran some water over it. Then, she washed it with slow and careful motions, before placing it away to dry. She hurried to her father on light steps, the smile still on her face.

"That means mother's getting better, right?" she asked him, sitting next to him.

"The doctor told me she's making considerable progress," he said, though his own smile had gone. He was too worried about his wife to enjoy the simple victory. The time it was taking her to recover was feeling too long to him, and he missed hearing her laughter. But he turned to his daughter and forced a small smile on his face. "She'll be back up sooner than you think," he told her. "Before you even notice it."

"I caught one," Mark called out with such glee in his voice that Richard felt bad not having invited him to fish together before then. He removed the fish from the hook and turned to his brother. "Look, Richard, I caught a big one!" Richard smiled to his little brother and pointed at the bucked near their feet.

"Put it away and we'll have Christina make us a great big lunch when we get home," he told him, and Mark's smile widened even more.

They resumed their positions next to the river, staring off at the waters.

"Who's going to work in the mine now?" Mark asked after a while. Richard had been thinking the same thing for quite some time.

"I don't know," he muttered. And he didn't want to ask their mother, considering how she was.

"Who can we ask?" Mark said, echoing Richard's own thoughts. They stayed silent for a long while, when Richard had an idea.

"Uncle Jimmy must know," he said. "I'll write him a letter when we get back. Remind me if I forget," he told his brother, who nodded.

They fished for a while, and Mark caught more fish than Richard did. When they were satisfied it would last them a few days, they packed their equipment and started on the way home.

The first thing Richard did when he got home was to write the letter to their uncle. He tried to write as clearly and correctly as he could, even though it felt he still had some issues, and then he put the letter in his coat, the one he always wore out, to avoid forgetting it.

The next day, he made a quick stop at the post office and mailed it off, asking the attendant to write out his uncle's name so that he didn't make any mistakes on such an important part as the address label. He returned to the mine then, satisfied he was done with that, but dreading the reply.

What if the mine was no longer theirs? What if they were suddenly without work? What could two boys and a drunk mother do to eat and pay their bills?

"No, I don't plan to pay for repairs," the man was shouting at Mr. Ansari. He was pointing vigorously at the parked wagon behind him, outside the store. "I just bought it from you. There's no way I will pay to have it fixed." His face was a furious red, and Faiz-ul could see spittle jumping towards his father every time the man spoke.

"You are selling defective wagons," he kept screaming and accusing. Mr. Ansari was at a loss and growing angrier by the second. This man had the audacity to scream at him in his own shop. If he was polite, they would have worked out a solution, but the more he screamed, the angrier he made Asrar.

Faiz-ul went out in quick steps and examined the damage. The wheel had broken, and the wagon did seem new. He remembered the man, he had come just a few days ago. The wood seemed to hold well, but it was strange that the wheel had been damaged so quickly. He briefly wondered if the man had done something to push the wagon more than it could take but decided against laying the blame on the customer. The wagon *was* brand new, after all.

He hurried back and checked the storeroom. There was a spare wheel lying on the wall, from when they had bought a few dozens and planned to sell them for such occasions.

"Of course I am not selling bloody defective products, of any kind," Asrar shouted back. He was about to add a few choice words, when Faiz-ul tugged at his tunic. Asrar saw that his son wanted to take control of the situation. He decided to allow him, and took a step back, disengaging from the man. He needed to cool off, too, before he did something he would later regret.

"I apologize for the inconvenience," Faiz-ul said, stepping in front of the man. "We do understand that the wagon was new, and it shouldn't have suffered that level of damage so quickly." The man seemed to deflate a bit, but his face was still red. "What we can offer, is this: we have a spare wheel, which we will give to you for free, as a token of our good will." He quickly brought the wheel from the storeroom. "Do you want me to help you put it on?"

The man took the wheel, and looked at Faiz-ul again, taking his measure, as if seeing him for the first time. "No, mate, I can do that much. Thank you for stepping up," he added, and looked at both Ansaris. "You have a good reputation around here, and for good reason, it seems. Good day," he said and departed, as quickly and abruptly as he had come.

"Those were some good diplomatic skills there, son," Asrar said as the man left. "You have proven your worth and that you're very reliable ten times over the last few weeks. I'm proud of you."

Faiz-ul beamed up to his father, pride filling his chest. "Thank you," he replied. He looked down, thinking. For the last few days, something had been in his mind. "There's something that I do want," he added a few moments later.

"What is it?" Asrar told him, still smiling widely.

"I want to go to the university," Faiz-ul said. "I want to study geology." His father didn't speak for a long moment, looking at his son, the smile slowly fading. Faiz-ul decided his father wanted a more detailed explanation and continued speaking. "I want to start a gold mine like the Hoaglands, and I need to study for it enough so I know what I'm doing."

"A gold mine right now is a sure way to go broke fast, or have an accident that will take your life," Asrar said. "You saw what happened with Mr. Hoagland, and we've been reading about miner deaths every day on the paper. It's an incredibly dangerous field to work in, and it rarely pays well."

"I understand that," Faiz-ul muttered, and then stood his full height. "But they are at least free to determine what they do each day, what they focus on. They don't slave away, doing the same thing again and again, like..." he paused, but in the end his frustration won. "Like us."

Asrar looked at his son, his eyes containing a mix of sadness and hurt, and a bit of anger. "I understand you feel like a slave. But we don't have the luxury to own a gold mine, not even to get started down that path. The reason we can't is that we have to pay off the debt we have already, and I need your help to make sure there's a constant flow of money coming in. That way, I can take care of your mother at home."

"I want to help," Faiz-ul said, putting an emphasis in his words, to make sure his father understood that he truly did. "But," he added after a moment, "I want to go to the university, or do something other than working in a hardware store for the rest of my life. I want something more... free."

His father stared at him for a long moment, and Faiz-ul saw his father's eyes getting wider, shinier with rage. He saw him trying to restrain himself, but then, he started shouting. "Do you understand our position, Faiz-ul?" he shouted, his face red, gesturing wildly with his hands. "We have travelled thousands of miles here from our home, to Australia. Do you remember how it was back home? It was easier, but it was worse, wasn't it?" He didn't wait for a reply and continued shouting.

"It's nicer here, the people are different, and we are respected. But I can't do anything alone. Do you remember what I told you before we left? We need to rely on each other, I can't do everything alone. The girls help back home, you and your brother are supposed to help with work, with the store, with anything we end up doing. We're in this together! You can't just go off alone, doing whatever you want. We need the store running fully to ensure we have the necessities of life. Only after your mother's well, and the store's running well, and the debt is paid off, can you even begin thinking of doing something different."

Faiz-ul was overwhelmed momentarily, staring at his enraged father. The man was slowly calming down, taking deep breaths, his face losing some of its red color.

"Alright," he couldn't help but mutter. What else could he say? "How long do you think it will take?" he asked, looking down.

"Until we are in a state good enough for you to run off?" his father said, a hint of sarcasm in his voice. Then, he took a few more breaths, and spoke more calmly. "I'd think about a decade. The debt is quite large, and the market is often unpredictable."

"A decade…" Faiz-ul muttered. That seemed like a lifetime. He continued looking down and shrugged. "Thanks," he said after a few moments and left his father standing in front of the counter. He took a broom and started sweeping the back of the shop. His father stared at his back for a while, rage giving way to hurt, to sadness, and then finally, to pity. But he steeled his eyes and turned to managing the finances of the shop. They were too long away from paying off the debt to consider such… luxuries, like choosing their fate for themselves.

"What's the date?" Mark said absentmindedly. "Is July spelled like this?"

"Yes, that's correct," Christina said to Mark, who smiled his thanks and returned to his homework. As Christina let her mind wander, considering the date and how she missed Johnny, and how long it had been since they saw each other, another thought suddenly popped in her head. She stood straighter, her eyes widening a little, though she kept her mouth shut, trying to avoid alerting Mark and Mrs. Hoagland.

How long had it been since she had her period? She tried to calculate, based on when she was last with Johnny. It had been more than three weeks… Four? Five? Was she late? They had been very… active with Johnny when he was here. She realized there was a high chance she was pregnant. Well, she would deal with that when she came to it.

Cathy stood up from the couch, taking the bottle of wine with her. How much had she drunk? This bottle was her second of the day, Christina knew. And she had been drinking for quite a while. They weren't in a financial state to allow for that.

As Cathy went towards the kitchen, probably to fix something quick to eat, Christina left Mark to his studies and approached her. Mark stood as well, eyeing his mother, and quickly fled to the back of the house, expecting a fight to break out.

"Mrs. Hoagland," she said, "do you think it is wise to drown your sorrows in alcohol?" The woman turned, her face growing angry. Before Cathy could explode to her, she quickly spoke more. "We need new plans. I want to help. How will we have money coming in?"

Mrs. Hoagland deflated, but her tone was still angry when she spoke. "Do you have any suggestions, or just criticism?"

"Yes, I would suggest you cut down on your drinking. Mourn your husband with your children. They are missing him as well."

"What do *you* know of mourning?" the woman said bitterly, her face turned into a sarcastic sneer. "I didn't ask for your opinion."

"I want to help," Christina insisted, even though the woman's bitterness and anger was irritating her. "And most of our income streams have dried up."

"And what do you suggest we do?" Cathy said, more sarcasm bleeding in her voice. "Sell that pretty body of yours?"

Christina's first thought was to slap the woman, though she knew it would end badly. Her rage did burn hot inside her, and a little spilled out.

"And what are *you* doing about it? You're just wasting what little gold dust your son brings in on booze. Not even making them food," Christina said, but she instantly regretted it. Cathy started shouting barely coherent bile at her, and Christina tried her best to calm her down, though not managing much.

"Where do you think Johnny is now?" Richard said, patting a chicken. Mark was sitting next to him in the chicken coop, staring up through the wire to the stars. They could faintly hear their mother fighting with Christina, the poor girl.

"He might be in France already," Mark muttered. "Fighting the Germans."

"I heard they sent them first to training, somewhere in Australia,"

Richard said. "At least that's what they were saying in town."

"He'll be alright, right?" Mark said, looking at his brother hopefully.

"Yes, he will," Richard told him, with more certainty than he felt. "And we will win the war. The good guys always win, right?"

"Right," Mark said, looking satisfied, though he did feel a shadow of a doubt. "The good guys always win."

CHAPTER EIGHT

"Congratulations," Sgt. Milat told the recruits, now privates. "You have finished your basic training and you are now ready to join the 175th Tunneling Company in France." He looked them over, one by one. "Do me proud out there. And do your country proud. Don't make the stupid mistakes you have made here.

"The 175th is over there, tunneling under France. You will join a warzone. Understand that things you had here will be considered luxuries. I don't want to read reports of you complaining about lack of food, as you did here," he eyed a few of them in particular, "nor reports of falling in unfilled trenches," he eyed others. "I want to receive reports of you being exemplary soldiers. Paragons of virtue. Perfect examples of our country." He took a step back before he grew angrier, and Lt. Kelly took a step forward to continue.

"You'll take the train from the station down by the town, and then you'll be taken to England by ship. It'll be a long and tough journey, but you're soldiers now, so everything will be tough. Good luck out there. Make us proud," he said, then he saluted them. They saluted back.

Johnny followed the other recruits to the trucks that would drive them to the train station. He had shouldered all his items, along with the rifle that he had learned to clean and maintain so meticulously. The drive to the station was quick, and the train was expecting them. To Johnny, it seemed like they were the only passengers, along with a few carriages of cargo going to the docks. They left as soon as everyone had boarded.

When they were off the train, a sergeant was waiting for them. He grabbed their attention, waiting until everyone got off the train, then led them to another pair of trucks. The trucks took them through populated areas to the dock, where Johnny saw the biggest ship he had ever seen. It was incredibly long and tall, and he saw so many people boarding that he couldn't even imagine how would they fit inside.

The trucks stopped near a ramp, and Johnny got off, along with the other soldiers. The sergeant that had come with them led them to the ramp, gave their codes to a couple of officers holding clipboards, and then motioned them in. He led them through tight metal corridors buzzing with activity to a cramped storage area near the bottom of the ship's interior. Johnny guessed it was used to carry cargo once, but was now full of bunk beds four stacks high. The space between each bed was too tight, and Johnny couldn't see where everyone would put their things.

On the way through the ship, he had seen many other soldiers, too. They were being led in groups by other officers or sailors, shoved in rooms similar to his own. He started counting the groups but soon lost count. The ship was probably carrying hundreds, if not thousands of recruits to England, at his estimate.

"This will be your room," the sergeant gestured. "Stay here. Keep out of the way of the sailors. Don't come on deck unless directed to come."

Johnny and the others looked at the beds in apprehension. He hurried to get into a ground-floor bed, and when the others realized what he was doing, hurried to get the remaining ground-floor beds. Soon they were gone, and the unlucky or slow soldiers started putting their stuff at the first, second, and some at the third floors of the bunk beds.

"Once the ship's ready, it will leave. I repeat, don't come on deck unless directed." He waited for them to acknowledge it and left quickly.

Johnny examined the space near the beds and saw that they could barely fit their four bags in the tight space over their heads. He placed his own bag there and gestured at his bunkmates to do the same. Then, not having to do anything for the first time in a few days, he grabbed his rifle and laid on the bed. He saw many others doing the same, probably thinking along the same lines. "Get all the rest you can get," hadn't they told them?

Their door was open, and Johnny saw an unbelievable number of sailors carrying cargo going back and forth, as well as lines of soldiers like him, newly trained recruits going to the war. He thought of his family, and of Christina—which, he guessed, counted as family now. They were married, after all. He decided he would write her a letter later, after the ship started. He wanted to tell her about his training and about the ship, to tell her that he had been missing her terribly, and so many other things. As he thought about her, he slowly fell asleep, hugging his rifle, like most of the other soldiers around him.

He was rudely awakened when the ship started moving with a lurch. He guessed it was early morning, judging from how rested he felt. The ship was moving slowly, and he felt a deep rumble through the metal frame, which had to be the engine. He saw more soldiers being woken by the movement and heard some groans. The door was closed, he noticed, but something was near it that hadn't been there earlier. It was a metal bucket. Johnny wondered what its purpose was when the ship lurched again.

As he felt increasingly distressed by the ship's movement, he thought about using the bucket to empty the contents of his stomach but held back. He tried to stay calm as much as he could. From the tiny windows, he saw occasional flickers of lightning and guessed they would be expecting rough seas.

He settled back down on the bed, trying to think of anything but his stomach. The ship was swaying hard now, as if he was in a hammock or a swing set. It moved side to side, probably being hit repeatedly by huge waves. He had no way of knowing, and they were expressly forbidden from going outside.

He closed his eyes tightly, thinking of Christina instead of the ship's movements. If he retreated deep into his own thoughts, he would probably manage to get through it. Probably.

And then, he heard the first retch. Then, hurried steps on the floor, and he saw someone grabbing the bucket. Then, more retching. The man truly emptied his stomach in the bucket, and Johnny wouldn't be surprised if he saw the bucket full of vomit and bile. He tried to ignore the smell and the sounds and turned his back to the door.

Another person jumped off his bed and hurried to the bucket. They were barely an hour out in the sea, and two people had already vomited. This didn't bode well, Johnny realized. Thankfully, some of the smell was escaping from the tiny windows, but it wasn't enough.

Over the next few hours, Johnny heard most of the soldiers rushing to the single bucket. What was initially dry steps on the floor soon changed to steps in warm liquid. The bucket had overflown, it had even been knocked over during one of the most difficult lurches and had emptied its own contents on the floor, as if the bucket itself had vomited on the ground. The whole room was smelling like the inside of a stomach, and Johnny had shoved his face in his coat, trying to put as many layers of fabric as a filter between the air and his nose as he could. Better to smell in his own sweat and dirt, than the smell of vomit that permeated the room.

The ship rolled left and right, jumped up and fell down, so many times during the night that it was impossible to count them. Johnny often found himself praying that it would hold, and he thankfully heard no strange sounds. The ship was groaning, the waves were making loud thuds sometimes, and he could hear the rain's patter when it was quiet, but he heard nothing too worrying.

The other soldiers mumbled between themselves occasionally. He heard a few say that it was their first time aboard a ship and wonder how sailors could stand working in these deathly conditions every day. Another guy joked about how lucky they were for not joining the navy, despite Sgt. Milat's beasting. The atmosphere was heavy, and no matter how many light-hearted jokes they cracked, the room smelled of vomit, and their beds lurched left and right.

Johnny stayed silent through the exchange. He kept thinking of Christina, of home, of everything he had left behind. He tried to think of what to write her, and in his mind's eye, he wrote three drafts before discarding all of them and deciding he would just write from the heart when the time came. When their door suddenly opened at what he guessed had to be about five or six in the morning, he doubted any of them had managed to sleep for more than an hour without being woken up by others vomiting or their own stomachs being upset.

"Good morning mates," the one who opened their door said, a

sergeant judging by his insignia. "Rise and shine." He took a step inside and the sound his boot made was wet. He looked down. "Bloody hell. You filled that bucket, didn't you?" he muttered.

The soldiers all stood, getting ready for inspection as they had gotten used to for so many days now, but the sergeant gestured for them to stop.

"At ease, soldiers. Today's not inspection day. I'll be your commanding officer for the duration of your stay on the ship. I'm sergeant Poomkah."

"Sgt. Poomkah," the soldiers saluted.

"Sgt. Pumpkin," Johnny said instead, and internally cursed himself. He had thought of the joke as the man had said his name, but he didn't intend to speak it just yet.

"Sgt. Pumpkin, that's a new one," Sgt. Poomkah said, smiling to himself. A few other soldiers dared to crack some smiles of their own. "Name's from Poland, but I've been living with all you Aussies for too long to remember." He looked around the room.

"Now that that's done, you'll be given your orders. You'll do endurance training on deck, get changed, washed up, breakfast, then lectures and drills. The weather's tough, but we'll figure something out. Someone will stay behind to guard the guns, and I'll have one of you bring him breakfast." His eyes scanned the room and then he pointed at a guy who looked worse than anyone else. "You, stay behind. No reason to cover the deck with your bile, too." A few laughed lightly, but they were all too exhausted to really laugh.

"The rest of you, follow me." Sgt. Poomkah left the room and Johnny, along with the others, followed out of the room, gingerly stepping around the vomit. The corridors smelled fresher, and on the way up, Johnny saw no sailors hanging over the railings, nor any recruits. Probably weren't allowed up, just like they hadn't been. Sgt. Poomkah said something to a sailor that Johnny didn't catch, and then they arrived on the upper deck.

"Line up here," the sergeant pointed, and the soldiers followed his orders. "Do as I do," he commanded, and started doing some light calisthenics, which gradually increased in intensity. The sergeant allowed no breaks, and when he saw the soldiers getting tired, he switched to lighter exercises again. Johnny had some trouble following the sergeant, who seemed to be in amazing shape, always jumping or moving his arms and feet in the strange patterns without pausing.

The exercise pushed them up against their limits, and when they were finally done, Johnny paused for a few minutes, trying to breathe normally again. After the sergeant had let them rest for a bit, he guided them down into the ship, back to their quarters, and showed them where the baths were. Then, he gave them a detailed explanation of how to reach one of the areas the army used to serve breakfast, and told them to hurry up and wash, and then go eat. He would be expecting them back in their quarters in an hour.

Washing up in the ship was a surprisingly mundane experience, and Johnny was wondering about all the various mechanisms that allowed for that. Was water stored for the long journey that would last for more than forty days, or did they somehow take advantage of the ocean's water? And what about the lavatory? Where did their trash and their refuse go? The thoughts occupied his mind while he rushed to eat, and then to prepare for the day ahead.

The sergeant led them through the ship again, to another room, which looked like a storeroom that was repurposed as a classroom. There was a corporal waiting for them, who without a preamble started a long lecture about hygiene and personal care. There were added details regarding what to do on the ship, which Johnny appreciated, and they went over what to do in the warzone once again.

Johnny was starting to doze off when the lecture finished, and another corporal started speaking about taking care of their rifles. Johnny had heard that what must be hundreds of times already, and as he tried to wake himself up and get ready for the boring speech, the corporal surprised them by making jokes out of the lecture material. He likened the rifle to a woman and started drawing parallels between the two, and the men woke up enough to pay attention.

Then, more drills topside. First, they went through a few rifle drills, setting it up and removing it quickly, for so long that Johnny's hands started aching. Then, they took advantage of a long empty portion of a deck and did some bayonet drills. They went through the motions of fixing and removing the bayonet, and how to move forward when given the order.

The sergeant was standing behind them and first had them fix and remove their bayonets a few times, and then, pointing forward, he ordered the bayonets to be affixed, and then the soldiers to charge. There was a specific way to move when holding what was essentially a short spear, and it was made doubly hard and dangerous by the ship's movements. Johnny barely avoided spearing through two of his mates, but not everyone was as dexterous. During a heavy lurch by the ship, one of the soldiers fell against another, bayonet cutting through parts of his clothes, drawing some blood.

"No more bayonet charges," Sgt. Poomkah muttered as he examined the damage, "at least during rough seas."

When Johnny finally laid down on his bed at the end of the day, he was exhausted. He had forced himself to wash up before sleeping, so it was even later when he managed to go to bed. It had been a tiring day, especially considering he had barely slept at all. He hoped this night would prove better.

The smell of vomit had vanished from the room by the ship's crew who had cleaned up while they were doing drills. There were also six buckets this time, and Johnny guessed the other buckets had been provided because the floor had been covered in vomit the night before. He saw some of the other soldiers set their canteen cups next to their pillows, as an intermediate vomit container between their stomach and the bucket, as he had heard a few sailors complain about having to wash vomit-covered sheets. Besides, who wanted to sleep in a pool of his own vomit?

Johnny stared at the planks supporting the bunkbed above his own. He was exhausted, but seas got rougher in the evening during their bayonet drills, and now the ship was moving wildly. He felt his stomach get distressed, but he had been dealing with that through the day, so he had grown more used to it. Many others hadn't, though, as was obvious from the sounds of retching around him.

He couldn't sleep. It wasn't due to the noise, he had lived with two younger brothers so he could sleep through most things, but it was the movement that kept him awake. There was still a part of his mind that didn't let him relax, thinking there was a danger to him being in a situation where he was being moved in an irregular fashion. He tried to let the movements of the ship relax him, but the more he tried, the more awake he became. At least he wasn't as nauseated as the other soldiers, who were already filling the buckets and their canteen cups.

Christina came to his mind, so he decided to start his letter to her. He took out a piece of paper and his pen, unscrewed the top, added an ink pellet and some water, and then folded his overcoat a few times to use as a writing surface. He thought he'd start it by writing about his trip so far, and about his experience on the boat, trying to leave out the most disgusting details.

Soon, he had a couple of pages filled and decided to leave it at that. He would think of more things to say, he was sure. After he packed everything up, he lied down again, and this time, sleep came easier.

Sgt. "Pumpkin" woke them up and they went through a similar routine the morning of the next day, leaving behind someone else to guard their guns, one of the soldiers who looked even worse than the one yesterday had. Then, the sergeant ordered them to get their rifles prepared. Today was rifle practice. Johnny couldn't imagine what they would shoot at, and as they went aft, saw the rough seas. The sergeant waited for a moment, letting them take in the sight.

The sky was dark and what little light shone through, only displayed the angry seas. His vision couldn't penetrate into the sea's depths, dark blue and terrifying. Huge waves added white highlights to the endless blue. It was easy to lose any sense of scale, thinking that the waves were like those hitting a beach playfully, when in truth, they were tall like buildings.

Johnny saw what he initially thought were tiny specs of trash, but then realized that they were wooden practice targets attached to ropes, jumping up and down the waves. He didn't like shooting much, and he liked shooting moving targets less, but he had to learn. He was going to war after all. They shot the targets for a while, and as the day grew darker, they did other drills, along with more endurance training. That night, the sea grew rougher. They were finally allowed to get outside, and even Johnny rushed to the deck.

There were many soldiers around him, emptying the contents of their stomachs in the rough sea below, as if to punish it for making them sick. Staring at the dark seas and the various soldiers that were doing chores around the ship, his mind wandered to his family. He wondered what they were doing, how was Richard doing at the mine, how was Mark at school, and how was his mother. Cathy was usually bad with booze, but after his father had died, she had been worse. Johnny hoped she found it in her to stop, at least for his brothers' sake. He would ask Christina about it in his letter, he decided.

He also had chores to do around the ship. Everyone did. But the weather was growing worse so he couldn't do much, and he was incapacitated because of his stomach. He knew that sooner or later, the sergeants would force them to do what was their duty, but it was still early in the trip, and they hadn't had the time to get used to the sea much.

The stars were hidden by clouds, but he could see the moon. He wondered if Christina was looking at it, as well.

CHAPTER NINE

Christina stole a glance at the moon as it shone through the clouds and thought of Johnny for a long moment before returning her attention to Mark and the open book on the table.

Richard stared at her from across the table. She was a stable presence, soothing. She felt like something between a friend and a mother to him. She was organizing the house better than Cathy ever did, and was thinking ahead, of tomorrow, and the day after. That affected him as well. He was starting to think about the future. He was still grieving about the loss of his father and Johnny's sudden disappearance, but he was starting to realize that life went on after those horrible events, and that he had to act.

The fire started to die out, and Richard stood quickly and hurried to the fireplace to put more fuel in. When he looked next to the fireplace, he realized they had to restock it.

"I'm going to get some firewood," Richard said, and Christina stood as well.

"I'm coming too, we need to stack some behind the house," she added. They went outside together and started moving the cut logs from the area they had been cutting them in, to the wall of the house, to be within reach. Richard was gathering the firewood, passing it to Christina, who was then stacking it against the wall.

"Thanks," Richard muttered at some point.

"We needed to stack it, no worries," Christina replied.

"No, I mean… For being here. Johnny chose well. Thank you for your help." He was embarrassed to speak out his mind, but he wanted to encourage her. "It's great to have you here."

"Thank you, Richard. And thank you for your hard work at the mine," Christina said. "Johnny would be glad to know you're so hardworking."

"I'd like to work more at the gold mine," Richard said, "but I don't like doing it alone. It's dangerous, and I don't know enough to work it by myself."

"Didn't your father have any people working with him?" she asked.

"No, but he had met another miner who he went to for advice, sometimes," Richard said thoughtfully. "He was called Evan Carter. I might go to him tomorrow, thanks for the suggestion!"

Christina smiled back and continued working silently. Soon, they were done, and had returned to the house.

The next day, Richard hurried to Evan Carter's mine. He found the man hard at work, a thawing kettle on the fire outside the entrance, while he was preparing his machinery.

"Hey Mr. Carter," Richard greeted the man, waving.

"Hello Richard," Evan said, leaving the machine and going to shake the boy's hand. "I saw you on the funeral but didn't get to speak to you. How's your family holding up?"

"Good enough, thanks," Richard muttered. "Johnny got enlisted. I've been working the mine, but I need help. Father didn't get to teach me everything before he... before the accident."

"That's understandable," Evan said, "mining is hard and dangerous work, though. How much do you know already?"

"A few things about how to handle the pickaxe, but nothing about explosives, or how to locate gold," Richard replied. Evan threw him a thoughtful look, considering the young man.

"It's much that you don't know, then. How about these?" he

pointed at the machine behind him.

"What's that?" Richard asked. Evan shook his head.

"It's much you don't know," Evan repeated, but his tone was sadder. "I can't get down to your mine and teach you. You should work under someone else, as an apprentice, if you can find someone that can afford to pay you…" Evan started, and saw the young man's eyes grow dark, disappointed. Then, he had an idea. "Or, you can ask your uncle. Jimmy's a great miner, you know. And the mine is his, right? It belonged to him and your father."

"You are right, I should do that," Richard said, sighing. He hoped that he would find a way to learn more about mining without having to rely too much on other people. And he knew that it would be hard to find someone to apprentice under. Even if there was such a position, he didn't even know how he'd get about starting to look for someone to take him.

"Thank you, Mr. Carter, good day and good luck," Richard said and left the man to his work. Evan stared after Richard for a while with a thoughtful look before returning to his work.

Richard went to the mine to take stock of the situation more calmly. He went underground and examined the tools he had left, making mental notes of everything he saw. He noticed some unlit lamps, as well as the area where they used to keep the dynamite. Then, he went outside, only then realizing he had been holding his hands in fists tightly and had been barely breathing. It was hard for him to go inside. He saw the machines outside, and other tools that he didn't know what they were used for.

He worked the creek for a while, and when it grew darker, he returned home. He wanted to discuss his thoughts with the others before making a decision. When he arrived home, he found Mark resting and Christina preparing dinner. He found his mother up, too, and he saw no empty bottles around her.

When he sat on the table, he narrated what happened with Mr. Carter, and his intentions to go to his uncle Jimmy, even though they weren't that close. His mother's lukewarm reaction proved that their father didn't have that much of a relationship with him either.

"I think that Jimmy will either teach me some things, or at least, help me find someone to apprentice under," Richard finished. His mother had snorted a few times, as if to show that she didn't think much of the man, but she didn't complain nor contradict him openly.

"I want to learn, too," Christina said.

"And me too," Mark added. "I want to help."

Richard nodded. That was what he had hoped for. He felt like a fish out of the water, but if he had at least his brother with him, it would be much easier. He felt like he could do more if he had the support of his family.

"I'd like to see the mine, too," Christina said after a moment. "Could we go over the weekend?" Richard nodded, and Christina turned to Cathy. "You could come too, if you'd like."

Cathy stared at the young woman for a long moment, before shaking her head. Christina thought that the woman's eyes seemed shinier for a moment, more wet than they had been, and Christina understood the woman's hesitation. Her husband had died there.

The next morning, Richard hurried to the mine, and told Mark to come get him after school. He worked the creek for a bit, and when his brother came, they went to their uncle's claim. Richard was barely sixteen, and Mark was fourteen, both feeling like boys who were suddenly called to become men. They wanted to help their family, but it was overwhelming looking at the mine and not knowing what to do. That was the worst of it, the total ignorance they felt they had.

They reached Jimmy's house and found him in his living room. The man hugged them, though he looked a bit distant.

"How's the family?" Jimmy asked.

"Johnny went to the war," Richard replied, looking down. Jimmy's face was covered by a shadow for a bit, but he shook his head and his face changed back to normal.

"He was talking about that for a while now, wasn't he?" he asked, and the boys nodded. "Well, good luck to him, and good luck to you. What can I do for you, my nephews?"

"We want to learn how to work in a mine," Richard said, and Mark looked up to his uncle, his eyes wide and eager. Jimmy examined them for a bit.

"Are you serious about this? Do you want to know how to run a mine or just work in one?"

"We want to run father's mine," Richard said. "I'm serious."

Mark looked as serious as his fourteen-year-old face could manage. "Me too. I want to help Richard."

Jimmy looked at them for a long moment more and nodded. "Alright. I'll teach you. Come here tomorrow morning, alright?"

The boys smiled widely and nodded. "Thank you, uncle!" They both said and hurried to give him a hug. Then, they left quickly.

Jimmy stared after them for a moment, and when they left, he hurried to his desk. He had much to teach them, and he had to start somewhere. There were some rocks around... He opened the desk's drawers and found a few rocks he had kept, as mementos and as teaching opportunities. He removed all of them, went through them, and sorted them in a box to show to the boys tomorrow. Then, he started writing a few ideas for lessons.

His wife found him writing at his desk later, and kept him company, smiling to herself.

The next day, Jimmy opened the door to see Mark's eager look, Richard's serious one, and Christina right behind them, trying her best to appear serious and not overwhelmed. She introduced herself as Christina Hoagland, Johnny's wife.

"I want to learn, too. I want to help," she said, which earned a look of approval from Jimmy. He thought that Johnny made a good choice, but he kept his thoughts to himself.

He guided them inside to the living room, which he had prepared the night before. He had the box down by the table, and had cleared a space behind it to stand. The boys and Christina sat on the sofa and the chairs he had arranged, and even his wife joined them, sitting aside and looking at her husband proudly.

"We will start from the basics, even though I know you boys have worked in the mine before. That's because back then you had your father keeping an eye on you. Now you need to keep an eye on yourselves and each other." The boys nodded, no hint of offense on their faces. "Good. There are many principles we need to go over. Stupid mistakes in the mines can be fatal. Pay attention, ask questions. Better to appear stupid for a moment, than to be dead by misjudging a situation," he added.

He went over the basic principles one by one, explaining what to pay attention to, what to don't ever do in the mine, and many other things. Richard had heard of most of them before, but he was now treating them differently. Not as a set of guidelines to follow, but as a system to enforce himself. With Johnny gone, he was now the head of the family, especially down at the mines. He had to keep his brother safe, and Christina as well, if did join them. It was up to him to guide everything, and he was realizing how being in the lead was completely different than just following orders.

Jimmy then laid out some rocks on the table. He pointed at each, explaining the type of rock it was, what it indicated, and what it hinted at.

"What is this rock? It looks pretty," Christina said at some point, pointing at a white stone lying on the table.

"That's quartz," Jimmy explained. "It's one of the most important rocks when it comes to mining, that's why I was going to go over it last. It's the most important rock to locate since gold is usually close by." He handed the rock over to Richard, who took it and examined it carefully, then passed it along to Mark and Christina. "Pay attention not just to its appearance, but to its texture as well. Use all your senses, as your hands are very sensitive, maybe more sensitive than your eyes. In the semi-lit mines, your eyes might betray you, but your fingers won't."

After Jimmy finished explaining the basics, he had them ask questions. Then, he asked them questions about everything he had said, testing them. He corrected them a few times, and he went over specific parts of his lesson some more times. When he was satisfied they had a good enough foundation, at least on a theoretical level, he decided to show them some things. By that time, his wife had left the room and was working in the kitchen.

A great smell came from the kitchen, and Jimmy realized that they had spent hours talking and it was getting late. "Let's take a break," Jimmy said. He gestured for them to come to the kitchen, and they all sat around the table as Jimmy's wife started serving them food. It smelled and tasted amazing, and Christina hurried to help her, though was rebuffed by the woman.

"You're a guest," she told her. "Sit down and enjoy."

Christina ate, feeling a little guilty, but was glad to see the boys attack their food ferociously. They enjoyed a decent lunch, rested for a bit while chatting, and then Jimmy stood.

"Now, let's move to practice," he said. "I'll take you to my personal claim to show you how a mine actually works." He gave his wife a kiss and took the boys and Christina out. They soon arrived at a well-kept mine, and Richard instantly felt bad about how he had kept his father's mine. There was another person there, he saw, a man older than Johnny but younger than Jimmy. He was probably around thirty, Richard guessed.

"That's Jessie," Jimmy pointed. The man saw them coming and stopped what he was doing, approaching them. As soon as he had come close enough, they realized he was missing half his left arm. "Jessie here fought in the war. He was dismissed, as you can see," Jimmy pointed at the man's arm. "But he's strong, and a good worker. He keeps the mine running, sometimes all by himself," Jimmy added, and patted the man on the back. Jessie smiled.

Richard's eyes were fixed on the man's arm. It was the first time he had seen a wounded veteran up close. The war always was a distant idea, a place where things happened, not something tangible.

But seeing the missing arm, it became real. His brother was there, fighting in the same war. How would he come back?

Jimmy showed them around while there was still sunlight, not yet going under the ground, but Richard's mind was on his brother. He wondered what he was doing at that moment, what he was about to do, and what waited for him in the war. What did Fate have in store for him? Richard knew that nowhere was truly safe; his own father had died working the mine. But that didn't mean that going to war wasn't going to be dangerous…

The tour was short, Jimmy was tired, as was Christina and the boys, and they decided to pick it up the next day. As they walked home, Richard's mind kept going back to Jessie and his missing arm, and as he later laid on his bed, trying to fall asleep, he couldn't help but imagine the different ways his brother would come back, most of them bad.

"Now, this is important," Jimmy pointed at the ground. Richard couldn't see anything important, just that it was rocky. Jimmy knelt and picked up a rock. "See here," he extended his arm, and Christina, Mark, and Richard brought their heads closer. "See this?" he pointed at a place on the rock that was highlighted with white. "That's quartz."

"So, that means there's gold nearby," Christina said, and Jimmy nodded.

They walked some more, going around the surface of the mine, while Jimmy spoke.

"Water is incredibly important, too. It's not always around, so it's a valuable resource in many ways. First, as drinking water, then for use in various mechanisms or contraptions like a thawing kettle, and of course to wash things. But one of the most important uses is that the water can bring out some of the minerals found in the mine. The claim you used to work in has a creek running through, which is great. It's a well-positioned claim. There can very well be gold in that creek, you know. Have you lads searched through it?"

"We've worked some areas with father," Richard replied, "but we haven't reached bedrock in some of them. There's still much work to be done there."

"That could be an excellent opportunity for you, then. It's much safer, and even though it generally is less efficient or rewarding, it's good work. It breaks up the routine, too," he added. "You know, speaking of the mine," Jimmy said after a moment, "it was under our two names. I got your letter, Richard," he said, "so let me explain how this works." He took a moment to gather his thoughts.

"The mine is under my control, now. When we got it, we had decided to share it, and share the yearly fee, if there is one. Even though now it's under my control, you can go, Richard, and work there freely, as well as Mark, and you Christina as well, if you decide to. Explore the creek for all its worth. Gather all gold or precious stones you find, it'll be good for your family."

"How do we discern what rocks are worth?" Richard asked.

"Anything with color should be examined. Search for color, and make sure you keep it. We'll examine everything later. Let's go over panning, for now," Jimmy said, and grabbed a pan. He demonstrated his technique, and then offered the pan to the others, going through it with everyone. When he was satisfied they got it, he put some dust in a pan, and had all of them go through it again.

"You should focus on this, I believe, at least initially. We'll get into mining soon too—today even—but since you have access to an excellent resource, the creek, you should start with this."

After a few more demonstrations, he checked the sun and got them near the mine's entrance. He indicated a couple of logs set around the fire and had them sit on them, then started heating up their lunch. They ate in silence, concentrating on their food. Jimmy mentally went over what he was about to teach them, while Christina and Richard thought about what they had learned, and Mark's thoughts jumped around, to school, to his brother, to his mother, and to how glad he was Christina was at least with them.

When they were done, Jimmy gestured to the mine's entrance. "Ready to go in?" They all sprang to their feet. On their way underground, Jimmy unhooked four kerosene lanterns and lit them. He gave them to the other three, and they went through the tunnels, using the lanterns to light their way.

Christina was the one who had the least experience, and was staring around, her eyes wide with interest. She could see different stones, she could see the markings of the tools used, and she was filled with wonder. It was obvious to her that this was a hard work, and one that needed a vast amount of expertise.

Jimmy led them to a tunnel and arrived at a dead end. On the left and right, there were white streaks on the stone. Christina instinctively reached out a hand and touched the white surface, realizing it was quartz.

"See here?" Jimmy said. "This is quartz. And remember what I told you about gold?"

"There has to be some nearby, right?" Mark said. Jimmy nodded and pointed at the wall. There was a faint but noticeable golden streak visible along the quartz vein.

"This is gold," Jimmy said. "And now that you found it, what do you do?" he asked. When they didn't reply, he went over some basic mining techniques. He showed them a few things they could do with a pickaxe, and then went on to one of the most common mining techniques, dynamite mining.

He grabbed a hammer and a chisel and showed them how to make holes on the wall large enough to fit a dynamite. He showed them a few holes they had already prepared on the wall, and then gave them hammers and chisels and had them try to make similar ones. Richard went at it furiously, having done it before in his father's mine, and Mark and Christina had more trouble. Jimmy corrected them a few times and let them wear themselves out after a few minutes.

"This can take days to complete, but when you're done, you stick the dynamite in and the whole wall comes down. In the end, you have gained more time than you lost, but it's a pain to carve." He took their tools and stored them in a bag he was carrying.

"But now, for one of the most important safety lessons. Air. Never, ever assume that the air quality down here is the same as on the surface. And that's not even taking into consideration the gasses that you might meet as you mine. Some miners use wind sails and rig them up on the entrances to their main shafts so that air can blow down into the mine. This allows for a constant flow of fresh air into the mine. Always remember the air when you are underground, and make sure it's recycled."

"It's very cold down here, too," Christina muttered. She had been feeling chilly all the time, and she guessed it was in part because of the moisture. It was winter, as well, and even though it wasn't snowing yet, snow would soon come.

"That's why you have these, right?" Richard pointed at a cage hanging from some timbers, near the lantern.

"Coal miners mainly use canaries as air quality detectors, that's right," Jimmy said, smiling. "I mostly keep them for company. It's an important lesson, though, and it's helpful to have an early warning device. We use them to test the oxygen, the air of the mine, because they need very clean air to live. When there's no clean air, these will be the first to notice."

Jimmy showed them more techniques, explained how to use timber to support the mine ceiling, then went through more of the industry's dangers. They spent quite some time in the mine before they started on their way to the surface, and back to Jimmy's house.

As the door opened, they were treated to a nice surprise. Cathy was sitting on the sofa, speaking with Jimmy's wife. She seemed in a good mood, and Christina was relieved to see her out of the house, socializing. It was good to do normal things, to make herself feel normal again. They sat around the table once again and ate a lovely dinner made by the two women. Cathy had brought something from home earlier, and along with Jimmy's wife, they had cooked through the day, waiting for Jimmy and his three students.

Christina stole glances at Cathy throughout dinner. The woman had an obvious edge to her voice and her movements were awkward, as she was still in the middle of grieving for her husband, but there was a glint in her eye and a tiny but noticeable note of enjoyment in her voice. She knew that it does good to be busy, to keep the mind from things. The last two days she had managed to keep her own worrying about Johnny to a level that was good enough for her to function, though every time she saw Jimmy's worker, the one who had lost his arm, it made her heart feel as if a cold hand was grabbing it.

They enjoyed their dinner, spent an hour more speaking and having a good time, and when Mark started nodding off, Christina suggested they leave. The Hoagland wagon was parked outside, and they got on it. Richard took the reins, guiding their horse, called Charlie, through the dark roads, to home. The horse knew where to step and what to avoid, and Richard thought that it even knew how to get home, so his own job was limited to overseeing the process.

The stars shone brightly in the cold night, where they were visible through the clouds. Christina stared up at them. Then, something fell against her face.

"It's snowing," she muttered. Mark woke up and looked to the sky, excited to see the little points of frozen water. He stared at the clouds dreamily and wondered if he would make a snowman this year. He remembered some time back, when they had all made a large snowman together, but now his dad was dead, and Johnny was gone to fight in the war. At least he had Richard, Christina, and his mom to play in the snow with. Mark hoped his mom would spend more time with them, and not with the wine bottle.

The wagon entered their yard, and the two women got off and hurried inside, to get the fire going. The house was cold and dark, and they set about methodically lighting it up, and preparing the fire in the hearth.

Mark and Richard took the horse off the wagon, and then carefully guided him into the small barn. They brushed him off, then made sure he had suffered no injuries during the day. Mark always felt bad about the animals out in the cold, and he and Richard took a heavy blanket and covered the horse, who neighed in what Mark interpreted as gratitude.

When they returned to the house, the fire was going strong, and they huddled in front of it to get the chill out, Mark dozing off on Richard's shoulder for a bit, before they left for their rooms.

CHAPTER TEN

"Good morning, Jessie," Richard greeted the man, as he entered the mine's area. He had dropped Mark off at the school before coming here, as he had been doing for the last couple of days. After the weekend's lessons, Richard was glad to be having some practice along with an expert miner, or at least a miner much more experienced than him.

"Hey Richard," Jessie greeted him. "Good day, mate. Ready to do some work?" Richard nodded excitedly. "Great. Let's get started with hauling today, alright? I've blasted a quartz wall earlier, and there's gold-bearing rocks to get to the crusher." Richard grabbed two buckets and Jessie grabbed one of his own, and the two men walked deep into the mine, where Jimmy had shown them the quartz vein a few days ago.

Richard first helped Jessie fill his own bucket, as it was hard to move rocks with one hand, and then filled his own two buckets. They carried them up, and Jessie started running the crusher. Hauling rocks was incredibly hard work, but work they did. Jessie alternated between working the crusher and panning through the dust, and Richard kept bringing up buckets of rock.

They had found quite a bit gold dust in the mine, a bit under four ounces. Jessie thought that if they could get some more, they might be able to pay Richard for his work, as well. That would have the double advantage of Jessie having help, as it was hard to work the mine with one arm, and Richard being able to support his family. When Jimmy came by for a quick inspection and to greet the men, Jessie told him his idea while Richard was inside the mine, and after Jimmy examined how much they had gathered, he agreed that it might be possible.

As they worked, Jessie caught Richard throwing him thoughtful looks, and then turning his eyes away. He thought that the boy wanted to ask something but was too scared to do so. The next time Richard brought a couple of buckets up, he gestured for him to get closer.

"Hey Richard, is there something on your mind?" he asked, keeping his voice even. Richard hesitated, fidgeting. "If you want to ask about my arm, go ahead," Jessie added and smiled sympathetically.

"No, that's not it," Richard said. "It's just… I am thinking about my brother. I wonder what he's going through, in the war." Jessie looked at Richard, realizing the immense worry the boy had for his brother.

"War is… war is hard," he said after a few moments. "No matter where you are, there's danger coming to you from every angle. Even when you are resting." He saw Richard's eyes grow wide. "I won't lie to you. There's death, noise, there's…" he paused, unwilling to go deeper in. There were things he saw and did back there, that he had buried deep inside him, and he didn't want them to get out again, to reach the surface.

"What part of the army did you serve in?" Richard ask after he realized the man wouldn't tell him more.

"I served in the infantry," Jessie said. "Bloody lucky to be alive, too. Where's your brother serving?"

"He's with the tunneling companies," Richard replied. "Is it as dangerous as the infantry?"

"All army positions are dangerous," Jessie said. "The Germans dig underground, searching for sappers. And they set mines, trying to blow our tunnels. The war is taking place on many levels, not just the ground." He paused for a moment before continuing.

"You know, that's how I lost my arm. I was in the tunnels the British had dug out before their attacks. I won't ever forget those tunnels… I still dream of them, often." He stopped speaking, trying to repress images that rose, unbidden, to his mind. He went to war a boy and returned *broken*. Some people had returned broken in body, as he had, and others had returned broken in spirit or mind. No one came back whole. No man he had served with had returned without some form of injury, internal or external. Or both.

"Thank you for your honesty," Richard said after he had allowed the man some time to think. "I appreciate it."

"I'll say a prayer for your brother," Jessie said suddenly. "A soldier's prayer. It is special, you know. It has the power to keep other soldiers alive. Remember that," he said. Richard nodded, his face solemn, as was the man's face. Without speaking more, he returned to gathering blown-up ore, bringing it up for Jessie who worked the rock crusher.

They worked in silence for quite a while, comfortable with each other. Having spoken their minds, they were more relaxed, especially Richard. He was worrying about his brother like crazy, but he was also resigned. He couldn't help but accept that there was always a risk of death. Besides, didn't his own father die working in the mine? Wasn't that supposed to be safer than going to war? And yet it had happened. There's always a risk of death, and he couldn't do anything about it. He channeled his frustration and his helplessness in his work, focusing on what he could control.

"There must be something we could do, as well, right?" Cathy said to Christina. "To start earning something, even enough to buy some bread."

Christina nodded. "I have some ideas."

"Me too, actually," Cathy said. "We should set up a garden in the back. We could have some vegetables to eat, and maybe some to sell if we grow enough."

"A cellar could go well with the garden, you know. We could use it for storage, and depending on the weather, maybe even try to make jams and other preserves," Christina added.

"As soon as it gets warmer, we should make that cellar," Cathy agreed. "An excellent idea. Do you have any more?"

"I've thought about knitting," Christina said. "We could make clothes and sell them, or repair worn clothing."

"That's good. Growing vegetables would go well with keeping more chickens and selling their eggs, too," Cathy added. "We could do all these things, but we should get started with the garden right away, don't you think?"

Christina thought that winter wouldn't be the best season to get started building a garden, but she didn't say it. Instead, she smiled and nodded.

Cathy looked out the window with interest. "We can ask Richard to dig up a garden in the back, so we can start planting."

When Richard came home, Cathy eagerly approached him. "Welcome home, Richard. We've been talking with Christine today, and we were looking for ways to earn a living. We thought to get started making a garden outside, growing some vegetables. Could you dig the ground up and help prepare the garden?"

Richard looked at his mother and smiled. "Sure will, mum. Right away." On his way out, he passed by Christine, and took her aside. "It's the wrong time of the year to plant, you know," he whispered. "But I don't want to stop mom. I'll get started on the garden and encourage her as much as possible." Christine, who had been thinking along the same lines, nodded in agreement.

Digging up the garden in the middle of winter was hard to do, the ground was frozen in places, and he was getting cold working in the wet ground. But he did work, to help his mother. He was happy she was thinking of earning a living finally. It took him a few days, and he couldn't go to the mine to help Jessie and his uncle, but at least with Mark's help, the yard was dug up a lot quicker. His mother spoke about the garden excitedly, and Christine was glad that the boy took the time to help. The week passed quickly, and Richard didn't manage to help in his uncle's mine any more than he had already done.

"Do you see this here?" Jessie pointed at a metal contraption. Mark and Richard took a couple of steps forward. It was an overcast Saturday morning, and it was the first day they managed to go to their uncle's mine after digging a garden for their mother.

The thing Jessie was pointing at was a thawing kettle. It was sitting on the ground, near the fire. It had a domed top, and its cylindrical body was mostly hollow. They had seen such devices before, and they knew they were used by miners to thaw their frozen dynamites without exposing them to fire directly.

Richard felt his legs weaken, and he saw Mark next to him take a couple of steps back. He saw his lips tremble a bit.

"Do you know what it is?" Jessie asked. Mark nodded.

"It's a thawing kettle," Richard said.

"And what does it do?" Jessie asked, observing them carefully.

"Thaws dynamite," Mark muttered.

"That's correct," Jessie said. "I know it's a tough subject for you guys. Those things can save your life, though." He looked at them meaningfully. "It cost the life of your father," he added, his voice softer. "If he had been using one of these..." he let his voice fade. "Let's teach you how to use it, then."

Jessie took it and opened it up, showing them what was inside. A smaller cylindrical chamber was connected with the opening on the top but had some distance from the kettle's walls. It could fit a few sticks of dynamite, Richard estimated. This one was smaller than others he had seen and should easily fit one stick; more would be tightly packed and dangerous.

"The water heats up," Jessie pointed, "and heats up the central chamber. When the water's boiling, it's best to remove it from the fire altogether, and then put the stick in. That way, the stick is protected from the fire even more. You do it one at a time."

Mark took the kettle in his hands and looked it over carefully. He judged the distance of the chamber from the wall wide enough, and the sticks protected from the fire with two covers, one of the main kettle, and one of the dynamite chamber.

Richard was standing still, not taking the item in his own hands, instead examining it as his brother did, barely keeping calm.

"Let me demonstrate," Jessie said, and walked them through the process. They watched carefully, and Jessie taught them about a lot of common mishaps. What could happen if the top was left open, or what could happen if you shoved too many sticks inside.

After that, they went back to mining basics. Richard had been learning a lot next to Jessie over the few days he worked here, and Mark was catching up. The boy had asked a few questions shyly and Jessie had always answered, happy to have help around the mine. They continued the work they had been doing a few days back, Jessie working the crusher and the two boys bringing up the ore.

As the boys walked around the mine, they heard a voice call out. Richard judged the time to be early afternoon, probably around four or five. It was a woman's voice, calling for Jessie. As the boys approached the source of the sound, they saw a woman come through the trees. She was wrapped in a heavy coat, but even through the thick material, the boys could see that she had a killer figure.

"Hey there," the woman greeted the boys. "You must be the Hoagland boys, right? Jessie spoke about you, ya know." Her voice was melodic and pretty, and Richard liked the way her hair was peeking out from under her hood. The woman was incredibly beautiful, now that he was seeing her up close.

"I'm Richard and this is Mark," Richard introduced them. He extended his hand and the woman shook it. She was taller than them, but not much.

"Nice to meet you boys, I'm Pauline Hanson," she said, smiling, and shook Mark's hand as well. Her smile made her face light up and Richard felt a sudden rush of blood to his own face. She was very pretty. "Where's Jessie?" she asked then, looking around.

"I'll get him," Mark said and hurried behind the rock crusher. The machine was making noise and there was no way Jessie would have been able to hear Pauline's calls. Richard saw Mark return with Jessie soon after, and the man smiled when he saw Pauline.

"Hey honey," he said, and kissed the woman lightly on her lips. He looked up at the sun, and back at the boys. "It's late, boys. Better wrap it up for today if you want to get home before dark."

Richard and Mark nodded, bid goodbye to the couple, and hurried off.

"She's very pretty," Mark muttered on the way home.

"She is, good for Jessie," Richard agreed. He was thinking that even though the man was missing an arm, he still had such a beautiful girlfriend. He was a good man, and it seemed that it counted for quite a bit. He felt somewhat relieved. In the back of his mind, he saw Jessie as Johnny's possible future, and it was good to see that being a good man still counted for something, even when one was lacking in other departments.

CHAPTER ELEVEN

Johnny heard his name being called amid the music of people vomiting in buckets. The three weeks he had spent on the ship thus far had taught him to filter out the vomit sounds from the useful sounds, and he heard his name immediately. He looked up to see private Michael Tilley, a man from his platoon, waving at him.

"It's time," the man told him, and motioned him up. Johnny got up from the bed, on the same time thankful for the distraction, but also bored of what was ahead. They hadn't been doing drills for days due to the rough seas, but now that he was called to hold watch on the empty deck, he felt that watching the rough sea would be even more boring than hearing soldiers throw up. Johnny left his rifle, as did Michael, and they hurried away.

As the two soldiers walked through the bunk beds, they took care to avoid stepping in vomit or in the full buckets arrayed around the beds. Johnny saw a man grab a half-full bucket laying by his bed and empty the remaining contents of his stomach inside, a gesture repeated many times around them. They entered the corridor, and Johnny asked the time.

"It's five past seven," Michael said.

"We're late, mate," Johnny told him. Tilley shrugged, saying nothing. When they arrived at the last stairs leading out, the ship lurched, hit by heavy waves lengthwise. They put out their arms in a practiced motion, keeping themselves steady against the walls of the corridor. They knew that another wave was coming so they remained still, and immediately after, another wave did come. The ship groaned and moved, and they had to push hard against the walls. More followed, and a few seconds later, when they passed, they continued.

When they got out, Johnny could see very little. The sun had hidden itself a while ago, and the moon rarely peeked from behind the clouds. The ship's lights shone against the wet deck and barely lit the rough seas. Despite the three weeks they had been sailing, Johnny had yet to grow accustomed to seeing the rough seas. The sight filled him with a combination of awe and terror, and he could only hope that the ship would hold, and that they would survive.

The two soldiers that were on watch before them, the ones that Johnny and Michael were sent to relieve, spotted them as they exited the door to the deck. When the pair arrived, Johnny saw they had sour looks on their faces.

"You're late," one of them grumbled. Michael shrugged and offered no reply again, but Johnny apologized. He knew that those minutes they were late would have felt like hours. They left quickly, relief obvious in their faces, and went back inside the ship where it was dry. Johnny could see they were soaked completely, shining under the ship's lights like the deck.

Michael and Johnny stood at the same place the other two soldiers had been standing, looking out at the sea, under some cover from the rain. It wasn't doing much, though, as the winds were making sure every inch of them was drenched. The minutes went by agonizingly slow, and every so often, they grabbed the railings, holding themselves steady against the huge waves.

"What are we going to do for two hours? There's no one around but us," Tilley said, boredom obvious in his voice. Johnny thought of a joke then.

"We should watch out for icebergs floating up from the Atlantic

Ocean, ya know," he said. A few seconds passed and Johnny realized that the man took him seriously. He could even see his eyes widening and focusing on the horizon more intently.

"Mate," Johnny said, "it's a joke. Don't worry."

"You got me there, mate," Tilley said, relief obvious in his voice. "I was so worried we'd be shoved against a wall of ice, and it would be all my fault," he said, and they both laughed for a moment.

"But standing here watching the sea for two hours is too boring," Johnny said after a few minutes. "I heard another guy in our platoon say that he walked around the ship, so we could do the same. Let's see if there are any windows damaged by the waves, ya know," he said. Michael nodded, and they made their way around the ship.

They moved slowly, making sure they held on to the railings as much as possible. The ship lurched and heaved, and Johnny felt as if she wanted them off her deck, like a wild animal. Despite the care they took, a rogue wave they didn't see coming hit the ship hard, spilling onto the deck. They held onto the railing for their lives and managed to avoid being washed overboard. They hurried back to the nook the previous soldiers had been standing in and sought its cover and protection. Johnny realized how dangerous being out in rough seas actually was and chose boredom instead of risking his life more.

When their two-hour shift was over and the next couple of soldiers came to relieve them, Johnny was deeply thankful they weren't late like he and Michael had been. They gratefully returned inside the dry ship, happy to be farther away from the dangerous waves. Back at their platoon's quarters, Michael went to sleep immediately, and Johnny laid on his bed, looking at the wooden boards of the bed above his own, as he so often did. He let his mind go to his family, and he was soon asleep.

The next day, as they were having breakfast, he overheard two soldiers speaking.

"I went to relieve the watch at four hundred hours in the morning and they weren't anywhere," the first one said. Johnny recognized him, as he belonged to his platoon. "I spoke with the sergeant, and after a headcount, it seems they were washed overboard. They aren't anywhere in the ship, no boats are missing, and their stuff is still in their bunkbeds."

"Bloody hell, I knew those guys," the other one said. They continued talking, but Johnny focused back on his food.

Just like that, two lives were lost. They weren't the only ones the rough seas had claimed, and they wouldn't be the last. It made Johnny feel powerless against the natural forces of the world. He was sure the two soldiers were doing the same thing he had been, that they were careful, and despite that, they were dead. Was there really anything anyone could do, if a huge wave hit against the ship, filling the deck with water?

When he returned to their quarters, he took out his pen and a piece of paper again and started writing another letter to Christina. He wrote her about the rough seas and what he had been doing to stay alive. He wrote about the two soldiers, trying to communicate his awe and not his terror. He didn't want her to worry too much. Having nothing else to write at the moment, he stowed the paper away, and lied on his back again.

His mind went to his father. He wished he was still alive, to share this experience with him. He still could not believe that he would never speak with him again, that he would never see him work the mine as he used to, that he would never even argue with him about what to do.

Tilley sat on Johnny's bed, obviously bored. Johnny sat up as well, his thoughts darker than his companion's.

"What's on your mind?" Michael asked, seeing his somber look. Johnny saw that a soldier from the next bed was also sitting facing them, serious. Johnny looked at Michael and the other guy, a private called Irwin, and decided to be honest.

"I joined the army to escape Bendigo, my town," he started. "My father had just died in the mine we worked. He was trying to thaw dynamite and it exploded, killing him. I couldn't work the mine anymore." He paused. "Everyone always told me that mining was safer than being a soldier, but it killed my father."

"Mate, I'm really sorry," Michael said, patting the man on his back once.

"I'm sorry," echoed Irwin from the other bed. A few other soldiers who had been listening mimicked them, and Johnny felt the camaraderie that soldiers who trained together felt.

"Thanks, mates," he muttered.

"You're not the only one running away," Tilley said then. "My parents are very strict, and I was supposed to enter my father's business after school. But I didn't want to live like he did, always working in the tannery. Do you know how much those places smell? After you work a few years in one, the smell doesn't leave your nostrils even after you go home." A few guys laughed, and Tilley continued.

"But I wasn't allowed to dream. One day, we had a huge fight and I said that I could decide my own life. My father insisted I could never do something on my own, so I enlisted the next day, to prove I could. I will keep my wages and start a business when I get back."

"What business?" came a question, though Johnny didn't see who spoke.

"I want to open a tavern," Tilley said.

"That's a good dream," Johnny said.

And just like that, another man took his turn and started sharing his own thoughts, just like they did back in training. They all spoke, and Johnny felt closer to them. He liked Michael and Irwin the most, and he enjoyed spending these moments with them, both in the ship and back at training.

"This area," Jimmy pointed at the riverbend, "can tell us many things." Richard and Mark were standing next to him, looking at the area.

"Father had us work this back when…" Richard said. "He suspected there could be gold here." It was late August and the weather was still too cold to simply jump into the river without direction. Jimmy looked determined, though, and removed his shoes and socks, getting his pan ready. Richard and Mark mimicked him, and they waded into the river, slowly, getting used to the cold.

"Let's see what we can find, alright mates?" Jimmy said. They started working under his directions, and they searched through the gravel until they could reach bedrock. They did that in various spots, and Jimmy was thinking of ways they could maximize their efficiency.

"If we could see the bedrock, it'd be easier to find something valuable," he muttered at some point, thinking as he dug.

"There's too much dust, and it's too deep in spots," Richard said back.

"What if we dived inside?" Jimmy said.

"Still too blurry, and I can't see that well in water," Richard replied in the same tone, absentmindedly panning the gravel.

"What if..." Jimmy started again. "What if we had diving masks to see better?" he asked.

Richard looked at Jimmy, taking him more seriously now. "They would need to be waterproof," he said. "Probably made from leather, to fit on our faces better." Jimmy was nodding, looking at his nephew with interest.

"I can find pieces of glass," he said, "and smoothed to avoid cutting into the leather. And I know of a leatherworker..." he let his voice fade. What had begun as a vague idea was slowly forming into a possible reality. "The leather can be treated for use underwater, and the points where glass meets leather can be glued..."

Jimmy got out of the water then and hurried to the shore, where he left his pan. "I'll go and see what I can get done," he said, and left with quick steps. Richard and Mark stayed behind, panning through wet rocks, looking for something precious.

Several hours passed before Richard saw Jimmy hurry back, holding something. Richard left the now terribly cold water along with Mark and they approached Jimmy. Their uncle presented his device.

It was a leather mask, with glass for the eyes to see through. The glass was clear, and even though it was glued to the leather, the lenses were kept untainted. Richard took the mask in his hands. It had some heft to it, the leather was of good quality, and the glass felt sturdy. It wouldn't break from any pressure they would encounter in the river, and it would probably hold even the pressure of the ocean. Leather covered most of the wearer's face, as well as his nose, and the mouth was left open to breathe through. Richard was glad for it, as water had a tendency to go up his nose.

"That's amazing, uncle," Richard said. Jimmy was nodding enthusiastically.

"The leatherworker liked my idea so much he started working immediately. He had that piece of leather lying around, he barely charged me anything. He told me that if it works, he'll make a dozen and sell it to the prospectors of the area."

"A very practical man," Richard muttered. He looked at the sun. "We'll try it tomorrow, probably."

"Yes, it's getting dark. And cold. Get back to your mother, boys, and I'll see you tomorrow morning, alright?" Jimmy said. Both boys nodded, and they all left quickly.

Richard was excited for the next day, but he fell asleep easily, as he was exhausted.

With first light, the boys were already at the mine, along with their uncle. Jimmy lit a good fire so that they could shake off the cold of the water, and Richard put on the mask. He had stripped down to his underwear, packing away his clothes near the fire, along with a clean pair of underwear he'd wear after diving.

He took a deep breath and dived in the cold water, which sent shocks through his body, but he withstood it. He was seeing clearly around himself. The mask was a genius idea, and he wished that Jimmy had patented it before giving the idea out, but it was too late. He swam awkwardly in the shallow river, and went to the deeper parts, looking at the river bottom. When he came up for a breath, he shared his excitement with Jimmy and Mark standing on the shore with a thumbs-up signal.

Then, he was back in the water. He shoved off the cold by moving vigorously, and he used larger rocks to anchor himself to the bottom of the river. Later, he saw Mark and Jimmy panning through the water, as well. Richard spent a good part of the day looking at the bedrock, but found nothing useful, and as they agreed, he exchanged the mask with Mark's pan, who stripped quickly and jumped into the water, with overflowing excitement. Richard sat by the fire for a bit, trying to get the cold out of his bones.

Mark swam more skillfully than Richard, and he was quicker. He went deep into the bottom of the river and scanned it quickly, looking for anything that might indicate the presence of valuable metals or gems, and when he saw little shiny spots, he focused his attention on them. After about an hour, he returned to Jimmy, holding a one-ounce nugget of gold. Richard laughed, relieved that they had found something, and Jimmy hugged his nephew tightly.

They spent some time panning and diving, but it was colder than the day before. When Jimmy realized they wouldn't be able to take full advantage of the day, he thought of another trick to use. He went through his late brother's things and found exactly what he was looking for: a couple of dowsing rods. They were made of metal, shaped like an "L", and Jimmy had made them for Mick. He didn't know if Mick had ever used them, but Jimmy had had success with them before, so he wanted to try again.

He held them in his hands and started walking along the riverside. Richard saw him, growing curious of the man's many ideas.

"What are you doing, uncle?" he shouted from the water.

"Stay with Mark, watch over him, and be careful, both of you. The waters are treacherous here, and you might slip. I'll be back soon, I'll be prospecting for a bit," he said, and went deeper into the bush. There were parts of the claim that he and Mick hadn't prospected deeply, and since the river wasn't the best place to hunt for gold in the winter, he wanted to give it a try.

As he walked, carefully observing the rods, his eyes caught some movement deeper in. Thinking it was a bird, he ignored it, but he realized it came from the ground. He looked towards it, hoping it wasn't a dangerous animal.

A couple of wallabies looked back, looking at Jimmy curiously. He smiled at them, and they hopped away quickly, hiding from the big bad man in the shade of a bush. He understood their hesitation, and went back to his dowsing, resuming his path.

Jimmy had created a mental map of the area, walking in tight lines along the river, and perpendicular to it, in a grid. He wanted to cover the most ground he could with the time he had available. Suddenly, the two rods moved. That could mean there was water underneath or solid mineral. He stopped dead in his tracks, and marked the ground clearly, then marked three trees around him, and even placed a heavy rock, also clearly marked. It would be bad to lose the spot.

When he returned to the riverbend, he found Mark and Richard still bravely fighting against the freezing waters. "Come out, boys," he called, and they quickly joined him. After they got warm enough to brave the bush, they armed themselves with shovels and followed his lead. They arrived at the spot he had marked, and under his instructions, they started digging.

The day grew darker and darker, but just before it became impossible to see, Richard exclaimed in excitement. Mark and Jimmy focused on where he had been digging and saw something shining in the dirt. Jimmy reached down to pick it up and exclaimed loudly.

"Fuck me dead," he muttered, before realizing there were kids around him. "Don't tell your mother I said that," he added. He lifted it up from the ground and tried to clean it up. Richard and Mark stared at a huge gold nugget, the size of a fist.

"To Mick's nugget," Richard started off the toast, and the group around him laughed. All the Hoaglands, both Jimmy's family and Cathy's family, had gathered the evening after the discovery in Jimmy's house, to celebrate. Cathy looked happier than Richard had seen her in weeks, Christina was smiling widely, a weight having been lifted off her shoulders. Jimmy's wife was proudly holding her husband's hand.

They had decided then to name the nugget in the honor of Jimmy's brother and the boys' father. Richard had felt it was a gift from his father, while Jimmy considered that the bad luck his brother had suffered was so that they could have good luck now.

"To Mick's nugget," the rest of the family raised their own glasses in response, and then they started attacking the food.

The gold nugget passed by every pair of hands, as everyone wanted to hold it and feel the weight. Jimmy had weighted it when he had returned home the day before and he had found it weighted twenty-one ounces, which would net them a huge sum. To Richard's mind, the money was inconceivable. It would feed them well for a time, and it would pay for everything his mother had been planning, easily.

The evening passed by pleasantly. After they ate, they went home, and Richard slept peacefully, not worrying about the next day for the first time after many weeks.

The next day, Jimmy hurried to the town, keeping a low profile. He went to a gold buyer and waited until all other miners had left the establishment having sold their little nuggets, before he approached the counter. He smiled at the man and leaned in, as if to whisper. The gold buyer also leaned in, used to the dealings of the miners here.

"Please refrain from showing surprise," Jimmy said in a low voice. "I have a huge nugget with me."

The gold buyer nodded and smiled an understanding smile, though it was obvious from the prideful way he raised his eyebrows and eyes that he didn't believe the miner had anything worthy of his surprise. Jimmy made sure they were alone and pulled out the nugget and left it on the counter. The gold buyer looked at it and his eyes grew wider, though to his credit he did not exclaim loudly.

"That's huge, indeed," he muttered. He checked it and then gave Jimmy an estimate. Jimmy nodded, and then suggested another amount, slightly lower.

"Consider the difference a personal tip," Jimmy said. "I don't want claim jumpers sneaking around my mine or my home, so buy yourself a few beers and keep this confidential."

"Aye, that's what I'll do, mate," the man said. "That's what I'll do."

"The good men have gone to war," Jimmy said thoughtfully, "and only the bad men have stayed behind." He gathered the money the buyer put out and left for his claim.

When he arrived, he saw Mark and Richard waiting. They jumped up the moment they saw him, and they met in the middle of the distance. Jimmy pulled out the money and the two boys gasped.

"I don't think I've seen this much money in a single place," Richard said.

"Well, here's half of it," Jimmy said. "It's yours."

"Thank you, uncle," Richard and Mark echoed excitedly.

"Thank you, too, for your hard work, boys," Jimmy said back.

"I don't feel that good carrying this much around, but there are some things we need to do," Richard said. "Do you mind if we left now uncle?"

"No, Richard. See you later," Jimmy said, and hurried off to his own house. He needed to put the money in his safe as soon as possible.

Richard and Mark left for the town. Richard had spent the previous day thinking about what to and planning things out with his mother and his brother, as well as Christina—who had become a permanent part of their family, and her opinion was important to him. As they entered the town, they walked closed together, their minds on their pockets and the significant sum hidden inside. Richard kept an arm down his side, pressing against the pocket, to constantly feel the little bulge and to keep himself from worrying too much.

The first things they ordered were materials to expand the chicken coop, with a quick stop at the Ansari shop. Then, the boys hurried to the clothier's shop, where they ordered clothes for everyone. Winter was still going strong, but summer would come soon, and both he and Mark were still growing. Johnny had left many of his clothes behind, but they were still too little to fit inside. And, besides, Richard didn't want to go through his brother's things. He might—no, he *would* return, and he would need them back.

Then, they bought a small surprise and hurried home. They entered the house and found their mother behind the house, working in the garden. Mark had been carrying the gift, and he proudly gave it to her, a full bouquet of beautiful flowers. Their mother's eyes grew wide when she saw them.

"Thank you, boys," she muttered, her eyes wet. She hadn't received flowers in so long. "That's very thoughtful of you." She went inside and put them on a vase, clearing tears from her eyes when the boys couldn't see them. They followed her a few moments later, and Richard put the money on the table.

"Here's what's left. What else is needed right away?" he asked, pretending he didn't see her wiping her tears.

"T-Timber," she muttered. "We need to make the root cellar. Food needs to be bought and bills need to be covered." She approached the table and looked over the money.

"That's for the timber," Richard pushed some of it aside. They had discussed how much would be needed, and he had asked around for an estimate.

"Then that's enough for at least two months," Cathy said, staring at the bills. She looked at the two boys. "I'm proud of you, boys. You did well. You'd make your father proud, if he could see you."

Richard heard his mother's voice getting strained but didn't say anything. He didn't trust his own voice, either.

CHAPTER TWELVE

"There," a soldier pointed, and the other soldier carrying the timbers, complied. He put the freshly cut logs onto a flat deck mini train car, and then returned to the pile that was nearby. He picked up another piece of timber and carried it to the transport, just as another soldier was leaving the one he had been carrying. The two soldiers, under the directions of the third, loaded the timber on the transport quickly. Then, the third one climbed into the front of the electric transport vehicle and drove into the tunnel entrance.

The main tunnel was wide enough so that the transport could fit with enough space around for a couple of men to pass through, though barely. As the timber transport continued through the main tunnel, it passed by two officers, judging by their insignia, going down the tunnel. When it reached them, the officers stopped walking, waiting for the slow tiny train-like transport to pass, before resuming their walking.

They soon passed by a large opening in the tunnels where men were loading crates onto another electric train car. The officers knew that the crates were full of ammunition, as was marked on their sides. When the train was filled, just as the officers were passing next to it, it started off towards another tunnel. There was a label drilled into the side of the tunnel, reading "Wombat Drive."

After a few short tunnels and series of rooms, the two officers arrived at the main briefing room. They entered, seeing the British Royal Engineers officers Major Moore already waiting to give them their morning briefing. When they saw him from the entrance, the officer on the back leaned in to whisper to the officer on the front. "M&M looks serious today." The one on the front nodded but made sure Major Moore didn't hear them calling him with his nickname.

Major Moore gestured for the two newcomers to sit, and the officers chose adjacent seats. More officers entered over the next few minutes, reaching twelve in total. Major Moore looked at the nine lieutenants and the three captains gathered before him, from both British and Australian forces. When all twelve had finally arrived, he started his briefing. After the usual greetings, he started giving them their orders.

"I received word from my senior commander, which you are to pass on to your soldiers. The 175th Tunneling Company will continue receiving training from the Royal Engineers before the Engineers leave for other parts of the front soon," he said. He knew that the Royal Engineers leaving would mean that the remaining troops would have more work to do, and less help. But these were the orders, unfortunately. And harder ones were still to come.

"We need to extend the Vimy tunnels towards Vimy Ridge. The Germans are underground looking for us over there, and they have fortified the ridgeline above the ground, but also below it. Vimy Sector will be extended up to twelve miles. We have the plans, and some points will need to go thirty feet deep." Some of the officers audibly gasped at that.

The British would soon be leaving the Australian 175th Tunneling Company to work on their own, the officers knew, and the amount of work was overwhelming. Major Moore saw one of the Australian officers half-raise his hand to ask a question, and then realizing that it was too soon for questions, he put it back down. He would ask after the major had finished his briefing, as was the correct procedure. The major saw the Australians get upset, and realized the morale hit they had taken, so he paused giving orders and gave out a few encouraging words.

"We will have more mining companies joining us to work on other sections of the Vimy Sector. Reinforcements have been dispatched from Australia already, and should be here soon, within weeks possibly." He saw them brightening up a bit at that, so he continued.

"Now listen closely here," he said. "We have a reason for this expansion. The Canadians will be coming soon. The tunnels need to be ready so that they can move safely undergrown, towards the Vimy Ridge position. They will get into position on the surface, bringing with them artillery weapons. The plan is to unleash the largest artillery barrage the Germans have ever seen, to keep their heads down.

"Nobody has taken Vimy Ridge until now, but the Canadians have a new type of artillery. The job of our sappers is to make the tunnels big enough so that they can house thousands of soldiers, along with their weapons, and the artillery guns. The tunnels will also be the main avenue of supplying the front lines with water, ammunition, and provisions. And, of course, we'll be getting the wounded back through them." He paused for a moment.

"So, I think you do understand we need the tunnels to be large, well-supported, and expertly made. The Royal Engineers have trained the tunneling companies enough, and the Australians know their job well. I have complete faith you'll all bring this mission to success. Any questions?" he asked and looked at the Australian officer who had almost interrupted him before.

"Will we have support from better electric systems?" the officer asked.

"Is there a problem with what we have now?" Major Moore asked.

"The electric engines and the pumps are unreliable. They often fail in the middle of a job, sometimes making a mess of things. If we are to expand so much, we'll need people for the new roles, as well as equipment that works and is reliable, ya know." He paused for a moment. "Without electricity, people are left surviving underground with candle lanterns, and working with picks, shovels, and buckets," he added. He had seen it happen, and he knew how hard that would make the huge undertaking they were to complete.

Major Moore examined the officer's face, and realized the man wasn't just making excuses. He was making a point based on his experience. Such issues would certainly prove disastrous, he knew. "List every piece of machinery you will need to sustain life here, underground, for the entire area. Give me your projections for the maximum scale of the project, too. Bring me the list within twenty-four hours and I'll see what I can do."

"Yes, sir," the man said. He was glad to help his men get better equipment. It was enough that they were risking their lives against enemy forces, and battling the very forces of nature as they dug, fighting against collapses, bad air, moisture, rot, and so many other issues; he didn't want to have them bear the added danger of equipment malfunction.

When no one else asked any questions, Major Moore dismissed them. The twelve officers left the briefing room, each thinking about the men under them.

Lieutenant Richard Hungerford, the platoon commander of the Third Platoon, from the 175th Tunneling Company, one of the companies tasked with expanding the tunnel system of the Vimy

Sector, walked through the system his company had proudly built, and reached his room. He had a little bunk space, where he sat, as he usually did when he wanted to think in peace.

He had forty-two men under him. He considered the plans, as laid out by Major Moore, and tried to understand what part of the tunnel system his men would soon start working in. His degree from the School of Mines back in Perth hadn't prepared him for war, but it had prepared him for engineering. As he went over his ideas in his mind, a plan was starting to take form.

"Come on, mate," one of the soldiers of the Third Platoon shook another one to awakening. They hurried to take their kits, and at seven in the morning, hurried through the tunnel system. Morning didn't mean much to the sappers, as they worked most of the time underground, not seeing the sun. But it separated work from sleep and defined eating times and the few rest times.

They arrived at the end of a tunnel and went to work, digging a new dugout, where they would construct a storage area. They prepared their candle lanterns and their pickaxes and started with removing the clay from the walls. As they worked, they were overseen by a British Sergeant of the Royal Engineers, Sgt. Bigsley.

Sgt. Bigsley watched them closely, seeing how they applied their training. He nodded to himself, satisfied that they were working smartly, avoiding silly mistakes. Then, he called a few of them over.

"Get your buckets and shovels," he ordered. "Form a chain, remove the soil before it builds up here." He pointed. "There's a train car there, which will be taking the soil outside."

The men nodded without comments to the sergeant, but as they started to form, he heard a wide variety of profanities. He was impressed by the extend of the Australians' vocabulary when it came to swearing. The men managed to create a schedule for themselves, to optimize their work and minimize how quickly they were getting exhausted. The sergeant saw the men working the pickaxes for fifteen minutes each, then switching to the bucket and shovel. The system was clever, and everyone worked in all the spots, with no one getting overworked.

The candle sputtered in the lantern and Sgt. Bigsley realized that the air smelled horribly. But it wasn't only the smell of the soldiers, many of whom had questionable hygiene at best, but the very air they were breathing out. They were deep in the tunnels, and there were many men here and elsewhere working, breathing out air that wasn't good for inhaling again. The sergeant gestured at one of the men, who promptly hurried to him.

"Go to Lt. Hungerford. Tell him there's an air issue," he ordered, and the private rushed off. A few minutes later, Sgt. Bigsley saw the lieutenant come back with his messenger. He saluted the sergeant, and then observed the workers.

"I understand what you meant," the lieutenant said after a few moments. "The air stinks."

"We need better air quality underground, especially if the tunnels are to expand," the sergeant told him. "Do you have any ideas?"

The man looked around for a few moments, thinking. Then he nodded. "We could do what miners have been doing in Australia since the 1800s," he said. The sergeant looked at him, not understanding. He wasn't familiar with centuries-old Australian miner techniques, but he also couldn't apply his modern engineering knowledge in such extreme conditions easily. So, he gave an encouraging nod to the man, so that he would explain what he meant.

"Australian miners use sails to encourage better airflow," Lt. Hungerford said, and the sergeant stared at him blankly. He couldn't even imagine how that would be done. "They put them up by the mine's entrance to bring more air in.

"Well, it's worth a shot, anyway," he added. "But we should not use white sails. Nothing that can be seen from afar. If we put up white sails, the Germans would be raining down artillery fire a few minutes later."

"Very well, sir," Sgt. Bigsley said. "Try your idea. Let me know how it goes."

Lt. Hungerford nodded and left, going for the quartermaster. After navigating the maze-like underground tunnels they had built, he reached the larger room the quartermaster used. He found the man noting down things in a large book. He looked up just as the lieutenant entered.

"Lt. Hungerford, how may I help you?" the quartermaster asked.

"I need canvas, like the one used for sails. But it has to be painted, not white, since I'll be using it outside," he said. The quartermaster looked around thoughtfully, then went through the book in front of him.

"Yes, I have exactly what you need," he said.

Lt. Hungerford took the canvas, thanked the man, and hurried back through the tunnels. He returned to the spot where the Australian soldiers were digging and called them to attention.

"Among all of you, who has worked in a mine back in Australia?"

he asked, and he saw many hands go up. "And who knows how to set up the airflow system that uses sails?" he added. Most hands went down, but a couple remained up. "You two, along with you," he pointed at a man who looked the strongest, "come with me. The rest, continue what you were doing."

The lieutenant took the three soldiers towards the tunnel entrance and explained his plan on the way. The two soldiers who had worked with the system before were nodding along, excited to be helping. When they arrived at the tunnel entrance, Hungerford left the canvas on the ground, and then sent out the soldiers to bring wood in the correct shape to hold the sails. He retrieved hammers and nails for them while they were gone, and then observed their work.

As the British soldiers went in and out of the tunnels, many paused for a few moments to examine what the Australians were doing. Lt. Hungerford saw the lack of understanding on their faces and heard them mutter between themselves in surprise and curiosity. The lieutenant saw that the three Australians were stealing glances at the muttering soldiers and saw them blushing more than once under the scrutiny. By the end of their work, they looked much less enthusiastic than they were before they began.

The three soldiers fastened the pieces of canvas well, and then made sure they were secured and that they wouldn't drop off with the first gust of wind. When they thought they were done, they saluted the lieutenant and retreated inside the tunnels, their faces lowered in embarrassment. Lt. Hungerford shared some of that embarrassment, thinking that he probably overestimated techniques that were decades old already.

He entered the tunnels, close behind them. After a few steps, he felt something unfamiliar. A slight breeze against the back of his neck. He turned his head to see the sails moving slightly. The system was working, after all. The soldiers in front of him were also looking around, touching their necks, before realizing what had happened. They shared laughter and friendly swear words and walked in a livelier rhythm.

When Hungerford and the three soldiers returned to the mining area, the soldiers returned to their work, speaking excitedly with the other soldiers. The lieutenant, and he was sure, everyone else, could still feel some of the breeze even this deep in the tunnels. Sgt. Bigsley looked at him expectantly and Lt. Hungerford explained that the project had been a success.

"Report to Major Moore, sir," the sergeant said. "He was worrying about poor air quality as well." Lt. Hungerford went to the major's office quickly. The major was impressed and wanted to inspect the sails himself, so he followed the lieutenant outside. He examined the sails carefully, pulling at places and pushing at others to ascertain that the structure could hold against stronger winds, too.

"This is brilliant work," Major Moore said. "I felt the improvement as we were coming, too. Congratulations." He turned to face the lieutenant. "If you have more suggestions about improving the air quality, let me know," he told him.

"I will get back to you shortly, sir," the lieutenant replied, and the major nodded, satisfied.

"Dismissed," the man told him, and Lt. Hungerford hurried away. He went straight back to the soldiers who were still digging for the new dugout and approached the three who had helped him. He saw that there was still a smile on their lips.

"Major Moore inspected your work," he told them, "and found it brilliant. Congratulations, you made a significant difference in the work conditions of you and your mates here." The three men looked so proud of themselves that even receiving a medal wouldn't have the same effect. Real, tangible benefits were always better than imagined or abstract ones.

"Thank you, sir," the three soldiers echoed, saluted, and returned to work.

Later that day, when the Australian miners were back in their bunks, they were in a better mood than they had been in weeks.

"That's Aussie logic for you, ya know," one of them said. "You got a problem, right? A British man just stares at the wall, silent, waiting for someone else to tell him what to do. An Aussie bastard, though, he applies good logic and solves it, eh?" The roaring laughter that followed ensured a stern look from an officer, but there was a smile hidden behind it. The Australians of the Third Platoon slept better than any other regiment that night.

CHAPTER THIRTEEN

The suits lying on Cathy's bed and on the chair looked new. She knew all of them were barely worn. Pairs of pants and shirts, some jackets, a few hats, all nice and in amazing condition. All of them belonged to her late husband, Mick, who had preferred more durable clothes for everyday wear, and had almost no reason to wear more formal clothes in the time they had been living here.

Cathy looked at them, Mick's closet behind her wide open and empty. She could sell them, if she had the courage to do it. Or she could donate them through the church to someone who could use them more than Mick would. Mick didn't have any more use of those clothes, wherever he was.

She put a hand in front of her mouth. She missed her husband terribly. A little sob escaped her as she touched one of his most favorite shirts. She remembered him wearing it. As it hung from the hanger, it was almost as if he was standing before her, in it. Her shoulders shook with another sob before she barely managed to stop herself from breaking down completely. She knew there was a… medicine for that. Cathy left the room and hurried to the pantry. As she passed next to the clock, she saw it was six in the evening, still too early for what she was about to do, but she needed something to dull her senses.

Taking the bottle, she opened it quickly. She took a few deep swigs, and made her way back to her room, ignoring the strict looks she received from Christina. The girl didn't yet know her pain. Cathy laid down on her bed, next to Mick's old suits, and drank some more. It would hide the pain in her heart, she knew. And she couldn't take it on that moment, she didn't have the courage to face a life without her husband. Maybe later.

The tears still came, though. Richard passed outside his mother's room later that evening and heard her sobs clearly. They were accompanied by slurred speech, and he realized how drunk his mother had gotten again. He sighed, disappointed in her; he had hoped it would pass, as she was finally busier and much more active and involved them before, when the hurt was still fresh.

It was late the next morning when the woman finally got up from the bed in a terrible stupor. Her head ached and she was incredibly thirsty. She hurried back down to drink some water and returned to her room. The suits were still there, waiting for her. She quickly left the room to do other things around the house, taking a couple of swigs of wine from a new bottle.

The day passed slowly, and her heart was heavy. When it was dark again, she went to the room to pack as many of the clothes as she could back inside the closet. She couldn't decide what to do with them just yet, she couldn't even imagine how she would live without Mick. When she thought she was finally finished, she sat back on the bed, taking a deep swig from the wine. Then, her eyes fell on her rocking chair. There were two suits still laying there, which she had forgotten out of the closet. She couldn't bring herself to stand up and get them away, though.

Cathy laid back down on the bed, staring at the ceiling. She thought about her life before Mick, and how better it had been when Mick was in it. She imagined how it would be if he was here, if he would help her with the garden, or if he would dig out the root cellar. How much better it would be if Johnny would also be helping him instead of fighting in a war half a world away.

She thought of Mick deeply, and she was crying before she even realized it. The bottle was empty while the moon and the stars were still shining, and another one had taken its place. Only when the sun had come up did Cathy finally find some rest, in a deep dreamless sleep. Christina knocked on her door at eight in the morning, and then again at nine. Cathy was too deep in her stupor to answer, and only when Christina opened the door at ten in the morning, hours after her usual wake-up time, did the woman manage to get up. She didn't dare look at the direction of the chair as she left the room.

"What is this?" Cathy screamed. Christina turned quickly to look at what the woman was pointing at.

"What is what?" she asked, not understanding what horrible thing had happened from the image she was seeing. Christina had set the table, had even put out the food.

"This," Cathy pointed at the stew.

"Vegetable stew," Christina muttered. "What do you mean?"

Cathy then started shouting, calling Christina names. She pointed at what she believed where faults in the woman's cooking—things that Christina couldn't see. Then, in her rage, she broke a plate, which she blamed on Richard who had been sitting nearby, that he had mislaid the plate in order to make her break it. Richard, familiar with his mother's moods, said nothing, but Christina didn't let it pass.

She argued with Cathy for a bit, defending the boys and herself, but the woman was louder, and Christina didn't want to scare Richard and Mark, who had been looking at her with wide eyes. She was at least happy that she took the drunk woman's attention away from her sons and onto herself, even though it was wearing her down.

That pattern slowly became familiar. The woman woke up late from her drinking the night before, then did a few things around the house, mostly busying herself with the projects she had started herself, and then picking up the bottle. The time she picked the bottle up was getting earlier every day. Then, she would find fault in everything everyone did. When Christina was around, she would fight, but Richard and Mark usually escaped silently.

A few days later, Richard was outside the house, trying to catch a chicken under Christina's request, when Mark joined him. The shouts that came from deeper into the house were all the indication Richard needed to understand what Mark was fleeing. They exchanged a look.

"Do you want to go for an adventure?" Mark said suddenly.

"What do you mean?" Richard asked.

"Let's go camping, the two of us," Mark suggested. "There," he pointed deeper in the bush. Richard knew there was a river deeper in, and a good camping spot where they had gone exploring often in the summer. It was cold for exploration, but they could light a small fire and be away from the shouting match for a bit.

Richard nodded, took a pack of matches and a small axe, and started walking deeper inside the forest. Mark followed him, his dog Bosco happily behind him, more excited than he had been earlier. They found the camping spot soon and gathered a few dry twigs. Richard cut a few pieces of wood, just to use his axe and get a bit of his frustration out on the poor wood.

They lit the fire and sat near it, almost hugging it. Mark was patting the dog slowly as she slept on his feet, and Richard was staring at the cold waters of the creek absentmindedly.

"What do you think Johnny is doing?" Mark said after a moment.

"Digging tunnels and killing Germans," Richard said automatically. He had thought about it himself, and that's what he had decided their brother was doing. Mark nodded, as if agreeing completely.

"What do you think we will do now?" Mark said after another long pause.

"What do you mean?" Richard said, his mind still far away.

"About… everything. About mom, about dad's mine, about…" he stopped. "I miss dad."

"I miss him too," Richard said. He turned to look at the fire, his mind more present. "I don't think a day passes when I don't miss him."

"I know mom misses him too. She has his clothes out and cries when she looks at them," Mark said. "I saw from the window."

"Yeah, I know," Richard said. "She took them out a few days ago."

"Dad loved the mine," Mark said. "He had told me we would never go hungry if we had it. That it was good, honest work."

"Sounds like dad," Richard muttered. He knew that it was too hopeful, but their father had always been hopeful and determined.

"We should go back to it," Mark said. "It would be his wish, I think."

"We should. Besides, we had found quartz, remember?" Richard said. His brother nodded emphatically without speaking. "We should tell uncle Jimmy," Richard added.

"Why do you think uncle Jimmy and dad didn't talk much?" Mark asked. Richard shrugged, unable to reply. How could he know?

Their father had been a private man, after all. He wondered if their mother even knew.

They stared at the fire longer, Mark asking strange questions about the future, which Richard didn't know how to answer. He didn't have all the answers, he didn't even know what he was supposed to do about their mother treating Christina, their brother's wife, so horribly. The poor girl would leave some day, he thought, and leave them with their drunk mother, and he wouldn't blame her at all.

Christina could hear the woman talking to herself, telling herself the usual story about how everyone was treating her badly. She didn't want to have another shouting match with her, and she was sure that if she entered the same room that Cathy was, the woman would attack her mercilessly. So, instead, she chose to hide in her own room, a guest room she had taken for herself weeks ago. She couldn't bring herself to move in and change Johnny's room, even though she knew he wouldn't have a problem with her living there.

She took her pen and paper and started out a letter. She often thought about writing to Johnny in her mind, and she wanted to write about his mother's new habit. She wrote how the boys were fleeing her, how she could barely stay at the house sometimes, and how Cathy had almost abandoned the projects she had started herself. Having access to more funds had only made her return to wine easier.

Christina missed Johnny and worried about him terribly, but she didn't want to let him know how much. He had his reasons for leaving, and she was finally understanding that, and she didn't want to burden him with her own issues. She ended up writing quite a large letter, the words pouring out of her, as if she was talking to him. Her writing hand's wrist was hurting by the end of it. She stood, stretched, and tried to listen to the telltale signs of Cathy's stupor.

No mutterings, only little sobs. So, the woman had returned to her grieving, probably in her own room, lying next to the unworn suits her late husband had left behind. Christina left her room and hurried to the kitchen to continue her work. She realized the boys had left, probably during their argument earlier today. She cleaned the kitchen and then started preparing a quick dinner for herself, the boys, and Cathy, should she get up before noon tomorrow.

When she was done, the boys had yet to return. She took a book and sat on an armchair in the living room, reading. It was after ten in the evening when she heard them open the door. She had dozed off a bit, but she quickly collected herself and hurried to the door.

"What time do you think it is?" she asked them. Despite her not being their mother, the two boys quickly lowered their eyes. They had grown to respect her, and her opinion mattered.

Richard glanced at the clock. "It's after ten," he muttered.

"Yes, and it's been dark out for hours. You should have been back when it was getting dark, not now." She tried to keep a stern face, as she had seen her own mother do so many times with her siblings and herself.

"You are right," said Richard. "Sorry, Christina." Christina turned to Mark.

"Sorry," he muttered, eyes lowered. "Time passed quickly."

She straightened her body, letting her stern look relax a little bit. "As long as you promise not to do it again," she said.

"I promise," they echoed at the same time.

"Good. Now go to bed," she told them. Richard turned to leave, but Mark remained.

"I need your help," he told her. She looked at him expectedly, waiting for him to explain. "I want to write a letter to Johnny. Can you help me?"

She smiled widely. "Of course I can, Mark. Go get your writing things," she told him, and he nodded and hurried away. A few moments later he was back and laid the things on the kitchen table. Christina encouraged him to get started, and then they discussed how to write the letter. She helped him with his spelling, and a few minutes ago they had the letter ready and in an envelope.

"We'll mail it tomorrow, alright?" she said. The boy nodded, hugged her goodnight, and hurried to his room. She looked at him leaving for a long moment, thinking how lucky she was that at least the two boys had accepted her, and weren't making her life as difficult as Cathy was.

The next morning, Christina and Mark went to the post office first thing in the morning. Mark had school and Christina didn't want him to be late. They entered the small building, which was pretty crowded already. She saw many women who she guessed were mothers, as well as younger girls who were probably in the same position she was, married to soldiers.

She stood in line until her turn came, where she gave the two letters and payment to the postmaster, a balding man called David Howl.

"Good morning, Christina," the man said. "Two today, huh?"

"Good morning Mr. Howl. Yes, Mark wrote to his brother, too," she told him, patting the boy's shoulder.

"You've been coming here often," he remarked.

"Yes," Christina replied, "and it seems that I'm not alone." She gestured around the room.

"Indeed. So many parents and siblings, or wives as yourself, sending their thoughts, their news, their love to their family members in the war."

"Let's pray everyone gets home safe," Christina told him, and the man nodded, then gestured for the next person to approach the counter.

Richard heard Jessie swearing from the mine site's entrance. He approached to see the one-handed man swearing at the rock crusher, kicking it.

"Damned machine, always jamming," he said.

"Good morning Jessie. Crusher's busted?" he asked.

"Hey Richard," Jessie said, his grimace breaking into a smile for a moment before returning to his scowl. "Yes, it's jammed. And I can't really do much," he gestured at his missing arm in explanation wordlessly.

"Can I be your hands, then?" Richard asked. Jessie looked at him appraisingly for a moment and nodded.

"But you need to follow my instructions to the letter, mate. You think you can do that?"

"Yes," Richard said, and approached the machine. Jessie gestured at a few places, explaining the procedure for opening the machine up, then pointed at where Richard should pull. Together, Jessie being the mind and Richard the arms, they unjammed the machine.

Richard patted himself off and offered a huge smile up to Jessie.

"That's the first time I fixed the rock crusher," he said. "Dad always used to do it, he told us it's too dangerous."

"It is, that's why I was so specific in my instructions," Jessie said. "Congratulations for your first time. It won't be the last, by far," he added. "These bloody things always jam."

"I'm not completely useless by myself, though," the boy said, a hint of protest in his voice. "Me and Mark helped dad lay tracks in our mine for ore carts, you know. But we didn't get to use them," he added, his eyes downcast. "We had just started using the ore carts when…"

"That's very good, though," Jessie said. "It's very helpful to have ore carts instead of having to bring the ore up in buckets." Richard nodded.

A few hours later, Jimmy passed by the mine, to see how Richard and Jessie were. The boy was ferrying ore up from the mine, with Jessie on the surface. Jessie called Jimmy and explained what Richard had told him.

"They had made quite a bit of infrastructure then," Jimmy said thoughtfully. "We should go and take a look soon, to make sure it's still there, ya know? Thieves love ripping out easy-to-grab metal like newly laid tracks. And if there was ore within reach, they might even take that."

Richard came up just then and greeted his uncle. He had heard them talking, as Jessie had turned the crusher off when Jimmy arrived. "We had just discovered a large quartz vein. Dad said there was gold there. We had found a bit in that vein before." Jessie's face lit up at the mention of a confirmed gold-bearing vein.

"All the more reason to go," Jessie said, looking at Jimmy.

"Alright. We'll go in a couple of days," Jimmy said. The boy and the one-handed man nodded, and they returned to work as Jimmy bid them goodbye and left.

The next couple of days passed quickly, Richard helping at his uncle's mine and getting paid a little for his help, and on the same time, getting to know more about running a mine. Then, when Richard arrived at the mine next morning, Jimmy was already there waiting for him, along with Jessie. They greeted each other and left for the other Hoagland claim.

As Richard neared the claim, a mix of nostalgia and apprehension filled him. He tried to steel his resolve. He couldn't be afraid of the mine and of dynamite mining forever if he wanted to work in the industry seriously. As they left the thick woods behind and entered into the clearing in front of the mine's entrance, they spotted a campfire. Jessie immediately placed a hand on Richard's shoulder protectively, as he and Jimmy's eyes started scanning the area.

Two men were sitting near the campfire. As the Hoaglands and Jessie broke through the trees, the two men spotted them almost on the same time they were spotted themselves. They bolted up and ran away before Jimmy or Jessie could do anything, leaving the fire and their breakfast behind.

The three men approached the campfire, looking it over.

"The thieves must have felt pretty comfortable, setting up camp with a fire," Jimmy said angrily, "even though it isn't their claim." He turned to Richard. "Let's take a look around." Richard nodded, and led the way around the mine's surface, as he was the most familiar with it. They noticed some tools missing. The rock crusher had more ore inside it than a month ago. And near a dried-out creek that ran through the claim, they found several new holes in the ground.

"The thieves tested the ground for gold or quartz before setting up camp," Jimmy said, pointing. He had an angry look on his face, getting more worked up by the minute. "Let's go inside the mine." Richard brought Jimmy back and then down, through the corridors he knew like the back of his hand, having worked with Johnny and his father for so long inside it.

As they walked around, they realized that the damned claim jumpers had had the audacity to blow out some of the quartz vein. Ore was missing, which was what Richard had seen up on the crusher. Deeper in, they discovered a completely new shaft, following another part of the quartz vein that Richard's father had never pursued. It went in more than fifteen feet.

Richard explained everything he was seeing, pointing at the differences between his memories and the image around them.

"This must have taken quite some time to dig," Jimmy noted, gesturing. "The claim jumper either had quite some time, or multiple friends." They went back to the surface, talking. "If they found gold, it would be a real threat. Gold is worth much, and they might get more daring. They could very well come back armed..." he let his voice fade as he thought, looking around the mine. He pointed at the entrance. "We need to board up the mine completely, right away, if we're not going to work it full time."

The boy nodded, and they went back to Jimmy's claim to work for the day, thinking on what they would do.

When Richard returned home, he found Mark studying with Christina, on the kitchen table. He didn't see his mother anywhere, and when he asked Christina about it, she said that the woman had already passed out on her bed. Richard sat with them.

"I went to dad's mine today," he said. "There were claim jumpers there. They had been working it while we were away." Mark's eyes grew wide, and Christina's face darkened. "We will board it up, probably, for now."

"I want to help," Mark said quickly. "You can't tell me no. I have worked there, too. I want to help." His last words ended in a whine.

"You can, you can," Richard replied, his hands out in a pacifying gesture, "but only on the weekend, alright? School's important. And don't tell mum, or you'll be staying at home for the rest of your life," he added.

"You promise to be careful," Christina said seriously. "Gold makes people crazy. Don't do something you might regret."

Both boys nodded, looking at the table. Then Mark looked up, his eyes shining. "I can't wait for the weekend. I wonder what the mine looks like inside," he muttered.

"But until then, homework," Christina told him, gesturing at their open book. "Let's go over this problem once more," she started. Richard went to the kitchen to find something to eat, leaving them to their studying.

On Saturday morning, Jimmy with his two nephews along with Jessie arrived at a thankfully empty mine. They cleaned up the campsite and set up their own, as they planned to stay for the whole weekend, if needed. They surveyed the site more carefully.

"The thieves haven't processed their ore yet," Jessie exclaimed suddenly. "There's good ore here!"

Jimmy approached the crusher to examine it himself. He saw that there were several good chunks of quartz with faint golden streaks. "Let's do it, then, before we board it up. Revenge for what the thieves have done. Besides, it's my claim, so it's my gold," he said, a mischievous grin on his face. He turned to Jessie. "Prepare the machine, mate." Then, he turned to the boys. "Let's get the ore up."

They brought up the mined ore in the cart, though they mostly used buckets for quicker trips as there was not much ore. Richard was loading the ore in the crusher, Mark bringing it up, and Jimmy helped in both positions, supervising the boys, and getting ready to board up the mine. They worked hard, as the sun first climbed up the sky, then slowly made its way to the other end of the horizon. When it was getting dark, they realized it was a two-day job, and prepared to sleep in the mine's campsite. Jimmy let the boys sleep peacefully, but he made sure to have a rotating watch with Jessie, to keep an eye out for the thieves.

The next day, they kept working on the ore, separating the gold from other useful minerals, and throwing away the useless materials. In the end of the day, the mine was boarded up, and they had several ounces of gold.

"Here," Jimmy split the gold into two piles, and offered the boys one half. "It's yours." The boys hesitated.

"Can you sell it and give me our cut next time I see you?" Richard voiced the thoughts in both of their heads.

"Sure will, mate," Jimmy said, smiling. "You did good work. Congratulations, boys. You're both on the way to become excellent miners." The boys smiled widely, glad for their uncle's praise, and proud for their work. Then, Jimmy grew more serious. "I need you to promise me something, though," he said.

"What?" Richard said, nodding along.

"The claim jumpers know there's gold down there," Jimmy gestured at the boarded-up mine. "They will be back, and they might even bring more friends. Promise me that you won't come here without at least either me or Jessie. It might be dangerous."

"I promise," the boys echoed. Jimmy nodded, satisfied, then they started on their way to home, all three Hoaglands and Jessie very satisfied with themselves and their weekend.

CHAPTER FOURTEEN

"We have reached England," Tilley said as he burst through the door. Johnny stood quickly, smiling widely, just like so many other soldiers around them. "They said we'll leave for France at seven hundred hours, tomorrow on the sixteenth," he added, "and that we can tour the port today." All the soldiers hurried to the door, excited to finally walk on land after weeks of being in the ship. As they passed Johnny, he heard that several of them planned to get drunk, and he was looking forward to paying a visit to a pub himself.

He and Tilley waited a few moments for the mob to pass them, and then they took their time walking off the boat. Johnny saw the crew loading crates, and he saw that there were many soldiers getting on the boat as well. New faces he hadn't seen, all heading to France like them.

When they were finally touching dry land, Johnny could kneel down and kiss it. It was so good standing on stable ground. He had grown used to the constant rocking of the boat but walking on something that wasn't moving felt incredibly more natural.

"Mate, I love the ground," Tilley muttered as they walked away from the port, echoing his own thoughts.

"Me too. I don't want to throw up for once in..." Johnny paused, trying to calculate the days, but gave up. "Weeks."

"Feels like a lifetime," Tilley said.

"Let's find somewhere to relax," Johnny said, looking around. They walked through the streets until they found a pretty park, with a few picnic tables laid around. They found one under the shade and sat down, relaxing for the first time in what felt like years.

"Hey, check them out," Tilley gestured with his head after a while. Johnny followed his gaze and saw a few groups of soldiers in uniform, like themselves, all walking in the same direction. They were talking among themselves, laughing, and Johnny had the sense that they were going somewhere specific. "Do you think they know something we don't?" Tilley asked, echoing once again his own thoughts.

"Let's follow them," Johnny suggested, and having nothing better to do, they hurried after the soldiers. They quickly led them through the narrow streets to an open pub. Johnny and Tilley exchanged an excited look. "Let's go for a beer!"

They entered and sat at a table in the corner. The pub was filled with soldiers like them, and Johnny could count at least four different uniform types. He saw that there were many from different countries, too. He spotted more Australians like themselves, a few English soldiers, and some he didn't recognize.

When they drank their first swig of beer, they let out a long sigh. First alcohol they had in a long time. They enjoyed the strange English brew, and it went down easily. With their second beer in hand, they turned their attention to the other soldiers.

Johnny observed an English soldier exchanging jests with some Australians. He saw that the Australians were in a good mood, but the Englishman was harsh, and what started as a joke slowly degraded into swearing. One of the Australians in particular was more involved, and the two soldiers stood, ready to exchange blows.

"Not inside," the pub manager called. "Or I'll tell your sergeants!" Laughter followed his words, but the two men looked determined to prove something that Johnny hadn't caught, and left the pub. Most soldiers followed, and a two-pints-drunk Tilley went with them.

Johnny drank his beer quickly and followed them out to a back alley.

The two men started circling each other, and other soldiers had formed a ring around them. As Johnny let his eyes wonder, he spotted a group of women nearby. They were one of the very few women other than the nurses on the ship he had seen in what felt like a century, and he enjoyed looking at them. As he let his eyes scan them, he realized two of them were looking at him and Tilley. He elbowed Tilley to grab his attention away from the fight, and gestured at the women, who were still looking at them, now smiling shyly.

"Mate, look." When Tilley realized that women were around, he straightened his body immediately, forgetting the fight completely.

"Let's go speak to them," he told Johnny. For about half a second, Johnny was about to follow, when he realized that he was a married man now.

"You can do whatever you want. I have a beautiful young wife waiting at home for me," Johnny said. He wondered if there truly was a hint of regret in his voice, or if he just missed Christina so much.

"Oh, the old ball and chain," Tilley teased him. "Do you write to her to take a piss, or are you allowed to do that by yourself?" He laughed at his own drunken joke. "But I'm a free man, so I'm going to get me an English woman." The alcohol running in his blood helped him find the courage to go to them by himself.

"Hey girls," he said as he neared them.

"Hey, soldier," one of the women said, approaching him and lightly placing her hand on his arm. "Having fun?"

"Sure do," Tilley said dumbly.

"You'd have more fun with us," the other woman said. "Do you want to go to a pub? We know a great place nearby, safer than this one."

Most of Tilley's thinking by that point was clouded by his hormones, his seemingly ages-long dry spell, and a generous amount of alcohol, and yet, a tiny logical part of his mind was still functioning. The women looked too forward, and Tilley was afraid they might be running some scheme, that they wanted to mug them. *A soldier in a foreign land can't be too careful*, the voice said. He wouldn't go anywhere without Johnny, who looked significantly more sober than he did, even though they had drunk the same amount of beer.

"Let's take my friend, too," he said, and the two women agreed. Tilley went back to him. "Mate, they said they knew a pub that's safer," he said in a low voice, "and they seem interested in us. But I have heard stories of women mugging stupid soldiers, and don't want to be one of them. Can you watch my back?"

"It's not a good idea, Tilley," Johnny said. "Let's not do it."

"How long until we have a chance like this again?" Tilley said. "Come on, mate. I need this."

Johnny couldn't deny his friend's request, so he simply nodded and followed him back to the two admittedly beautiful women who were not shy in the slightest in their behavior. One of them took hold of Tilley's arm, pushing it against her chest, and the other grabbed Johnny.

"Do you want to go to a pub," the one holding Tilley asked, leaving her voice to fade suggestively before continuing, "or take you somewhere more *secluded?*" She emphasized the last word, sending shivers down Johnny's spine. Still having his wits about him, he looked around quickly. There was no one following him, there was no one paying them any attention, in fact. He realized Tilley was waiting for his confirmation, which he gave with a slight nod.

"S-Sure," Tilley muttered, and the woman holding onto him pushed his arm even harder against herself. Johnny was glad the girl holding onto himself was calmer, since he didn't want to push his willpower further. They gently led them through the streets and into a nearby barn. The barn was empty save for themselves, and Johnny saw that there were horse stalls that were full of fresh hay. The smell of hay brought back certain memories of Christina, which made him both more excited, and boosted his willpower.

The woman that had been holding Johnny's arm left him and took a step back, looking him over suggestively and allowing him to take a better look at her. She had an ample chest, and her eyes shone with intelligence. Despite her killer figure, it was her face that drew him in the most. It was sharp and looked pretty, and Johnny saw that she had accented her natural features with expertly applied makeup. She smiled mischievously, and Johnny realized no woman had been so seductive with him before. He tried his best to keep his mind on Christina, though not having had sex in weeks wasn't making things any easier.

"I'm Teresa May," the woman told him, "and this is Suzanne Ray," she gestured at the woman who was still holding onto Tilley. Teresa had a more seductive, sexy look at her, while Suzanne looked sweeter and kinder. Johnny wasn't sure which he would have preferred, if he was given a choice. "You can have some fun before you're sent off to war…" she let her suggestion hang in the air for a moment, making Tilley's eyes grow noticeably wider, "for the right price," she added in the end.

Tilley turned to Suzanne, who nodded at him. He touched her hand, and she took it in her own. "Do you want to have some fun, honey?" Suzanne asked him, and Tilley melted before Johnny's eyes. Johnny thought that the man had lost the battle before it had even begun, back in the alley.

"Sure do," the man said stupidly again. Johnny threw him an angry stare.

"Tilley," Johnny muttered, trying to warn him against it, but the man didn't even hear him. Suzanne led him to one of the horse stalls. The door closed forcefully, and Johnny could hear the woman making suggestive noises.

"What about you, handsome?" Teresa said, taking a step towards Johnny. She placed her hand on his chest and looked at him through her eyelashes. "I want to see if you are the silent, brooding type in bed, as well." Johnny briefly wondered how much a man could take.

"Sorry, but I'm not interested. You're incredibly attractive, but I'm married," he said. His voice came out more forced than he had expected, louder than he wanted to, and he sounded unsure even to himself.

Teresa's face fell and she clicked her tongue. "You waste my time, you damn Aussie—" she started muttering under her breath, then took out a cigarette from somewhere in her clothes. She put it in her mouth, cutting her swearing off, and lit it with a match, in a practiced motion. She threw him one last look of disapproval and stormed out of the barn. Johnny was left alone for a moment, then heard Tilley's and Suzanne's moans, and followed her out.

He saw her take a few steps away and into a more populated street, and then she stood more provocatively, throwing meaningful glances at the men who passed. Johnny found a good spot to sit down and laid against a building, waiting for his friend.

As the time passed, he grew more impressed with his friend. In the time Tilley took to finish, Teresa worked with three men. Tilley spent about an hour with Suzanne, and when he did come out of the barn, he had the widest smile Johnny had ever seen on his friend's face. He said his goodbyes to Suzanne, who looked equally glad about what had transpired, and Johnny waved at Teresa, who was in a better mood and waved back.

"Mate, it was amazing," Tilley started saying as soon as they started walking towards the harbor. "I can't even remember when my last time was, ya know. And Suzanne, mate," Tilley paused for effect, "she knew some tricks. She did something with her tongue, oh, I can't even describe it."

Johnny smiled at his friend. He had a good time, too. It was nice to flirt with a woman, and even though Teresa was justifiably angry with him for wasting her time, he had enjoyed what little of it they spent together. He had enjoyed looking up at sky sitting down and not rocking about, too. On the rest of the way to the ship, Tilley went over several details of his encounter, and how much better women were, compared to his hand.

"I did not miss this," Tilley muttered, holding onto the railing. The ship had left the harbor a few minutes earlier, at seven in the morning. The sun was shining through dark clouds, but it was still enough to see by clearly.

The deck was full of soldiers. Johnny counted at least two hundred men with full packs and their rifles. There was no room inside the ship, so the newcomers would have to tough it out on the deck.

Tilley was looking at the men with Johnny, having the same grimace. They had both a look of anxiety.

"Mate, if we meet rough seas," Tilley started, then paused. He almost did not want to say it, for fear of making it come true. But his anxiousness overcame his superstitions. "These men will be in trouble. I don't want to see more honest men getting washed overboard."

"And these are infantrymen," Johnny added. "They're good, honest people. They are the ones fighting for their country with nothing but their rifle." He shook his head and prayed for the best.

They slowly made their way back inside the ship. "We got more soldiers for the 175th Tunneling company, did you hear?" Tilley said.

"Aye," said Johnny. "I heard that most of them were injured in the field. Instead of sending them back home to Australia, they let them recover in England, and now they're shipping them back to France."

"Tunnelers must be in short supply," Tilley mused.

"There was a guy saying that he had a cracked skull that took a full six months to heal," added Johnny.

"Did you hear about the venereal diseases?" Tilley said, a smile breaking on his face despite the seriousness of the issue.

"Yeah. So many men went with prostitutes while they were staying here that the issue of venereal diseases reached the high command," Johnny said.

"They even made it into a self-inflicted wound," Tilley added, breaking into a short laughter. "Not only do you get the clap, but you also get a fine and extra duties. Not to mention that everyone learns it."

"And yet, they still went for it," Johnny said.

Tilley smiled to himself. "Can't say I blame them, though," he muttered. "It was still a stupid idea, probably." They shook their heads at the situation and entered the cabin.

The two men spotted about thirty new faces. They had brought in more beds and the bunks were more squeezed together. Johnny went for his own bunk bed and sat down, with Tilley sitting next to him.

"At least the trip to France won't be like the one from Australia," Tilley muttered, changing the subject. One of the new faces turned to look at them.

"How was your trip from Australia?" he asked, and Johnny detected the man's Australian accent. He was probably one of the wounded Tunnelers being sent back into the fray.

"Horrible," said Johnny. "Rough seas all the way. Two men were washed overboard, presumed drown."

"Did you hear about that other bloke?" Tilley added. "I only just did, myself. They weren't allowing the story to go around. The bloke was so seasick that he vomited himself to death," he said, shaking his head. "He presumably had preexisting ulcers, the doctor said, and by the end he was vomiting more blood than bile."

The other man looked at Tilley, his eyes wide. "Damn." He sat at a bunk bed, one of the new neighbors they had brought next to Johnny.

"I'm private Michael Tilley," Tilley said, extending his hand to the new soldier. "What's your story, mate?" he asked, ever curious.

"I'm Corporal Winston Taylor," the man introduced himself. He shook hands with Johnny, too, after Johnny said his own name. "I've been with the 175th since it arrived in France. My own voyage to France is certainly something I will never forget."

"Why is that?" asked Tilley, his eyes shining, eager for stories.

"A man hung himself in the showers. We didn't know why, he left no note behind." He shrugged. "We also passed through rough seas, and some crates in the hold crashed three soldiers to death. I got my hand crushed and had to be treated by the ship doctor. I was seasick, and on the same time, had a crushed hand I had to mind so that it could heal properly. It was a hard few days."

"Must have been," echoed Johnny. He was also curious about the man and his experience at war, just less upfront about than Tilley.

"Then, France," said Taylor, saving him the embarrassment of asking. "I was repairing pumps underground when I was caught in an explosion. It was nine months after arriving there. The Germans were doing offensive mining at the time, listening for us. Then, they blew up an area nearby, killing twelve men." He paused. "I don't know which is worse, dying straight away or staying alive underground, buried, listening to the other survivors talk." Johnny saw the man shiver as he remembered the experience.

"You couldn't even see your nose. There was no way to tell if it was day or night. It was dark, cold, and wet. The pumps weren't working, and the area was flooding. I thought I would drown or die from hypothermia. Fortunately, the rescue units came to the collapsed area to dig us out. Those guys are the real heroes."

The man stopped speaking, and even though he hadn't been speaking for long, both Johnny and Tilley had been completely invested in his story. Johnny realized that more men were listening, too, curious to see how war truly was. They would soon find out first-hand, they knew, but hearing someone else talking about his experience was helpful. Even the bad stories were sometimes better than the ones they had cooked up in their heads.

Another soldier started speaking then, a friend of Taylor's who patted the man on his back before starting. He shared his own story, and it went like that for most of the day. Johnny was thankful the experienced soldiers had shared their stories, and by the time he was lying on his bed to sleep, he was feeling less anxiety than he had been in the morning. War was terrifying, but it was less unknown now.

"Follow me," shouted Cpl. Taylor once again, waving his hands wildly in the madness that was the ship disembarking in France. "The reinforcements for the 175th Tunneling Company gather on me." Johnny had known the man only for the two days of their trip, but he liked him already.

Cpl. Taylor was standing off the ship, in an open area on the docks. The soldiers around him had their things on the ground, looking around with curiosity. Johnny observed the infantry reinforcements as they passed them by, walking deeper in the harbor, probably to be moved by trucks or trains towards the front lines. All soldiers, Tunnelers and infantry alike, had the same apprehension on their faces. No one knew where they were going.

The corporal saluted someone suddenly. "Lt. Hungerford!" The experienced Tunnelers snapped to attention, and the new reinforcements took a couple of seconds longer, but also focused on the superior officer, saluting as they had done so many times in their training.

"I am lieutenant Hungerford," the man said. "I will be taking you to where we'll be working. We won't go empty-handed, you'll be bringing our rations along." He pointed at some wooden crates off in the distance. Johnny noticed they had rope handles on each side. "Each of you will grab one side."

Some soldiers started moving towards the crates, then hesitated. Others scrambled around trying to take their kits with them. Yet others looked at the lieutenant with wide eyes, confused. The man sighed.

"Corporals, come here," he ordered. A few men walked away from the group and stood behind him. "Good. I want those of you fresh off the boat to gather there," he pointed. About ninety men, Johnny and Tilley among them, gathered in a small square three rows deep, like in their training. "Our wounded soldiers who are here to fight more, gather there." He pointed again, and about thirty men gathered in the spot. Cpl. Taylor was behind the lieutenant, Johnny realized, as he was an officer.

"Good." He turned to the new soldiers. "Welcome to the 175th company. You are no longer Privates, you are all Sappers from now on. Be proud of that title, because even if it ranks the same as a private, you are very important to the army, important enough to be sent back here after a serious injury." He waited for a few moments, so they could settle down and be more attentive.

"We will take the rations and drop them off six miles down the road. Then, you will be assigned to your dugout, where you'll be sleeping, and to your platoon." He paused and looked over the men. "Any questions?" No one spoke up, so he pointed at the ration boxes. "Take your kit, each one grab a handle, and let's get moving." As the sappers rushed to the boxes, he gestured at the corporals. "Go behind the men, and on their sides. I want no one falling out of line. Pay attention of the men, to catch any issues before they become problems."

In a tight formation, Lt. Hungerford, the corporals, and the sappers all started marching. Johnny felt his apprehension growing but having to juggle his kit and the heavy box helped divert his attention for a bit.

CHAPTER FIFTEEN

Richard felt the bump in his pocket once more, half to make sure it was still there, and half because he was so excited. He pushed the door to his house open and entered to see Christina's back, as she was working in the kitchen. His eyes fell on her middle. *Was Christina always this chubby or did she gain weight recently?* he thought to himself. *Maybe she's eating too much.*

Then, he realized that Christina was speaking to him already, greeting him, and he withdrew his eyes from her waist. He was a little embarrassed and started at the ceiling as he spoke. He returned her greetings and sat on the table, and he fingered the bump ins his pocket again.

"You look happy," Christina said after observing him for a moment.

"Uncle Jimmy paid me," he said excitedly. "Is mum around?"

"No, she has gone into town to buy canning jars," Christina told him.

"That's alright." Richard stayed on the chair for a few more moments, but then felt a void in his stomach. He was hungry. He stood and got something to eat. His mind went to his brother, then. "How is Mark doing at school? I see you helping him study more," he said.

"He's doing well in his studies," Christina said thoughtfully, "but he's been having trouble. There's a kid that's been picking on him."

"Dad told me how to deal with bullies, once, when I had a similar problem," Richard said, with the barest hit of strain in his voice. "You look for at least three vulnerable points on your bully's body and hit them all as hard as you can. Next time he sees you, he'll remember the pain, and he'll think twice before doing anything."

"Did that work?" Christina asked.

"It did. Johnny stopped picking on me," Richard said nonchalantly. Christina smiled and shook her head. Her own mind returned once again to Johnny. She wondered how her husband was doing. As her thoughts slowly grew darker, she shook her head to clear them, then tried to focus her chores.

"Good evening, Mr. Ansari," he heard a voice call behind him as he was closing the windows. He turned to see a woman he seldom saw, the wife of the late Mick Hoagland, Cathy Hoagland. "Are you still open?" she asked, smiling.

"How can I help you?" he said, as he motioned her in. The woman followed him in and approached the counter.

"First, how much do we still owe on our account?" she asked. Mr. Ansari went over his books and found the last entry.

"It's five pounds," he said. Cathy, glad for the work her sons had done, pulled out enough cash to cover the debt, with some left over to buy what she wanted.

"I want canning jars and some hard rock candy," she told him, pushing him a piece of paper with details on it. "Put them here, please," he pointed at a wheeled cart she had brought with her, one she would later pull behind her. The jars were heavy, and she wouldn't be able to carry them otherwise.

"Right away," Mr. Ansari said, smiling, and went to the back of the store to bring out her things.

Cathy browsed around the store and her eyes fell on a pretty hat. She hadn't bought a hat in such a long time, but she couldn't afford to right on that moment. Then, she saw a pair of drapes Mr. Ansari had put on one of his windows and realized the color and texture would go excellently in the house. She would certainly buy both the drapes and the hat as soon as she could afford to, she decided.

"Your order's ready, Mrs. Hoagland," she heard from back in the store. She hurried back. Mr. Ansari had already loaded her cart. She paid him happily, bid him goodbye, and left.

Mr. Ansari stared after her, wishing the woman truly was as happy as she seemed, but doubting it. He shook his head to himself, threw a quick prayer of good luck for both the Hoaglands and his own family, and returned to closing up. When he had finally closed the front of the store, he went back, where his eldest was packing the wagon with the orders they would have to take out on the next day.

He didn't speak immediately, examining his son. It was late in the evening, and they had been working through the day. He was very tired, though Faiz-ul seemed still energetic. He was working hard, despite the hour. He felt a bit of pride, though he then realized his son's face was frowned in concentration. He seemed distressed.

"Everything alright, son?"

Faiz-ul shook his head, not lifting his eyes from the boxes he was moving. "I think I screwed up on one of the orders."

"What's wrong?"

"I can't find a box of bullets. Remember a prospector ordering a box of special caliber bullets that we had to get from outside of Victoria? I can't find it."

Mr. Ansari shook his head in disappointment. "You must find it today, before you come home. The costumer has ordered them three months ago, if you recall. We can't have him waiting anymore, he'll be angry, and justifiably so." He saw Faiz-ul lowered his head in shame.

"You are right," he said simply, and started unloading all the orders he had packed already. "I'll go through everything."

Mr. Ansari nodded. "I've closed off in the front. Remember to lock everything before you leave." He went to the counter, made sure everything was marked in the books, and then left Faiz-ul alone.

Faiz-ul unloaded every single box he had packed in the wagon, opening it, and checking inside. It took him quite a while to undo the work he had done throughout the evening, and yet he did not find the bullets anywhere. He placed the boxes back up on the utility wagon to be taken out the next day, and to separate them from everything he hadn't checked yet. And then, he set to work on the rest of the store, intending to check every nook and cranny.

When the front door opened, Asrar checked the clock. It was almost eight in the evening. Faiz-ul must have been searching for almost three hours. The door closed, but it brought a heavy gust of cold air inside, and Asrar saw that it was completely dark.

"Come here, son," he called at Faiz-ul, who promptly entered the living room. "Have a seat," he set his newspaper aside and pointed at the chair facing him. "Did you manage to find the bullets?"

"Yes, father. They were under the driver's seat. I had stored them away for safekeeping, but I forgot. I looked through the whole store before I found them," he said, his shoulders slumped. He looked tired, and much more disheartened than he had looked back in the store.

"You must be careful, son," Asrar said. "We carry goods that are often dangerous. You mustn't be careless, or it could cost us heavily," he said, his voice serious.

Faiz-ul nodded, stood, and left the room. Asrar heard him as he went up the stairs, and then went to the bathroom. He sighed, took his newspaper, and resumed his reading.

Richard heard his mother's shoes on the stone path and hurried to the door. Mark must have heard her too, as he rushed to his side. They opened the door and saw Cathy pulling her cart carefully down the stone path that led to the entrance of the house. They left the door open and hurried to their mother's side, each boy picking up one end of the cart and carrying it inside. They set it down in the hall and closed the door behind their mother as she entered after them.

"Welcome home, mum," Richard said. "You bought some useful things," he remarked, seeing the jars. They would be useful when the produce was ready, for storage, but also for other things as well.

"And I have a surprise for you, too," she said. The boys smiled widely, but Cathy detected a hint of something else, as if they had something to share with her, too. They stood side by side, waiting for her to get out of her coat, their eyes happy and a little bit mischievous. Boys that had a surprise for their mother. She removed her coat and then turned to them and put her hands on her hips. "So? What is going on?"

Richard pulled something out of his pocket and put it in her hand, something of a strange texture. She judged it weighed about half an ounce. She looked at it and realized it was a gold nugget.

"I discovered it today on uncle Jimmy's mine site. He also paid me in cash for the work I've done," he patted his other pocket. "He said he wanted to help us with the bills too."

"And I have something to show you, too," said Mark excitedly. He pulled a jar from behind his back and gave it to Cathy. It felt heavier, she judged that it was carrying about two ounces of fine gold dust. "This is from dad's claim."

"Congratulations, my boys," she said. She gave them the gold back and patted their heads. Mark received her affections more gladly, and Richard stayed still, accepting it silently. "How should we sell it? I fear that I'll be robbed if I went to town with so much gold on me."

"We were thinking of going with you. I need to get used to selling gold, especially if we work on dad's mine more."

"That's a good idea," Cathy said, smiling. She took a few steps deeper into the house, towards the kitchen. "Have you eaten anything?"

"Christina made fish," Mark said excitedly as he followed her. "We have left some over for you, if you want."

"I do," Cathy said. Richard followed her in as well, pointing at where the leftovers were lying.

"Hey Mark," Richard surprised his brother while the boy was counting the chickens in the coop.

"Hey Richard. You made me lose count," Mark said, throwing his brother an irritated look. "I need to start again, now. One, two..." Richard wanted to speak with his brother for a bit, so he waited until he finished his count. "Good, all here," Mark muttered, then turned towards his brother. "What did you want?"

"How's school?" Richard asked, trying to approach the subject from another angle. His brother simply shrugged, offering no explanation. "Are you having any trouble?"

Mark looked at the ground for a few moments before speaking. "Yeah. There's a boy who's been pestering me recently. Robert Bishop."

"I know him. The guy's a dick. I knew his older brother more." He paused, thinking.

"He sucks at sports, but somehow he's good at boxing, and has been attacking me," Mark added in a lower voice.

"His brother was the same," Richard said. He paused again. "I think the best plan of attack would be to embarrass him."

"How can I embarrass him?" Mark asked, looking up at his older brother with hope in his eyes.

"He sucks at sports," Richard muttered, repeating what his brother had said. "Maybe we could use that against him."

"How?"

"If you were good at a sport, you'd have a reputation for it, right? The other kids would know you. Bullies don't mess with the popular kids."

Mark stared at his brother for a long moment, then nodded. "That's a good idea, Richard. Thanks."

"Do you have any sport that interests you?" his brother asked.

"I don't know yet. I'll think about it," Mark said, and then started walking towards the house.

"Come in!" Christina called, answering the knock on her door. The door opened to reveal Cathy, holding something in her hand. The woman took a step inside and extended her arm, offering

Christina the stick of hard rock candy she had been holding.

"I bought a piece for each of you," Cathy said. Christina took it and smiled widely, thanking the woman. She put it in her mouth, tasting the sweetness. It was very sweet, and she enjoyed it.

"We'll go shopping tomorrow afternoon," Cathy said after a moment. "I was thinking of taking all of you. I want to get new curtains and I want your opinion on that, and I'd like us to have better food. Let's also see if we can get at least two more chickens for the coop."

"That's a great idea," Christina said, her voice excited. She liked seeing Cathy more active, and they certainly needed better food. Today's food wasn't even bought. "Did you like the fish? The boys caught them down at the river, you know."

"It was very tasty, and I really appreciate the boys doing that," Cathy said, smiling. "Good night, Christina, see you tomorrow," she said finally and closed the door behind her as she left.

Christina turned back to her desk, to the letter she had been writing to Johnny. She let her eyes wander as she thought about what else to write when she noticed herself in the mirror. She stood and approached it, turning this way and that. From the front, she looked normal, as she did from the back. But from the side, she saw that the bump on her stomach was noticeable. She still had no idea what she would do. And she had yet to tell Johnny about it. She turned back to the letter. Should she tell him now? She pondered the question for a bit, biting at the back of her pen.

CHAPTER SIXTEEN

Jessie stepped away from the rock crusher, brushing sweat from his brow. Despite the snow, heavy work still made him sweat, and he needed a break. He took a few steps away from it and followed the excited voices he could hear towards the main open area of the mine surface.

It was Saturday, so Mark and Richard were running around shouting excitedly. The boys had decided to master cricket, for some reason they explained to Jessie but he couldn't quite recall. He approached them and waved.

"Can I join?" he asked. The boring and repeating job of working the rock crusher made him go crazy with boredom sometimes, and he wanted to do something more fun. The boys nodded vigorously, and he entered their game. Jimmy was already playing with them, and they quickly took their spots.

Jessie threw the ball to Mark, who was ready to make a hit, while Jimmy was to respond. The snowing was making the game even more interesting than usual. Mark missed the pitch, and it hit one of three posts on the ground behind him. It didn't knock the blocks off, which would mean Mark would have lost is chance to bat and they would have changed positions.

Richard hurried to his brother and pushed his shoulders and knees. "You have to stand *this* way," he said, and mimicked his stance. "It's more suited to batting." He grabbed the ball and threw it back to Jessie, who took his original spot again and prepared for the next pitch.

Jessie ran and pitched the ball, and Mark managed to connect with his bat, sending the ball along the ground towards his uncle. Richard cheered and Mark stared after the ball, his eyes wide with a mix of surprise and excitement. The hit looked good and he was glad about himself. But he was so surprised he forgot he had to run.

Jimmy hadn't forgotten, and he ran after the ball. Richard's yelling brought Mark out of his reverie a few moments later and he sprinted towards the ball.

On the other side of the area, a wagon pushed through the snow-covered trees, pulled by horses. Faiz-ul, sitting on the driver's seat, stopped the horses as soon as he saw the Hoaglands and Jessie.

First, he thought they were doing chores, but a moment later he realized they were playing cricket. Mark was running as fast as he could to catch his uncle, Faiz-ul saw, but Jimmy reached the ball first, and then he threw it to Jessie. Jessie couldn't do anything, though, as Mark arrived back where he started. Richard was jumping up and down, yelling so loudly that even Faiz-ul could hear him despite the distance and the snow absorbing some of the sound.

"Time out!" Faiz-ul heard Jimmy shout, and he turned towards the wagon. Jimmy knew there were a few boxes and some timber waiting for him in the back. The boys rushed towards their canteens, took them, and sat down with large sighs of relief.

"Hello, Faiz-ul," Jimmy greeted the man as he approached. "Good morning, mate. Thank you for coming out here."

"Just doing my job, Mr. Hoagland," Faiz-ul said, smiling. "Where do you want them?"

"Over there's fine," Jimmy said, pointing. Faiz-ul directed the horses through the open area and reached the point Jimmy had indicated, then jumped off the wagon. Jimmy started towards the wagon, but Faiz-ul was already unloading the goods before he had even offered his help. He did help him, but the young man ended up doing most of the work. It took them a good quarter of an hour. At the end, as the young man was about to get back to his seat, Jimmy looked him over for a long moment.

"Mate, would you be available to work as a laborer in a mine?" he asked him. He always appreciated the young man's work ethic, and from their interactions, he had gathered that he was a good-natured man.

Faiz-ul paused in thought for a moment. "You know, I haven't thought about working for anyone but my father," he said. "What exactly do you have in mind?"

"I'm a man short. I have Jessie and Richard working this mine, and I want myself and another man working the other claim that my brother used to work." He paused, thinking if he wanted to explain further. He decided to give out a little more information. "I'm worried about claim jumpers. They might discover the other mine isn't being worked right now. I want to change that, I've... made some interesting discoveries." He didn't want to reveal the whole truth, only enough to keep the young man interested.

"That's—" Faiz-ul started, but then, he recalled something. He stopped talking and opened a bag he had left on the driver's seat. He rummaged inside, then retrieved a cardboard box that contained three smaller boxes. "Here. These are the bullets you wanted."

"Thank you, mate," Jimmy said, receiving the order. "Hope they didn't give you too much trouble. My rifle's a bit special."

"No trouble at all, Mr. Hoagland."

"Back to my proposition, if you accepted, we could work the mine whenever it suited you. But I'd need your decision within a couple of days. I have another person I might ask, if you decide against it."

"Thank you for considering me," Faiz-ul said, smiling widely. Working in a mine, getting experience so he could run his own one day… He had been thinking about that for a while now. "I will need to talk with my father, you understand."

"I do understand," Jimmy said, nodding. It was good that the young man respected his father. Jimmy's attention was drawn by Mark and Richard who were running around the mine's surface, playing cricket. "Ya know, you could stay and play outfield with us for a bit, if you want," Jimmy invited him.

Faiz-ul looked at the boys and realized that he wanted to. He hadn't played any sort of sport in a while. "Sure. I can't stay for long, but I have a few minutes."

The Hoaglands, Jessie, and Faiz-ul played for about half an hour, with some stops to coach Mark. Faiz-ul thought the boy looked determined and he appreciated that. He liked that family and he enjoyed his time. In the end, they stroke out first Mark and then Richard, and as Jimmy and Jessie took their place as batters, Faiz-ul bid them goodbye and left.

He had more orders to deliver, and it took him a good couple of hours before he was back at the town. As he made his way on the bumpy road towards the store, he passed by the open square. An army recruiter had taken over the central area of the square, Faiz-ul saw, sitting behind a desk with a large design on the front. The sign indicated they were recruiting miners for the war effort, as tunnelers and sappers. That brought Johnny to his mind.

Where was he? He hadn't heard anything about him in a while. What kind of adventures was the man having? Were they dark, as the wounded veterans said, or bright and glorious, as the recruiters insisted?

He turned the corner behind the store and guided the horses into the stables. He got off, unhitched them from the wagon, and pulled the water trough near them. When he entered the store from the back door, he saw his brother Praveen. The boy was concentrating on his work, packing the orders that would go out tomorrow, on Sunday. There were more prospectors outside of Bendigo who had ordered supplies, and Faiz-ul would drive out to them first thing in the morning. Faiz-ul greeted his brother and continued towards the front of the store.

His father was standing behind the counter, talking with a man. Faiz-ul didn't want to disrupt him, so he took a broom and started sweeping the dust that had already built up throughout the day. It took a good while before the man had finished with his purchase, had paid, and left the store. Faiz-ul put the broom aside and greeted his father.

"Hello, son," Asrar told him, happy to see him back from the deliveries. "How did the delivery to Mr. Hoagland go?"

"Without a hitch, father," Faiz-ul said. He paused for a moment, looking at his father's face, debating whether it was a good idea to mention the job offer Mr. Hoagland had made him or not. He decided against it. "I stayed for a bit longer. They were playing cricket and they invited me to play with them."

Mr. Ansari laughed and patted his son on his shoulder. "That's good!" he said, smiling widely. "They are good men, all of them. And honest."

Faiz-ul nodded, and once again thought of his friend, Johnny.

What could he be doing?

Sapper Johnny listened intently at the instruments. Sapper Tilley had a similar apparatus, a variation of the geophone, next to him, pointed at a slightly different location. They had volunteered to work as active listeners for enemy digging, and were sitting in a spot further away from their activities, so that they wouldn't mistake their own sappers for Germans.

Johnny stared at his friend. The man was absentminded and was scratching himself at his genitals often. Every now and then, his hand would go down, scratch, and then return to the instrument. Johnny's eyes slowly left his mate and turned away, his mind going back home. Tilley tapped Johnny's shoulder to get his attention at some point, pulling him out of his thoughts. Johnny removed the earbuds and turned to him.

"I'll be right back, alright?" Tilley said.

"What's wrong?" Johnny asked.

"I need to take a piss," the man said. He let his instrument down, then hurried towards a bucket Lt. Hungerford had given them. The man was their commanding officer now they were in Third Platoon, in the 175th Tunneling Company. After a few moments of loud urination and more sounds of scratching, Tilley returned to his post.

Time passed by tensely, until two men came into their post to relieve them. Johnny and Tilley left the nook and returned to the dugout where they had been assigned their beds. They saw the two men sleeping in their bunks, and they shook them awake so they could take their turn. The men thanked them and left for their own duties.

Following their training, Tilley and Johnny took a bucket each, filled it with water, and hurried to the washing area. There were more men around them, all using bars of soap and the tepid water to wash up for sleep, and the two Australians mimicked them. Johnny kept an eye on Tilley, and saw that he paid more attention to his privates, trying to wash himself thoroughly, and on the same time, sneak a scratch in when he thought that no one was looking.

Afterwards, they hurried to their beds. Johnny hoped he could get a couple of hours of uninterrupted sleep, but he didn't really believe he would be able to. He got under the covers and closed his eyes.

A man shook him awake after what felt like barely a minute. Johnny opened his eyes to see private O'Reilly, who then moved on to shake another soldier awake. "Does anyone of you know how to fix a pump?" he kept repeating.

"I do," Tilley said. Johnny went back to sleep quickly, relieved. Tilley, on the other hand, hadn't been sleeping. He hadn't even been able to sleep. There was an unbearable itching in his underarms, one like nothing he had ever experienced. He put his boots on, threw his blanket back over the bed, and hurried away.

Another sapper woke Johnny a few hours after his first awakening; he found himself more rested, but also itchier. He got up from the bed and put on his boots, and he scratched himself vigorously. His eyes fell on Sapper Moran, who had been sleeping in Tilley's bed. He was putting on his pants, half-asleep, but scratching his genitals without realizing it.

Moran got out of his bed, put on his boots, and took a few unsteady steps towards the bucket. Johnny saw that the man was barely awake, as were most of them when woken up. He opened his pants, took a long piss, then buttoned himself up again. In the same unsteady way, he turned to leave, but his boot caught on the bucket's handle. The bucket turned over.

"You idiot!" a soldier shouted from a bunk as the bucket flooded the floor, and more men joined in booing him. Moran apologized and got started cleaning it up, but the damage was done, and the whole floor was drenched with piss. The smell was overwhelming, and most sappers left Moran to clean the dugout alone.

That evening, Lt. Hungerford called them together to deal with the incident.

"That bucket has to be emptied," he insisted. "It's part of your duties. One of you will be assigned to it every day. Hygiene is important." The soldiers groaned, not because they were bored, but because they knew how dangerous leaving their tunnels was. But Lt. Hungerford went over it a few times until he was sure that everyone had understood the importance of keeping the bucket as empty as possible, and then he left.

Even after a few days, the dugout still smelled of piss. The soldier in charge of keeping the bucket empty did an excellent job pushed by the reminder that still hung in the air. Johnny had one of the first turns at it.

On that night, he took the bucket during the cover of the night, as they had been ordered. He took a few tentative steps outside of the tunnels, hurried down the path marked from hundreds of feet, and reached the dump spot that had been assigned for human waste. He emptied the bucket in one quick motion.

Suddenly, he heard gunfire. The sound was far away, not aimed at him, but the persistent and repeated noise filled him with terror.

He ran through the night towards the tunnel entrance, not minding where he stepped and tripped once. When he entered the tunnels, he felt significantly safer and wished to never hear such sounds again.

Another sapper was assigned the next night. Johnny was lying in his bed, trying to sleep through the noises of the camp, when he heard an unmistakable sound. A loud and piercing bang, the marking of a sniper rifle. The next morning, he woke to take a piss and saw the bucket missing. His suspicions were confirmed later.

"He was killed by a German sniper," everyone was muttering. "The demons can see even in the dark."

CHAPTER SEVENTEEN

"Good morning, sir," Cpl. Taylor saluted his platoon commander, Lt. Hungerford. The calendar on the desk read that today was the twenty-fourth of September, though that made little sense to the corporal. Time didn't really exist when you lived underground, only shifts existed.

"Good morning corporal," the lieutenant greeted him. "You needed to tell me something urgently?"

"I do, sir. Something needs to be done in the forward areas, regarding hygiene, sir." He paused for a moment. "If I may be frank, there are many incidents of full piss buckets spilling over. The stink stays in the dugouts for days, sir. And it's increasingly hard to keep ourselves and the living areas clean."

Lt. Hungerford nodded. He had heard similar complaints. Initially, he had hoped the soldiers would find a way to manage it, but it seemed more impossible with each day. He stood. "Show me."

Taylor lead the officer through the tunnels into the dugout 3 Platoon was using for bunking. Lt. Hungerford took a step inside and was shocked by how crowded it was, and how bad it smelled. It reminded him of stables or pigsties. Something needed to be done, quickly. He relieved the corporal and, deep in thought, started walking back towards his office.

"Lt. Hungerford," a call came, pulling him out of his thoughts. He turned to see a medic waving at him, and he paused, waiting for the soldier to catch up to him. "Sir, I need to report something important," the man said. He threw a look around quickly to make sure they wouldn't be overheard, took a tentative step towards him, and spoke again in a lower voice.

"I think we have a crabs infestation."

"Crabs," said Lt. Hungerford, dazed. Another incredibly serious issue.

"Yes. It might be lice, but I think it's crabs. Sapper Tilley came to see me earlier, with all the symptoms. He admitted that he went with a hooker when their ship was docked in England."

"Crabs," repeated Lt. Hungerford, now angry. He had lost men to venereal diseases before. The whole army had issues with venereal diseases picked up by horny soldiers and often transmitted to whole platoons. He needed to make sure his platoon was safe, and he needed to act fast.

"I want all soldiers inspected," Lt. Hungerford started. "Stop all work. Get started." The medic nodded and left, while Lt. Hungerford hurried away. He had to report to his superior, and he dreaded it.

"Major," he greeted his superior. The man looked busy and irritated, so Lt. Hungerford was quick in his explanation, listing the details he had managed to discover.

"I want whoever brought the disease here charged," the major started, his eyes shining angrily. "Everyone who is infected will be sent to the hospital. And everyone who brought the infection here…" he let his voice fade with unspoken menace. "Bring me a doctor. I need to discuss the issue in depth." Lt. Hungerford saluted and left in a hurry to comply.

On the way back, he found a corporal and had him bring Sapper Tilley over, then waited for the sapper in his office.

"Sir," Tilley said, saluting. The lieutenant saw fear in the man's eyes. He must have seen the anger in his own.

"Do you have a venereal disease, Sapper Tilley?" Lt. Hungerford asked.

"Not sure, sir," the man replied. "I've been itchy for days, though."

"Did you have sex with a hooker in England?" Lt. Hungerford asked bluntly.

"Yes, sir." To his credit, he didn't hesitate, nor did he evade the question.

The lieutenant sighed and turned to the doctor. "I want you to examine him and make a certain diagnosis. I had some medics prepare a dugout as an examination area." The three men walked to it and the doctor took Tilley inside. Lt. Hungerford stayed outside to give the man his privacy. As the lieutenant waited, he saw a man coming towards him.

"Sir," Sgt. Hudson saluted. "The men are waiting for the inspection."

"Take me there," Lt. Hungerford said, and followed the sergeant to the sleeping quarters of Third Platoon. The men had lined up inside the sleeping quarters, a few spilling outside as the dugout wasn't designed to hold the whole platoon all at once. They were anxious, and the lieutenant spotted a few of them scratching themselves.

"I will speak to you plainly," Lt. Hungerford started. "There's a venereal disease spreading among the members of the platoon. Those diseases, by themselves, are very dangerous and disruptive. However, when they appear on people who work underground, in extremely close quarters, with little access to hygiene facilities, they can halt work and make production stop completely.

"Every single soldier is going to the doctor to be checked up.

Any soldier with symptoms of any venereal disease must speak to the doctor plainly. Do you understand that?" He paused. "I want no one to lie, nor hide anything. If one of you hides something, and it's later discovered, the punishment will be much more severe." He paused for a bit longer, to drive the point in. "It is not acceptable to be carrying venereal diseases while underground. We are on a time-sensitive mission and you are soldiers with a duty. This issue will be dealt with immediately, and with maximum efficiency."

He nodded to Sgt. Hudson, who had the men line up towards the dugout used for the examinations.

"While you wait," Lt. Hungerford said, turning to Cpl. Taylor, "let's go ahead and get the mail delivered."

Cpl. Taylor was holding a sack full of letters and was pulling out the envelopes one by one, calling out the name written on it. All soldiers were paying attention to the man, as they were all anxious to receive news from home. Most soldiers who received their letters did so with a huge smile on their faces, though Johnny noticed a couple that seemed to dread the envelopes they were holding.

Most of the soldiers had already received letters, and Johnny was losing hope of receiving one now. Then, he heard his name called out. He hurried to Cpl. Taylor, took the letter, and hurried back to his spot in the queue. When he recognized the handwriting on the envelope to be Christina's, he opened it hastily. The letter was somewhat older, so he would be reading older news, but it would be news to him.

Christina wrote him about many things. The letter was three pages long. The first thing she wrote was how much she missed him, which warmed his heart, despite the situation going on around him. Then, she went on to write him that it had started snowing in Bendigo and that it was a cold winter, but they had found some gold and were able to pay for several things. Finally, she wrote about something she overheard from Richard and Mark. His two brothers were working in the chicken coop—which was being upgraded on his mother's initiative—and they said that there were claim jumpers on their dad's claim.

Johnny grew angry about it and wished he could do something. He also feared for his brothers. Claim jumpers wouldn't hesitate to harm them, even though they were just boys. In the end, he read the whole thing three times, pleased to have a connection with home.

As the soldiers waited for their turn to be inspected, Lt. Hungerford took Sgt. Hudson and went to the forward areas of Vimy Sector. Several soldiers were manning the listening posts, and they wouldn't have been alerted about the inspection. When he arrived at each pair, he quietly sent them back to the dugout where the inspection was taking place, repeating his statement that they needed to tell the truth, no matter how bad it was.

After the soldiers of the listening posts had been sent back, the lieutenant and the sergeant inspected the space.

"We need better hygiene. If we had it, the whole thing wouldn't have spread so easily," the sergeant said.

"We do. We'd need water tanks and better facilities," Lt. Hungerford agreed.

"We could excavate a dugout here," Sgt. Hudson pointed. "Or here."

"I have the full plans in my office," Lt. Hungerford said. "I'll put together a proposal for the major. Do you have any suggestions?"

Sgt. Hudson thought for a moment, then pointed at three more good places for hygiene facilities, and one for water tanks that could serve them. Hungerford made mental notes, wanting to make sure he'd include everything in his proposals. He sent the sergeant to keep an eye on the inspections and went to his office, to prepare for the meeting with his superior.

As he examined the maps, he realized there were various suitable points, and drafted several suggestions for the major. He put them all on paper so the man could examine them thoroughly, then took them and went to his office. As he arrived, he saw that the doctor the major had called was getting started to brief him, and as he debated getting in the office or coming back later, the major called him in. He entered and sat near his superior's desk.

"Go on, doctor," Major Moore said. "You were saying we have some bad news." He looked at the desk with a huge frown on his face, and Hungerford saw several maps and data sheets on the man's desk.

"We have confirmed that there is more than one venereal disease among our soldiers," the doctor said. "Three men have gonorrhea. One man seems to have an advanced stage of syphilis. And at least ten of our sappers have crabs."

The major shook his head in disappointment. "That's fourteen soldiers we need to remove either temporary or permanently, isn't it?"

"Yes, Major. They need to be taken to the hospital immediately."

"That's a quarter of my platoon strength," muttered Lt. Hungerford.

The major hit the desk with his fist. "Work will slow down

significantly, and because, what? Because a few soldiers were lonely and fucked some whores in England?"

"That's not all, Major," the doctor said. "Being underground and so close to each other complicates things. All clothes in the platoon need to be burned, immediately. All beds and bedsheets, along with blankets, as well. The soldiers need completely new clothes and blankets."

"Of course," the major said. "We need to make sure it doesn't spread. On that note, I will have all platoons of the 175th be inspected. I'll inform all company commanders in the *sector* that there are venereal diseases confirmed among our men." He shook his head again, his frown deepening. "Have you confirmed that our soldiers contracted the diseases from prostitutes?"

"Yes, Major. They were coming back from the hospitals of England and they admitted they had sex with prostitutes during their stay there, as you said."

Major Moore stood abruptly, pushing his chair back. He kicked the leg of his desk, which withstood it silently. "Despite our warnings, despite the issues already caused by this, they did it?" The doctor didn't say anything and just nodded. "This isn't just a single stupid soldier. Things are getting out of hand. I'll personally inform the hospitals in England about this. From this point on, I will treat all of them as self-inflicted wounds. They will be fined, and I will keep the possibility of imprisonment open. This won't go on." The major remained standing, fuming, for a long moment as he tried to calm down. He pulled his chair up violently and sat.

"Thank you, doctor," he dismissed him, and the doctor left quickly. He knew the major's anger wasn't directed at him, but he didn't want to be around it either. Major Moore then spent a few moments breathing deeply, looking over his papers. Lt. Hungerford saw the man's face visibly relax, the deep frown turning into an impassive look. "What do you have for me, lieutenant?" he said finally.

"We have serious hygiene deficiencies, which is one of the reasons the disease spread like wildfire." He listed the suggestions he had come up by himself and with the help of his sergeant, and then gave him the papers he had prepared. The major looked them over carefully, nodding along. When the lieutenant finished, he remained silent for a few minutes, examining the proposals.

"We will go with this one," he said finally, showing Lt. Hungerford the proposal he had picked, which was what the lieutenant would have picked himself. "I want new water-storing facilities in forward areas and special areas for washing. I want all soldiers to wash themselves and their clothing daily. I want everyone on the lookout for any kind of bugs, especially lice, in either their bunks or their persons. Any such discoveries are to be reported immediately, and if they're not, tell the soldiers that they should expect the worst."

"Yes, Major," Lt. Hungerford said. "You will find the list of the materials," he pointed at the paper the major was holding. "If you can get them for me, I can start making them."

"With a quarter of your workforce missing, it will be hard," the major said. "Venereal diseases are causing our war effort significant problems." He sighed. "We need to deal with this, decisively."

"I can't believe we have such a… *variety* of diseases," Lt. Hungerford said, shaking his head. "This is not acceptable. Maybe we should be holding in-depth classes about what diseases prostitutes can carry, and how damaging they are to the war effort."

"Remember to burn all clothing and blankets, and get new ones issued," Moore said. "Have all soldiers go through decontamination first, though. And have them do it as soon as the doctor is ready."

Lt. Hungerford nodded. The major looked over the papers some more, before speaking again. "I will lay tracks for the electric carts through some of the tunnels of Third Platoon," he said. "I want them to be removing sanitation and bringing in fresh water every day."

"I agree, sir. It should be a priority."

"And it will be." He paused, then finally stood up. "Go and tell your men what charges they will be facing. Have them go to the hospital. The doctor has more information about where it is, as we'll be making it away from the tunnels."

"Yes sir," Hungerford said and left quickly. He asked the doctor for the names of the infected and those who had started the infection, and then gathered them in his office. The men were nervous, and the lieutenant could read on their faces that they were expecting to be in trouble.

He stared at them for a long moment. "Those of you who brought the diseases here will be facing the charge of a self-inflicted wound, per the orders of the major. You will be represented by an officer shortly. If you are found guilty, you will be fined. The major will consider imprisonment, as well." His gaze pierced them, making them go white. Sapper Tilley in particular looked ready to faint. Other sappers, like Hoagland, who were found to have contracted the disease, but knew they hadn't done anything wrong, had a mix of indignation and irritation on their faces.

"Of course, those of you who have simply contracted the disease, won't be charged. You will be removed from the work areas, though, as we want to prevent further spreading of the crab lice. Now go with Sgt. Hudson. He will take you to the hospital. Get ready for some walking," he added meaningfully. Johnny, Tilley, and the rest left the room and found the sergeant. The moment he saw them, his face turned red.

"Do you understand what you have done? You have single-handedly caused more damage to the Vimy Sector than the Germans have done today," he screamed at them. "The loss of manpower will set us back days, even weeks. We need to divert personnel and resources to face this issue, and all because you were horny!" He paused for breath, then continued screaming. "You should all be bloody ashamed of yourselves! Go," he gestured, and they scrambled away through the tunnels towards the exit of the system.

The sergeant led them through the tunnels and then to an area that was further away from the main paths the soldiers used. They walked for a while before reaching a private spot near the hospital. Then, he had them arrayed for the next step of the plan. "Strip!" he shouted, and the soldiers complied immediately. Under his directions, they threw their clothes in a big pile. The sergeant had them douse the pile with a can of petrol, and then he lit it up.

As they watched the fire for a moment, Johnny turned to Tilley next to him. He looked at him square in the eye. "I told you, Tilley," he said. "I told you not to fuck that prostitute back in England. And now you even got me scratching." He wanted to swear more, but he saw the regret in his friend's eyes. There was no point in pushing him more, it was obvious he had gotten it.

"Now wash up," the sergeant told them. They each got a bar of a special soap and water from cans, and were directed to wash themselves three times, especially in their pubic areas. They dried up and a medic covered them in some kind of powder. Then, they put on hospital clothing and shoes. "This way," the medic directed them to cots.

The hospital was in an empty area at the foot of a hillside, hidden by the Germans. It was a simple tent, Johnny saw, with cots arrayed in lines. He settled in his cot, being on the lookout for any new itching. He spotted others who were still itching, but he felt better. The rest of the day passed slowly, but the night's winds blew against the tent, slipping through. The soldiers didn't dare complain, sensing the anger of their superiors, and they passed the night shaking from the cold. After a few days, some had a low fever, while others complained of stomach pains.

The medics examined those with the new symptoms and realized that they had gotten sick with the flu. They admonished them for not speaking up sooner and reinforced the insulation of the tent. They slept better that night.

Over the duration of his stay, Johnny paid attention to the men around him. The sapper who had syphilis was the first to leave, shipped to England on the first ship out, but the medics spent time on him while waiting. Johnny didn't know the techniques used on him, but the man didn't seem to enjoy his time.

They also discovered that Tilley had gonorrhea along with crabs. He, along with the other two that shared the condition, were treated by the medics and Johnny saw they did not enjoy their methods in the slightest. The more he observed his fellow patients, the more thankful he was for Christina, for marrying him, and for indirectly preventing him from having sex with a prostitute and picking up similar *souvenirs*.

CHAPTER EIGHTEEN

Jimmy observed Richard kicking another useless rock away, and then sighing. It was the sixth time the boy had done that. His face looked sullen and his eyes had been downcast the entire time he had been working in the mine today.

"Is everything alright, Richard?" Jimmy asked hesitantly. He wasn't good with kids, never had any of his own, and didn't know how to approach them besides as pint-sized adults.

"It's my brother," Richard replied. Jimmy nodded knowingly, though he didn't really know what to say. "He hasn't sent me a letter yet," he said as an explanation a few moments later. Jimmy understood more now.

"He left without saying much in the way of goodbye either, right?" Jimmy said.

"It's more than that," Richard muttered. "He's written to Christina and Mark already."

"Ah," Jimmy said. "You know, grief is a strange thing. It often changes a person." He shook his head slowly. "You must have seen almost all of your family go through this on their own by now, right? Your mother is another example." Richard nodded. Jimmy paused, thinking of what to say. "Everyone mourns on their own pace. It won't do good to push them, even if their anger is misdirected."

"I just can't understand why my brother's angry with me," Richard said. "Is it my fault dad died?"

"It's most certainly *not* your fault, Richard," Jimmy said forcefully. "People die in mines all the time. It's almost expected. You work the mine until you either die or can't work it anymore due to a sickness you pick up here."

Richard looked at the ground, not satisfied.

"Look," Jimmy said. "Don't take your brother's anger as him being angry with you, alright?" Richard looked up. "He misses your father. We all do. That's all."

"You're right, uncle," Richard said after a long moment. He picked up the two buckets again. "I'll go bring up more ore, alright?"

Jimmy observed his nephew as he walked away, thinking about Mick and his family. The man had left a void, felt by everyone, and they did their best to manage it. It's bad enough losing a family member, he didn't want to imagine how it would feel to lose a father at such an age. He shook his head and resumed working the crusher, the machine's noise putting him in a trance, his thoughts traveling away.

Mark walked as quickly as his little legs could take him, hurrying away from the school. The sun was hidden behind clouds and it felt gloomy, and Mark wanted to be home. A voice called his name then, the voice belonging to the very person Mark wanted to avoid. Robert Bishop, the big boy who had been harassing him.

To make things worse, the voice was coming from in front of him, so he couldn't even hurry away pretending he hadn't heard him. Mark raised his eyes and saw Robert and his two henchmen blocking his way.

"Hello little crybaby," Robert said. Once, Mark hadn't been able to suppress his tears at the boy's harassing and the nickname had stuck as they tend to do; the worse a nickname is, the more durable it is to the passing of time.

"Leave me alone, Robert," Mark said, trying to go around him.

The henchman to the boy's left blocked his way.

"Leave me alone," Robert mimicked, mocking him. He made his hands into fists and moved them as if to dry away tears. "What are you going to do, cry?" He had his laugh, the henchmen had their laughs, and then, Robert pushed Mark's shoulder. Mark knew that the bully wanted to provoke him into a fistfight, having the excuse of doing it in self-defense. It hadn't been the first time, and Mark didn't dare hope it would be the last. But now, he had a plan.

Mark took a couple of steps back, staring at the bully in his eyes. He wanted to issue his challenge head-on, to try to intimidate the bully, as Richard had said that bullies were essentially cowards.

"I challenge you, Robert," Mark said, trying to keep his voice from shaking. His hands were shaking, but he hoped the boy would interpret it as rage instead of fear. "A game of cricket. Your team against mine."

Robert's eyes widened, and his foot slid back a few inches, as if he was about to take a step back. Instead of that, though, his eyes hardened. "You're a silly crybaby," he said, his voice cruel. "I accept your silly challenge." Mark was momentarily dazed, not sure how to proceed from there.

"Sunday, at one in the afternoon," Robert added then. "In the park in Bendigo the school took us to in the summer." Mark knew the park, it was in fact the one he would have suggested himself. "Looking forward to crushing your silly team of crybabies," Robert finished, then nodded at his henchmen and left. The boys scrambled after him, and Mark was left alone, with no new bruises. That *was* an improvement.

The momentary glee he got from having avoided the fight was

short-lived as he realized he had to beat Robert in the game of cricket. Mark had been training, but now he had to assemble a team, and train more. He took off towards the house, eager to talk with his brother about what to do. Richard would know, he had suggested the cricket idea himself.

When he arrived home, he saw that Richard had probably not returned from the mine yet. He sprinted through the house, barely greeted Christina and his mother, and when he confirmed his brother had indeed not returned, he left his bag and went off again. By now, he knew the way to Jimmy's mine well enough, so he followed the simple path. He pushed the fence gate open and entered the mine's surface, to find Richard carrying buckets of ore. Mark waved at him, and Richard left the buckets down, his face turning into a frown.

It was strange for Mark to visit on a school day. The boy should be back at the house resting, doing his homework, having dinner—not here at the mine. Unless something had happened. Richard ran towards his brother.

"Everything alright, Mark?" he asked quickly when they met in the middle of the distance.

"I challenged Robert Bishop to a cricket game," Mark said, out of breath.

"When's the game?" Richard asked, his face suddenly changing from worried to determined.

"Sunday, at one."

"We need a team, we don't have much time," Richard said, "and we need to train more." He hurried away, going deeper into the mine. Mark followed him. "Jessie?" Richard called. "Mark's cricket game is on Sunday. Can you help us train after work today?"

Mark heard the man reply from deeper in. "Gladly!" He saw the man come out of a tunnel a few moments later, smiling widely. He put his hand on the boy's shoulder. "We'll make you into a magnificent batter, mate."

"They're late," Cathy said, looking at the clock, the dinner already laid on the table. Then, she realized there was no one around to hear her. She took a deep swig of her drink, feeling the alcohol numb her. Her nerves poked through the haze, though. Her foot was tapping against the floor, her fingers drumming against the table, and she felt close to bursting.

She heard the door open and stood quickly, going to the door, ready to pick a fight. It was Christina who entered, carrying what Cathy judged to be new clothes. They looked cheap to her eyes, and significantly larger in size. The woman had developed a belly in the duration of her stay in their house, Cathy had seen it grow progressively larger as the weeks passed.

A small smirk grew on her face as she saw her, thinking of how Johnny would react to his wife being fatter when he got back. Would he seek his satisfaction elsewhere, in the whores around town and in the pubs? Would he shout or get angry? She was so lost in her musings that she didn't speak to Christina at all as the woman looked at her, then shook her head and left.

She grew angry at the dismissive attitude she saw on Christina's face, and went back to her drink. She took a few good swigs, then started calling her names in her head. She was slowly leaning towards Mrs. Piggy, as the woman's pale-pink face could easily be mistaken for a pig the fatter she grew. How long had she been growing fat for, again?

Cathy had seen the first signs a few weeks after Johnny had left. And the progress had been gradual. As if she was growing a little bit every day. Suddenly, she realized that she knew this pattern of getting fatter. She had gone through it herself three times. Her thighs hadn't been growing, as far as Cathy could ascertain, nor did her arms. Her face looked normal, too. Christina had not been getting fatter, Christina was pregnant!

She took another swig and hurried to the woman's room. She knocked and opened the door immediately without waiting for an answer.

"You're pregnant!" she said, in an accusatory tone, as if the woman was at fault. "How long did you expect to hide it?"

"I never did, you just didn't ask," Christina shot back.

"Don't talk back to me, you little girl. Is that how you married my son?" Cathy said, staring daggers at the woman. "You tricked him into it, didn't you?"

"I discovered it after he was gone," Christina said defensively. "And there was no *trick*, we both had control of our senses when *that* happened."

"Men are easy to manipulate if you're a slut," Cathy said. "What is it you want from my son? Why did you trick him into marrying you?"

"I *love* him, that's why I married him," Christina said, her voice rising in pitch and intensity. "And he loves me!"

"That's what they all think when you open your legs easily enough," Cathy sneered.

Christina stared at her, unsure what to do. "All that wine must have messed with your brain," she said after a moment. She pushed past her and went towards the front door. She couldn't stay here with the drunk woman spewing her poison at that moment. She didn't really know what to do, only feeling that she wanted to leave, so she simply opened the front door and got out.

Mark and Richard pushed open the front yard door, talking excitedly between themselves. They were discussing possible teammates when they saw Christina leave the house in a hurry, having opened the front door just as they entered the front yard.

"That's not a good omen," Richard muttered as Christina hurried away without greeting them, tears in her eyes glistening to the moonlight. The boys exchanged a look and entered the house carefully. The table was laid with a tasty-looking dinner and the two boys checked around the living room. They saw no one, and then exchanged another look.

"Should we...?" Richard started, nodding towards the table.

"It's lying here, so it's for us, right?" Mark said. They stared at the table once more and then each nodded, having decided the meal was for them. They hurried to the bathroom to wash away the dirt from practicing cricket and then started eating.

Cathy stared at Christina's empty room for quite a while, fuming and cursing the woman in her head. No one had any respect for her in this house. No one cared nor understood her. She could only count on herself. Cathy turned away, leaving the door open as Christina had left it, and started down the stairs. She heard the sound of forks against plates and realized the boys were probably back. She looked at the clock. It was after seven in the evening.

"Don't you know when it's dinner time?" Cathy said as she entered the room. The boys looked up from their cold food, knowing that it was way earlier than seven. "Why can't you show up for dinner on time?" She crossed her hands in front of her chest, staring at them. "It's rude behavior, and worse, it shows you don't appreciate me slaving away to keep you fed."

"Sorry, mum," Richard said. "But there's a good reason we were late."

"And what is that?" Cathy said. She had a frown on her face and her anger was still boiling from her fight with Christina moments earlier, so she was staring daggers at the boys as if they had done a horrible crime—in her mind, being so unappreciative to her *was* a crime, and there weren't many things that could excuse such a crime.

"We've been training with Jessie," Richard said, looking at Mark. "Mark has a cricket game this weekend, and we need to practice."

Cathy untied her arms and looked at her son with curiosity in her face, a hopeful omen of the storm breaking. "I didn't know you were interested in cricket."

"I like it," Mark muttered. "I want to practice some more after dinner, too." His voice was low, fearful, but it made Cathy's anger flare up again.

"No way," she said matter-of-factly. "You have homework, don't you?"

Mark thought for a moment. "I have some Math and English assignments, but they can wait," he said, but before he could add anything more, his mother interrupted him.

"No. After dinner, you will go to your room and you will finish your assignment. I know you aren't doing everything you can to achieve higher grades."

"But mum," Mark said, "high grades are for sissies!" He had been called that quite a few times, and by now knew what Robert had been saying about him to the whole school.

"I'm not in the mood for arguments. You won't go anywhere until you've done your homework."

Richard, who had been silent until that point, stood up from his seat. He couldn't take it anymore.

"Why do you drink, mum?" he said. He stared at her eyes, trying use his rage to muster as much courage as he could to finally speak his mind. Cathy was so shocked by the sudden question that she didn't reply immediately. "When you drink, you go around picking fights, and that makes living here not very fun."

Cathy's face contorted with wrath as she raised her arm and brought her hand against Richard's face. The sound from the slap was like a clap of thunder filling the room. It wasn't targeted well as Cathy was not far from black-out drunk, and it found Richard against the ear as much as the cheek. The skin turned an angry red and the sting that Richard felt brought tears in his eyes automatically. He stared at his mother with blurry eyes then left the table. He walked to the front door, opened it, and left, closing it behind himself.

The woman turned to Mark then, her eyes filled with such rage that Mark averted his own out of fear of appearing too confrontational.

"Go to your room and study," she told him through her clenched teeth, and Mark shot up and ran away to his room. Cathy sat at the table, which was still covered in food, took a deep swig from her glass, and started crying.

The cold made Richard's tears sting against his skin as he walked through the dark towards his father's mine. He wanted to work, to do something to take his mind off his mother and his own empty stomach. Jimmy was probably at the mine, working it with Faiz-ul or by himself.

In the barely lit environment, he spotted something moving, and he turned his head towards it by instinct. A person was sitting by a creek on a rock. Richard could see only the person's back, but it seemed familiar. He took a couple of silent steps towards the creek and realized that it was Christina. On the rest of the way, he walked normally, so that he wouldn't scare the woman by suddenly appearing beside her. When he was halfway there, she turned her head and spotted him, a slight smile breaking what Richard realized was a deep frown.

"Hello Christina," Richard muttered when he was near her. The woman nodded, not speaking, and when Richard had arrived at her side, he saw that her eyes were red and puffy. She had been crying. "Mum's pushed you out of there, too, eh?" he said, trying to appear nonchalant.

Christina nodded, then dried a few new tears. Richard could see that they weren't sad tears but angry ones, as the light burning behind the woman's eyes was far from self-pitying. He knew rage well enough by now, having lived with his drunk mother for so long.

"What happened?" he asked again after a few moments of silence. He saw that the woman battled an inner fight before she spoke with a strained voice.

"Cathy was a mean drunk. She said bad things about me and Johnny, and that I was a slut for..." she hesitated, then looked at Richard straight in the eyes. "For getting pregnant by him."

Richard was shocked, and then realized it made so much sense. Christina hadn't been eating that much, and yet he had noticed she had put on some weight. It wasn't fat, it was a baby!

"You're not a... slut," Richard said, nodding. "You're his wife. It makes sense to have his baby."

Christina smiled through her tears, and Richard realized she was relieved. She was worried he would share his mother's views. He knew, though, that those words didn't even belong to his mother. It was the alcohol that spoke, and that was the worst of it—she was doing so much damage to her family, and it wasn't even because she was a bad woman. It was because she was a coward. Richard grew angry again but didn't speak.

"Thanks," Christina said when she was calm enough to speak. "But I want to be alone for a bit." Richard nodded, bid her goodnight, and left, continuing his search for his uncle.

As he turned towards his father's mine, he smelled smoke. He entered the mine's surface but realized the fire wasn't burning where Jimmy usually lit it. The spot was dark, no light filtering through. The smoke was coming from the other side of the claim. Richard wondered why his uncle had decided to change the place where he lit the fire as he approached it.

Just as he turned by the side of a cliff, he saw the flame, and instantly froze in his tracks. There were two people he didn't know. They were by the creek, ankle-deep, prospecting in the cold, dark waters. Richard lowered his body and moved as quietly as he could through the property, hiding behind some thick bushes a few feet away from the fire.

These were the claim jumpers, and he wanted to see them clearly. They were stealing from his family. If he saw their faces well enough, he would remember them and then he'd tell his uncle. He would know what to do.

As Richard watched them, he realized they were working in rather harsh conditions. He was getting cold himself and he wasn't ankle-deep in freezing water. They had their backs to the fire and no matter how he craned his neck, he couldn't catch a good glimpse of them.

A shot echoed through the open area, making Richard jump. The pot that had been slowly boiling over the fire clanged loudly and was thrown away, spinning in the air. Richard saw the two men abandoning everything and running as fast as they could, barefooted, through the river and into the woods further away. Richard stayed completely still then, waiting to see who was behind the shooting. A familiar figure appeared a few minutes later, his uncle Jimmy, holding a long, strange rifle.

Jimmy bent to examine the contents of the two bags by the fire, satisfied that he had scared the claim jumpers enough to dissuade them from returning immediately. Richard stood from behind the bush and started walking towards Jimmy, when the man heard him and raised his rifle to his direction. Richard raised his arms, taken by surprise, and stayed still.

"Who goes—" Jimmy started, then squinted at his nephew. "Richard?"

"Hi uncle," Richard muttered.

"You idiot boy, I would have shot you if I didn't want to waste these bullets!" Jimmy shouted. "They cost more than I care to throw away."

"Sorry uncle," Richard said.

"What were you even doing here?" Jimmy asked.

"I was looking for you, that's why I came here. When I saw that the fire didn't belong to you, I hid. I wanted to see what they were doing, and to remember their faces."

Jimmy stared at him for a few moments, thinking. "Your idea was good but dangerous. I told you to stay away and not come here unless you're with either me or Jessie."

"You are right," Richard sighed. "I'm really sorry."

"What's done is done," Jimmy muttered and knelt again, opening the bag. "Let's see what we can figure out about those thieves."

They browsed through the contents of the bag silently for a few moments. There was some uncooked food that had probably been waiting for the water to boil completely, a few tools, and, to Jimmy's excitement, a notebook. He pulled it out and opened it. Richard moved his head so he could sneak a look over his uncle's shoulder.

The notebook was filled with names, Richard realized. They were contact information to the claim jumper's friends. And as Jimmy leafed through it, he stopped in the page right after the cover. There, handwritten by the claim jumper himself, were identification details, titled "if found, please return to." They had found exactly what they were looking for.

Jimmy smiled widely as he stood, putting the notebook in his pocket. "We have them," he muttered, more to himself than to Richard. He had found enough to push things to the next step, though he didn't yet know what the next step was. He approached the fire and started putting it out, and Richard hurried to help him, pushing dirt over it along with his uncle.

When they had extinguished the flames, Jimmy shot towards the trees twice, "to make a point" as he said, and then walked towards the mine's entrance. Since Faiz-ul had started helping Jimmy, they had removed the boards, and Jimmy wanted to see what they had taken, or if they had more of their stuff left inside. They explored the mine quickly and found no tools.

"I will stay here tonight," Jimmy said after they finished their exploration. "They might return. I'll be ready for them," he gestured at his rifle. He found a comfortable spot from which he could see the entrance, still inside the mine, and huddled down.

"I want to stay, too," Richard said, sitting next to him. Jimmy looked at his nephew, his eyes betraying that he wanted to ask him to go away, but then realized that the boy was too serious. Something might have happened at home. He said nothing and Richard laid back, more relaxed. A few moments passed before Richard spoke again.

"Mark challenged that bully Bishop to a cricket game," he said. "Do you think Faiz-ul and Praveen might know how to play?"

"I might ask them next time I see them, if you like," Jimmy said. "You should get some more coaching from Jessie while you have the chance," he added. "Ya know, he used to play cricket before the war. He was on a team, even. He was pretty good, I'm told."

"I didn't know that!" Richard said. "Though it does seem obvious now, in retrospect," he added after a few moments, thinking. "He always has great advice and knows the game perfectly. He could spot any move or trick we used."

"So, ask him to help you," Jimmy said. Richard nodded and they passed a few more moments in silence.

"How are things going at dad's mine?" Richard broke the silence again. He gestured around vaguely.

"Faiz-ul doesn't know a lot about the methods we use, but he knows the names of the tools, at least, and can describe their use, so he's halfway there. He is a good learner, and keen to learn more."

"That's good," Richard nodded. He had much respect for the man.

"It's hard work, and he is slowly realizing that. It doesn't seem like he's about to quit any time soon, though."

"When will you see Faiz-ul again?" Richard asked.

"We've arranged for him to come over next Saturday," Jimmy replied.

"That's too long away…" Richard muttered. "I need to get a team together, now."

"If you want them to be part of your team, then just go over to their store and ask them," Jimmy said. "I believe they'd be interested, at least judging from how much fun Faiz-ul seemed to have when he played with us."

"That's what I'll do, then," Richard said. "Do you have any other kids in mind?"

"I've seen a few playing around," Jimmy said. "I could give you some suggestions. And I'm sure that Jessie would be able to put together an entire team for you, if you asked. However, I'd suggest you handle that part yourself."

"You are right, but I'd like to hear the kids you have in mind, as well as see what Jessie would think. This is important to me."

"It's good that you care about your brother," Jimmy said after a few moments.

"Mother's too drunk to care, Johnny's at the war, so Mark and you are all the blood family I have left that cares about me. I could count Christina there, too, even if we're not related by blood," Richard muttered. "You need to take care of family, ya know?"

Christina hesitantly opened the front door to the house. It was way after eight in the evening, and most of the houses she passed on her way were already dark. She entered, hoping to see no trace of Cathy. She was glad to see that the woman had retreated to her own room for the evening. She closed the front door behind her silently then hurried up to her own room.

As she closed the room's door, she unwittingly brought Cathy out of her daze. The drunk woman left her bed and made her way towards the living room for some more wine, checking the two boys' rooms on her way. Mark was asleep, Richard was still missing. Where had the stupid boy gone?

She poured herself a good glass of wine and stumbled towards her rocking chair. After she turned it to look at the front door, she sat down, waiting for Richard to return while sipping her wine. She refilled her glass more times through the night, before passing out on the chair.

Hours later, a bit after sunrise, Christina made her way to the kitchen, preparing breakfast for the boys. She was as silent as she could to avoid waking Cathy up and starting another argument. The woman was snoring, oblivious to the world, to Christina's delight. Later, Mark made his way downstairs, dressed for school. He immediately saw his mother and started tiptoeing around. He waved at Christina instead of speaking, ate, and left for school.

"Sun's up," Jimmy woke Richard up. The boy had been snoozing for a bit, and Jimmy didn't want to wake him up. He'd need his strength.

"Morning, uncle," Richard muttered standing up and stretching. His body felt sore and tired, since sleeping against the mine's wall wasn't really comfortable.

"Good morning to you, too. I have some breakfast stew ready. Then, we'll get started with the day's work." Jimmy led the boy to the campfire by the mine's entrance and gestured at the pot. Richard felt his mouth salivating at the smell, realizing he was incredibly hungry. He poured himself a bowl and started eating ferociously.

"What will we do today?" he asked between mouthfuls.

"Drilling in this site. There's a quartz vein I'm chasing, which shows a lot of promise."

"Great," Richard said. He liked the mindless work of preparing a wall to be blown up with dynamite. "But I need to go to the other site too. Jessie needs me."

"I know," Jimmy said. "Let's work on this one for a bit, and we'll talk about that later."

"Alright, uncle," Richard nodded. He finished his bowl quickly, then stood. "Let's go." Jimmy led the boy through the mine. As they walked, they came upon various pieces of wood that were taking up space along the corridors.

"Let's tidy up a bit first," Jimmy said thoughtfully. "We need to clear the space, so we don't have an accident."

"You're right," Richard agreed. They picked up as many of the boards as they could and moved them to a storage area outside of the mine. On the way, they saw other piles they needed to tidy up, so they made a plan and started moving stuff around. It took them a few hours but by the end of the time, the mine was significantly tidier and the danger of tripping against unwanted objects was minimized. Then, it was finally time to go to the vein.

Jimmy went deeper into the mine with Richard, towards the newer areas, and stopped in front of a wall. He showed his nephew the vein, a large quartz streak against the wall that had one or two yellow markings that spoke of gold. It was a big one and Richard was impressed. It did show a lot of promise. He saw a few holes already drilled.

"I want to have at least eight more," Jimmy said, and pointed at little marks along the surface of the wall. "I've marked where I want them. I don't expect we'll be done by today, don't worry," he added, seeing Richard frown. He nodded, took his tools and started working with an efficiency that impressed Jimmy. The boy was already an experienced miner despite his age.

When they got hungry again, they ate a quick lunch and discussed their plans once more.

"It's noon by now," Richard said, staring at the overcast sky. "Is it time to go to the other site?"

"You can go," Jimmy agreed, "but I want you to run an errand for me."

"Sure, what do you need?"

"I want you to go into town and pick up a new lantern for me. A couple broke and I need replacements. I want you to get me a few supplies, too. Give me a moment," Jimmy said, and pulled a piece of paper from his bag, which he offered to Richard. "I made a list yesterday." Richard took it and looked it over, and then nodded. "Have the items charged to my account."

Richard stood then. "Anything else?"

"No, mate. Go on your way."

"See you later, uncle," Richard said and left the site. He walked fast, keen to go to the other site where Jessie worked and talk to him about the challenge, as well as to speak with Faiz-ul about joining their team, so he took little time to arrive.

Passing through the streets, he saw an army recruiter having set up a desk in the town square, with a large sign that was requesting miners to join the war effort as sappers, working underground. Richard was amazed that they had come up to Bendigo. He looked at him, trying to make out what kind of man he was, but when the soldier looked back at Richard, the boy looked away and hurried off.

The Ansari shop was open, and Richard entered, seeing Mr. Ansari talking to a customer. There was a crate of goods on the counter, and the stranger was paying Mr. Ansari. Richard didn't see any of the man's sons around, so he waited for his turn. When the stranger left with his crate, Richard approached the counter.

"Good evening, Mr. Ansari," Richard greeted him.

"Hello, Richard," the man said. "How's the Hoagland mine going?" he asked conversely. Richard was pleasantly surprised the man remembered him.

"Going well, sir, thank you. My uncle needs some things," he pulled out his list. "A kerosene lantern," he started reading, "some kerosene, and food supplies." He ordered certain quantities of coffee, salt, beer, a kettle, a frying pan, some butter, flour, bacon, a good amount of smoked jerky, and Richard was surprised to see some tobacco for his pipe and some bullets for his rifle on the list as well.

While Richard spoke, Mr. Ansari was marking things on a piece of paper of his own. "I have everything you need," he said afterwards. "Even the bullets. When your uncle ordered the last time, I got a few crates more, so I could hold them in stock, ya know?" the man said, satisfied with his foresight. "Will you take all these with you?" he asked, craning his neck to see if there was a wagon or a trolley outside. "Or will one of my sons bring them to your uncle's claim?"

"Please bring them over," Richard said. "I can't carry all these on my own, I'm just making the order."

"Excellent. And everything charged to your uncle's account, right?"

"That's right Mr. Ansari, thank you," Richard said.

"Thank you too," the man replied, and noted down a few more details. Richard stayed put, waiting for him to finish before speaking again. "Is there something else you need, Richard?" he said, raising his head.

"Yes, sir. I wanted to ask you something about your sons."

"Go ahead," Mr. Ansari said, his curiosity piqued.

"My brother has got a cricket game soon. Do your sons know how to play the game?"

"Both Faiz-ul and Praveen know," Mr. Ansari said proudly. "They're quite good, too."

"Do you think they'd want to play on our team this coming weekend?" He explained where it was taking place and when, and

Mr. Ansari nodded.

"I think they'd be glad to play with you. Faiz-ul had enjoyed his time when he practiced with you a few days ago," Mr. Ansari said, smiling. "They're out on deliveries right now, but when they return, I'll tell them about it."

"Thank you," Richard said. "If you can, tell them they should come to my uncle's mine. The one where the one-armed man is. We will be practicing there on Thursday, on Friday, and on Saturday, since the game's on Sunday."

"I will," Mr. Ansari said.

"Thank you so much, sir," Richard said, smiling widely. He left quickly, excited that he would have to new members for his brother's team. The excitement brought him quickly to the mine, and he sought out Jessie. The one-armed man was on his knees next to a wooden contraption, swearing so much that Richard thought he would make even a sailor blush.

Jessie was holding a tool on his one hand, pulling and pushing at a spot of the contraption, but Richard realized that with a helping hand, it would be much easier. He rushed next to him and knelt, grabbing hold of the wooden thing. Jessie greeted him through his teeth and guided him verbally, telling him where to hold, where to pull, where to push.

There were ropes and pieces of fabric attached to wooden beams, and as they worked in perfect sync, Richard slowly realized they were making something like a sail of a boat.

At some point, Jessie told him they were finished, and Richard stood. He pulled up the contraption under Jessie's directions and carried it towards the mine's entrance. Then, they put it up, and fixed it against the cliff wall, on holding rings that Jessie had prepared earlier. Richard tied it well and opened the sail.

"The damned thing was giving me hell," Jessie muttered. "Yesterday's wind destroyed the previous sail and I was making a new one. I was about to throw the damned thing over the fire and be done with it when you came. Thank you, mate."

"I would have come earlier, but Jimmy needed help at the other site," Richard said. "I have news about the cricket game!" Richard added excitedly. "I got us two more members, and I need more advice from you!"

"Sure," Jessie said back. "Let's get started hauling ore, and you'll tell me all about it."

CHAPTER NINETEEN

"Hey, crybaby," Mark heard Robert Bishop's voice coming from somewhere behind him. The three boys that were sitting around Mark as they ate lunch looked at him with sad eyes. Mark felt as if the schoolyard had gone more silent, waiting to see what would happen. Mark, his terror blunted by a newfound confidence he had acquired thanks to his progress in cricket, ignored the bully for a moment.

"Are you deaf and a crybaby" Robert said, nearer now. Mark stood then, turning towards him. He was standing a couple of steps away, his two henchmen next to him as always.

"No, I just was in no mood to see your face," Mark said. Robert stared at him and Mark saw that he barely held himself back. There was a teacher standing by the school's door, looking over curiously, and Mark knew that it was the only thing holding him back.

"You talk big for someone who's about to lose in cricket," Robert said through clenched teeth. "We'll see how you'll be talking after Sunday."

"Did you interrupt my lunch just for empty threats?" Mark said. Anger flashed in the boy's eyes and Mark felt like he was pushing his luck to its limits. He decided to stop provoking him and see what the boy wanted to say.

"My threats are never empty, as you're about to see. I came to clear the rules regarding our teams," he said, a hint of a sardonic smile on his lips.

"Go ahead," Mark said hesitantly.

"We'll set the bar at school age," Robert said.

"You need to be more specific, there are multiple levels of

schooling."

"Twenty-two years at most, then," Robert said. Mark briefly wondered if the boy had assembled a full team of twenty-two-year-olds, but remembered what he had heard, that he had trouble with assembling a full team, just like Mark himself had. Many kids wanted to avoid taking sides in the confrontation, and there weren't that many cricket players under twenty-two around. Thankfully, Faiz-ul could still play, as he was within the age bracket.

"I agree," Mark said officially.

"It wasn't a discussion," said Robert. He turned to leave, but then stopped. Another sinister smile appeared on the boy's face as he turned back. "Let's make it more interesting, shall we?" he said.

"How?" Mark asked, a sense of dread filling him.

"Let's make a bet, you and me," Robert said. "Winner gets two pounds."

Two Australian pounds was about a week's wages for most workers, and Mark wasn't a worker. He didn't have that much money readily available, he would have to borrow or somehow make the money, if he lost. Robert saw his hesitation and his smile grew.

"What's the matter? Do you have so little faith in your team that you won't take a tiny bet?"

Mark realized that his friends were listening in, and they would talk. If he wasn't confident in their abilities, their morale would fall, and they might even quit the team. The match would be lost before it was even played.

"I have complete confidence in my team," Mark said with bravado, even if he felt his stomach dropping. "I agree to the bet," he added in the same formal tone he had used before.

Mark's acting convinced Robert whose smile turned upside down. "See you Sunday," the bully said and turned away, his two henchmen falling in on each side. Mark returned to his lunch. He joked around with his friends for a moment with a lightness he didn't really feel and ate his food quickly. "Ready for some bowling practice?" he asked them, and they all nodded.

They went to a clear area near the school and started throwing a cricket ball around, getting some practice in for the match. Mark's mind was on the bet, though. Two pounds was a lot of money, especially for someone who had no income, like Mark. He would have to speak with Richard later, who had a much more stable income than he did. If he needed to, he would even go ask his uncle for some money, and he would work them off over several weekends. Besides, he didn't mind working the mine.

His friends seemed to notice he was preoccupied because they gave him more encouragement when he did well. He smiled widely when he realized, thankful to have such good friends. He focused completely on the practice, momentarily putting everything else out of his mind.

As Cathy pushed the house's back door open, she realized something was different. There was something near the front door, and the door was open. She entered the house and made her way deeper in. Two packed suitcases were next to the door. They looked familiar, and as she approached, remembered that they were the suitcases Christina had used when she brought in her things.

Christina passed in front of her as she entered the room, walking to her things. There was an envelope sitting on the kitchen table with

Christina's writing on it, addressed to Cathy. The woman stared at it and then turned her eyes to Christina. Christina stared back at her, first in shame and then in defiance. She grabbed her things, threw one last look at the woman that contained a hit of regret, then walked out the front door.

The woman stared after her for a few long moments. Christina was walking away. Two things slowly came to focus on her mind.

First, Christina was bearing her grandchild. Even if Cathy was mad at her for getting pregnant—though she was significantly madder at Johnny for that—the child was her blood, too. And second, the woman was leaving because of her. She had fucked up, majorly. The blame was on her shoulders, and on no one else's.

While the realization felt like a blazing brand on her skin, there was also significant resistance. If the woman wanted to leave, she was free to leave. What would Cathy do, beg her to stay? The woman had come here on her own initiative. She had been trying to set things up differently than Cathy, too. She had made so many changes around the house, and she had been picking fights with her.

Her internal fight lasted for what felt like ages but was probably about two minutes. There was an incredibly strong push to go after her, while there was also her own pride, acting as an incredibly strong force holding her back. In the end, a single thought won out. The child was her own blood. She flew through the open door, hurrying after the departing woman.

Cathy caught up with her. Christina, a pregnant woman carrying two bags, walked slower than Cathy, a middle-aged woman that was in good physical condition, ran, so it wasn't a close call at all.

"Christina, wait," Cathy called out. The woman hesitated and then stopped, turning towards her.

"What do you want?" she asked. She was still holding on to her things, though her eyes looked less aggressive and more sad. Cathy stood in front of her, staring at her, trying to put her feelings in words.

"Come back to the house," she finally said.

"No." Christina's tone had a finality that made Cathy's stomach drop further.

"Look, whatever it was that I did, I apologize," she said. Christina's eyes grew harder.

"That's not going to cut it," she threw back, and turned her back to Cathy. She took a few steps before the woman found the words to speak.

"The child is my blood, too," she muttered. There was a hesitation in her voice, and Cathy's introspective ability was too lacking to understand why. Christina heard it, and heard the sincerity behind it, as well. She paused and turned back to the woman.

"They why do you act like you hate me and the baby?" she spat back. There was a flood of emotions inside her that couldn't be contained. "Why do you keep doing everything in your power to hurt us?"

Cathy took a step back, her eyes opening wide in shock. She hadn't expected such an outburst from the woman. "I don't hate you," she said, her voice containing a mix of shock and defensiveness.

"You certainly fooled me," Christina said ironically. "All you do is drink and pick fights with me and your own sons."

The cold wind blew through the trees, Bendigo's cold winter still in full swing. It would soon break into spring, but for now, the dirty road and the trees around them were cold, as were the two women.

Cathy lowered her head. "I miss Mick," she said, and Christina thought she saw tears in the woman's eyes. Her heart softened a little, but she had been hurt too much to simply give in at the first sign of tears.

"Drinking to dull the pain isn't the solution," Christina said, making her voice as cold as she could. "Mick's gone. Life goes on. You need to focus on your sons, or they'll go away because of you."

Cathy hesitated for a long moment before she spoke again. "I know." Christina stared at the woman for a long while, saying nothing. She had to judge how sincere the woman was, and if there was a chance she would change her ways. Cathy raised her head then and looked at the younger woman in her eyes. "In truth, I am angrier with Johnny than I am with you," she said. "You can't knock up a woman and go to war half a world away."

"I'm angry at Johnny, too, to some degree," Christina replied. "He abandoned his family out of fear."

"But you do love him," Cathy said. There was a tone of realization in her words, as if she had had an epiphany. "You are angry at him, but you love him."

"Yes," Christina said. "And you're angry at Mick, aren't you?"

"I am," Cathy replied, her words hollow. "I think I am more angry than sad."

"But the solution isn't at the bottom of the wine bottle," Christina interrupted the woman's thoughts, bringing them back to the issue at hand. "Your anger, your sadness, they are emotions you must work out on your own, and not take out on those who want to help you."

"Yes. I understand that," Cathy said. Christina stared at her again, her eyes boring holes in the woman's face, looking for clues. When she found what she was looking for, her shoulders relaxed, and she let out a long sigh.

"I don't want to leave, not really. I like Mark and Richard, and I like you when you're not drinking. But you need to work with me, and you need to leave alcohol behind for good."

"I can't promise that," Cathy said slowly, "but I can promise that I will limit it. And I will try to stop taking out my own sadness on you."

Christina nodded. "Then, I won't promise that I will stay forever. But I will come back for now."

Cathy's whole body felt like a strung bow full of tension, and Christina's words released it immediately. She felt her neck relax, her breathing turned from short and shallow to more even, and she could think significantly more clearly. The cold wind pierced through her clothes and she longed for their hearth.

"Let's get away from this bloody weather, then," she said, shivering.

"Say, Richard," Mark said, leaning against the idle rock crusher. "Do you have any money?"

Richard let the buckets on the ground, his eyes widening in surprise. "What? Why? What happened?"

"Relax, mate," Mark said, his feigned ease disappearing. "Nothing serious happened. It's just a bet..." he started, but his voice faded uncertainly.

"A bet?" Richard said, his eyebrows shooting up. That was even worse than what he had expected, which was that the bullies had taken Mark's lunch. "Where did you find a gambling den? And why did they let you in?"

"No, no gabling," Mark said, even more anxious. "Robert Bishop made me bet two pounds on the match."

"Come on, mate," Richard said loudly, "you had me shitting my pants here. That's nothing!"

"But I don't have any money," Mark retorted. "So, for me, it is something."

"I have a pound saved up, and Jessie is going to pay me soon, after we sell this gold," Richard said, gesturing at the buckets with his head. The quartz rocks had golden lines shooting through them. "You focus on practicing, alright? Besides, we're not going to lose."

"But two pounds is a lot of money," Mark muttered. "Mum would kill me if I lost so much."

"Don't worry, mate," Richard said, patting his brother's shoulder. "You aren't going to lose. In fact," he emptied his buckets in the rocket crusher, "I think I'll have my break and start practicing right now." He turned to the mine's entrance. "Hey, Jessie," he called, and the man poked his head from the mine.

"What?"

"I'll go practice with Mark for a bit, alright?"

"Sure thing, mate," Jessie shot back and ducked inside again.

"Come, I'll be the batter and you'll be the bowler, and then we switch," he told his brother as they grabbed bat and ball and retreated towards the empty part of the mine's surface.

The suitcase was lying on Christina's bed, open, and Christina was slowly making her way through it, putting her clothes in the closet.

Her mind was distant as she went through the motions, thinking about Johnny and her family.

If someone saw her belly, they'd think that she was getting chubby. She knew that Richard had been surprised when she told him about it, so he hadn't expected it. But if her parents saw, they'd instantly recognize that she was pregnant. The few times she had met them after Johnny had left, she had been wearing clothes to hide her body, but it was getting harder to hide.

There was no shame in her for being pregnant. She always wanted to have a couple of children herself, at some point. And Johnny was a good man, whom she loved. But she knew that people would get angry with Johnny, just like she and his own mother both were angry with him. The man had left her here, pregnant, and alone, while he was off half a world away.

She was glad she had managed to avoid going to her parents' farm. It would create many more problems than it would solve, in the end. And if she managed to strike a truce with Cathy at the same time, all the better.

A knock on her door brought her out of her reverie. She turned to see Cathy standing at the doorway.

"Finished unpacking?"

"Just about," she replied, closing her closet. "Something wrong?"

"I wanted to continue our previous conversation about money," she said. She took a step back and Cathy followed her to the living room, where they sat at the kitchen table. Cathy had prepared some fish and Christina took a few bites as the woman talked.

"I want to discuss a new idea," she said. "I was thinking of asking Jimmy if we could help out at the mine."

"Mining is hard work," Christina interjected.

"I know," Cathy said. "I wasn't talking about working in the mine itself. Besides, I'm not sure if I can go where..." her voice trailed off and Christina saw that the woman threw a glance at the wine bottle. She pulled herself together again and continued speaking after a moment. "I was thinking of prospecting in the river or digging around for gems."

"That's a good idea," Christina said. "However, I think your original idea for making a garden and selling the produce is better. It's something we can do, by ourselves, and it's something that can help the family. You can't eat gems, but even if we have leftover produce, we can eat that."

"We will do that, as soon as the weather clears. And we could expand our farm to include animals like sheep or goats," Cathy said.

"Animal husbandry is a lot of work, you know. My father has animals, and he usually works with them throughout the day, every day. But it's a great idea. A cow or a few sheep would help the household, besides providing a source of income."

"And we need to get started on the house expansion. I want to finish the root cellar."

"We could ask Richard and Mark to help with the work," Christina said, "and even ask Jimmy for help with the planning and the materials."

Cathy nodded, a smile on her face. What started as idle dreaming were now taking form. The boys had helped them already with the garden outside, and the completion of the root cellar was much more tangible than it was when they first imagined it.

The week flew by and on Saturday, Mark and Richard were standing on a clearing inside the forest, surrounded by their chosen ten players. They were about to have their last practice, a rehearsal for the match. Faiz-ul and Praveen were there, as well as a couple of Mark's friends from school, and old friends from Richard's school. Two kids that worked in a mine neighboring the mine they had been working with their father had also come. They always greeted each other on the way to work, and as it turned out, they were good cricket players, so Richard had invited them.

A couple of the boys around them, Richard had met through Jessie. The one-handed man had put out a good word for them, and several people approached them. Two of them were young enough to join and Richard had invited them. They were good players, on their way to being professional. Mark had spent quite a few sleepless nights, trying to figure out a plan that worked to the best of everyone's abilities, and as he explained, Richard was impressed with his brother.

The boy had focused on something, for probably the first time in his life, and he had become quite good at it. He had grasped the rules and the basic strategies of the game quickly and had formulated good plans. Richard briefly wondered if he could ever become a professional, before his attention was pulled back to the present.

"Take your places," Mark shouted, and they ran to their spots. Their final practice had begun.

"Hey Jessie," Faiz-ul greeted the man.

"Hey mate," Jimmy returned. "Shouldn't you be at practice?"

"We're done for the day. It went well, and resting is as important as practicing, sometimes," he replied.

"But you're not here to rest," Jimmy smiled. "Or at least, I hope you're not. I'm not paying you to."

"No, you're not paying me to rest," Faiz-ul said and smiled back. "So, what's the plan?"

"Ore hauling. We'll use the ore cart system that my brother built."

"Show me how, and I'll do it," Faiz-ul said.

Jimmy guided him down into the mine. Faiz-ul saw that the man had used explosives recently and there was a new opening on a wall, with ore strewn about. The tracks ended a few feet from the opening and there was a cart already sitting on them, where Jimmy had put a few buckets. They used the buckets to fill the cart, and Faiz-ul admired the skills of the cart's maker. It was durable and well-made, simple, and without any extraneous parts.

They pushed the first cart up and emptied it into the crusher, then hurried back down. The sun was slowly making its way through the sky, peeking from behind the clouds often. The days were getting longer as the winter was breaking into spring.

After the third cart, they stood some distance away from the crusher, while the machine worked through what they had brought up. They sat on a log, taking a small break and snacking on salted fish.

"So, how is the team?" Jimmy asked.

"As ready as we're going to get," Faiz-ul replied. "It's going to be an all-day game and the winner will get bragging rights for years. I've heard people talking about it in the shop, as well as on the street."

"Do you know anything about the enemy team?" Jimmy asked,

and Faiz-ul shrugged. "Haven't Mark or Richard spied on them? I would have," he added.

"Sometimes it's best to focus on your own abilities and improve, instead of trying to copy or sabotage others," Faiz-ul muttered, more to himself than to Jimmy.

"Right you are, mate," Jimmy said. He stood and stretched. "Let's get on, there's still some ore down there, and I don't want any claim jumpers stealing the ore *my* dynamite extracted. I'll work the crusher and you work the cart, alright?"

Faiz-ul nodded and hurried off. The rock crusher was making a lot of noise as it worked, but Jimmy had his attention to his surroundings. He didn't let his guard down when he was at the mine, for two reasons. First, it was where his brother had died, and he didn't want to make the same mistakes. Second, the claim jumper knew there was gold here, and he might return. So, since he was paying attention, he saw Christina coming through the trees before the woman called out to him.

She looked chubby to his eyes and he briefly considered if the woman was pregnant. He did some mental math and realized that she could very well be, considering when Johnny was here last. A stray thought entered his mind unbidden, and he wondered if the child was truly Johnny's. It was not rare for wives of soldiers to cheat while their husbands were away. He did not make any judgment, though, deciding he would look into it only if he had more concrete clues.

"Hello Mr. Hoagland," Christina greeted him when she was within earshot. They took a few steps away from the crusher so they could talk without shouting.

"Hello Christina, good evening. Is there something wrong?"

"No, I just wanted to talk to you about something."

"Go ahead, then," he said.

"Cathy wanted your help to figure out how to make a root cellar at her house, either below the house or next to it," she said.

"Why she didn't come to ask me herself?" Jimmy asked with curiosity.

"Well, you must understand why she might not be able to, since this is where Mick died," Christina said, gesturing towards the mine. "It's difficult for her, coming here."

"That's understandable," Jimmy replied. "So, a root cellar. Who will be building it?"

"The boys mostly," Christina said. She touched her belly. "I'm with child, as you can see, and I don't think I can be of much help. It's Johnny's," she added hastily to Jimmy's unspoken question. "I think I was already pregnant when he left.

"So, Cathy's going to be a grandma," Jimmy smiled. "I'll draft something up for the root cellar. The Ansari store will have all the materials you're going to need. But it's going to require quite a bit of work. I hope the boys are ready for it."

"We'll help as much as we can, too," Christina said. "Cathy's determined to build it soon."

"Good, good," Jimmy said. He was worried about Cathy. There was something unstable in her eyes every time he saw her, like the eyes of a captured animal. She remined him of the times his wife woke up during a nightmare, the dream still alive inside her mind, and her eyes half-crazy with fear. He hoped things turned out alright for them.

"Thank you, Mr. Hoagland," Christina said sincerely. "I'll pass on your answer to Cathy."

"And tell her about the game," Jimmy said. On that moment, Faiz-ul appeared with the ore cart. "Christina, if you wait for a moment, I'll take you home on my cart," Jimmy said, and hurried off.

"Thank you, Mr. Hoagland," Christina said again, and stood aside, watching the men work. They emptied the cart in the crusher as the machine rumbled along, turning the thick ore chunks into fine dust. They worked the dust for a bit, afterwards.

Faiz-ul dusted himself off when the crusher was empty, as did Jimmy. "Thank you for your help, mate," Jimmy said to Faiz-ul. "Tomorrow's a day off, alright? Good luck at the game."

"Thank you, sir," Faiz-ul said, smiling widely. He was dead tired, but he was also excited about tomorrow.

Jimmy locked up, then turned to Faiz-ul and Christina. "Come," Jimmy said, and gestured with his head towards the wagon. They got on it and Jimmy silently led the way towards Christina's home.

"Your stop," Jimmy said to Christina and the woman jumped off.

"Thank you, Mr. Hoagland," the woman said. She waved them goodbye as they left. Faiz-ul sat silently, waiting for his own turn to get off.

"Faiz-ul, your help has been greatly appreciated," Jimmy said when they were alone. "I wouldn't be able to work as efficiently without you. Here's a fair wage for your time," he said, and extended an envelope towards the younger man.

"Thank you," Faiz-ul muttered, surprised. He peeked inside and saw more money than he had expected. The man had paid him fair wages indeed.

"Is this spot good enough?" Jimmy asked. "If I go deeper into town, I'd have trouble turning around."

"No, that's alright, thank you, sir," Faiz-ul replied quickly and jumped off. "Have a good trip home."

"Take care, see you at the game tomorrow," Jimmy waved, and turned the wagon around.

Faiz-ul waved back and hurried through the empty streets. It was dark and cold and he wanted to get home. He opened the door to his house, and the first thing he saw was his father, lowering his newspaper. He had a serious look about him.

"Where were you?" Mr. Ansari asked.

"I was at the Hoagland mine, the claim Mr. Mick used to work."

"What do you think you're doing there? You should be helping your family earn a living instead of... enjoying a *hobby*," the man asked, putting his newspaper aside. His eyes were hard. Faiz-ul felt a wave of rage building up, but he pushed it down. There was no reason to fight with his father. He pulled out the envelope Jimmy had given him and gave it to his mother.

"I am," Faiz-ul said. The woman opened the envelope and her eyes shone. "I won't be working in the store forever, don't forget that."

Mr. Ansari exchanged a look with his wife, who nodded appreciatively. He laid back and his face relaxed.

"One more thing," Faiz-ul said. "Me and my friends have been practicing hard for the cricket game tomorrow. Praveen is playing as well. You're invited to come."

"Of course we will," Mr. Ansari said, nodding. Faiz-ul nodded back and left the room, a small smile playing on his lips. The feeling of having achieved a victory over his father was incredibly satisfying. It felt like he was making a step towards earning his freedom.

The few chickens that were awake were clucking at Mark, probably hoping to get a snack. The sky was dark and it was past nine, Mark knew, but he couldn't sleep. He found the chickens' sounds soothing, as this coop had been his refuge for a while now, and he hoped that they would soothe him this time as well. He spoke to them in low tones, and when the creatures realized he was not going to feed them, they returned to their nests. It was cold out for them.

Mark stared at the stars. He was as excited for tomorrow as he was afraid. The game was going to be huge. It was already the talk of the town. He felt the immense pressure, but he also felt a finality, like things were about to finally be over. He hoped the bully wouldn't pay any more attention to him after it.

But there was nothing he could achieve by worrying about it. He sighed, relaxed back against the fence, and stared at the stars, wishing good luck for himself, and for the rest of his family.

The horses knew the way even though it was dark, and they took care on the road, avoiding their well-known holes and large rocks. Jimmy led them easily to his mine, and they entered through the gate going towards the place he usually had them wait. As soon as they arrived at the makeshift stable, Jimmy jumped off the wagon and hurried to the crusher.

"Good evening, mates," he called to Richard and Jessie. The rock crusher was silent so that probably meant the ore had been crushed and they were shifting through the results of the day's work.

"Hey mate," Jessie called back, and Richard waved.

"What do you have here?" Jimmy said as he knelt by the crusher's opening. There was some gold dust inside.

"That's the last bit," Jessie said, shifting. "Along with what we found earlier today, it should be at least nine ounces, maybe more."

Richard was smiling widely. The good result from the day's work meant that he could borrow some money to cover the bet Mark had been forced to agree with.

"Say, uncle," Richard approached the subject. "Could I borrow a pound?"

"Sure," Jimmy said, but his brows came closer together. "Is everything alright?"

"Yes," Richard said quickly. "It's just that Mark's bully forced him to make a bet for two pounds. I had one, but I'd like to borrow one more from you, to cover the bet, just in case. Though I don't expect us to lose," he added.

"Ah, I understand," Jimmy said. He felt a little awkward interrogating his nephew, but he wanted to make sure the money wasn't used for less… healthy adventures. "Here," he offered the money, and Richard took it gratefully.

"Thank you, uncle. You can deduct it from what you would pay me after the gold is sold," he said.

"That's good with me," Jimmy replied. "Listen, have you heard from your brother Johnny yet? I wonder how he's doing." He instantly regretted his question when he saw that Richard's face took on a weird look. It was obvious it was a sensitive subject.

"No," Richard said, trying to appear nonchalant, but instead clearly showing how uncomfortable he was. His eyes turned aside, he took on a more guarded stance by putting his hands across his chest, and Jimmy saw that even his eyes hardened. "I haven't heard of anything. Ask Christina or Mark, they might know more."

Jimmy didn't know what to do, so he shrugged it off. He was about to call it a day, when Jessie salvaged the situation.

"Are you ready for the game tomorrow, mate?" he asked Richard. The young man's whole stance changed immediately, and he smiled to the one-handed man. His smile was nervous and shaky, but it was a different nervousness than the one he had displayed before.

"As ready as I'm ever going to be. I only wonder how Mark's going to do under all this pressure." His voice had an edge to it, and Jimmy realized that the boy was more nervous than he was showing.

"I'm sure you'll both do well," Jimmy said, patting his nephew's shoulder. "You've practiced much, and your team is sound."

Richard smiled up to his uncle and nodded. "It is going to be a game that everyone will be talking about for a while," he said.

CHAPTER TWENTY

The papers were piling next to Lt. Hungerford's writing space. There were reports to be made and orders to be signed, especially now that they were under such strict timelines. His desk barely supported the weight, as it was just four planks standing on ammo crates. The little storage room around him was all Third Platoon could afford to give him.

"Sir," came a voice from the entrance and Lt. Hungerford raised his eyes. Sgt. Hudson was waiting to for permission to come in.

"Enter," Lt. Hungerford said. The sergeant entered quickly and saluted, and the lieutenant stopped writing. He really hoped the man had good news.

"There's a problem with the extra manpower we brought in from the British, sir," the man said, immediately dispelling Lt. Hungerford's hopes.

"So, we lost a quarter of our forces to crabs, and you tell me that the temporary replacements are also problematic?" the lieutenant said.

"Unfortunately, yes, sir."

"I was sincerely hoping you would tell me we had finally returned to the expected productivity levels," Lt. Hungerford muttered.

"There's been some improvement in this area, but there's also been a new problem that's affecting the morale of the troops."

"So, what is it?"

"There's been a thief among the men. The first report was about a pocketknife being stolen, but now there's been a report of stolen money."

"A thief?" Lt. Hungerford said. Then he stood, his face turning red. "A thief, here? How can a soldier steal from his fellow mates? Especially here, in enemy territory, under such conditions? I want that man found right now, I want every soldier's kit inspected, and when you find him, I want him—"

"Just a second, sir, if I may," Sgt. Hudson interrupted. "It is not a wise idea."

Lt. Hungerford deflated and sat back down. "Why is that, sergeant?"

"It will send the thief into hiding. It would be better to examine during which shifts things were stolen and lay some traps for him."

"You are right," Hungerford said. "You have my permission to do that. Catch the bloody thief in the act." He took a deep breath. "How many incidents have been reported?"

"Four, sir. The first case was reported right after the British infantry units were assigned to help with the shortage of our own men. They're sleeping in the same area as Third Platoon, sir."

"Do you think it might be those bloody British?"

"Or someone trying to shift the blame, sir," Sgt. Hudson said.

"When are our men coming back?" Lt. Hungerford asked.

"Some are already back," the sergeant said. "At least the ones who aren't in prison."

"So, the Major really did it," the lieutenant muttered. He read about it in a report but couldn't believe it.

"Yes, Sapper Tilley and several others, sir. They've been charged and sentenced to three days in military confinement for self-inflicted wounds. They have two more days to go. Ten of our men have returned, though, and I plan to have them go through their things to see if there's something missing."

"Good," Hungerford said. "Send them back to work as soon as possible and get the quartermaster to supply them rations and everything they need. Since we have most of our men back, the British troops won't stay for long, but they'll stay for at least a couple of days, until we've caught up with the tunnel system objectives the Major has set out for us. Major Moore has been pushing everyone, as we're in a strict timeline, and our mission is vital to the war effort."

"Yes, sir," Sgt. Hudson said. "Permission to be dismissed, sir. I need to get started on those traps."

"Yes, of course. Go. Thank you for the briefing. Keep the men working, at the highest level of productivity you can achieve."

"Aye, sir," Hudson said and left the lieutenant's little office quickly. He hurried down the tunnel system, going around carts bringing waste or soil to be dumped outside, and catching snippets of conversation from the soldiers around him resting in their bunks or working in the tunnels. He turned a corner and reached the ten soldiers that had been waiting for him, as he had ordered them, sitting with their backs against the wall.

"Sir," they said as he stopped before them and stood, saluting. They were the Australians who had returned from the hospital.

"Sit," he ordered, and they sat back down. He looked at them seriously, his eyes pinning them to the ground. "While you were at the hospital getting treated for venereal diseases, Third Platoon was left with their dicks hanging in the wind," he started, and his look didn't allow them to smile, even if the phrase seemed funny to them. It was clear the man wasn't joking.

"Because of your mistakes, your superior officers were forced to borrow troops from the British infantry to keep up with the platoon's objectives. The British have been moving soil out the tunnels, with one casualty to sniper fire so far, and they've been monitoring for countermining activities. Both are duties that belong to our platoon, but we have been so much behind, that we needed to ask for help."

He paused and took a quick look around to make sure they were relatively alone. He saw no British troops. The tunnels immediately around them were empty on that moment. He lowered his voice and continued. "They've been sleeping in our areas, too." His face was gravely serious. "Stuff has been going missing while you were gone."

In the pause that followed, the soldiers gasped. Johnny couldn't believe his ears. Another soldier spoke in a low tone, his voice dripping with rage. "A fucking thief?"

"Yes. The platoon commander is informed about it and has given us permission to find out who the thief is. When you get to your bunk space, look through your kit and if you find anything missing let me or Cpl. Taylor know right away. Make sure you're not overhead, though. Keep all this to yourselves," he added, looking them over. They weren't suspects, since they've been missing. The British were the main suspects, but he still considered the chance the thief was a member of the platoon using the British as cover.

"We will set traps for the thief—or thieves. If you have any ideas, let me know." He looked around. "Now, do I have a volunteer?" he asked, and he saw a hand immediately shoot up. "Sapper Hoagland, right?"

"Yes sir," Johnny replied. He had almost gone crazy from boredom during his hospital stay. He would do anything for some action.

"That's the spirit," Sgt. Hudson said, smiling widely. "I want you all to have the same enthusiasm as Hoagland. Because of your misbehavior, the 175th Tunneling Company is the laughingstock of the army, and you need to make things right. I want you to put more than your all into your work."

The soldiers had serious looks on their faces, the sergeant was glad to see. He saw a few of them nodding along to his words, as well. That was a good sign.

"And you need to rebuild the trust you lost when you let your platoon commander down," he continued. "Lt. Hungerford received a reprimand from the Major and the only reason he wasn't relieved of his command was that other soldiers from other companies also suffered from venereal diseases. So, until further notice, women are off-limits for you, if you get injured and need to go back to England. No more prostitutes, is that clear?"

"Yes, sir," came the reply from most, and he saw that the others at least nodded.

"If a soldier is caught with another venereal disease from this point on, a month-long prison sentence will be waiting for him when he returns, with no pay." He paused. "Are there any questions?" No reply came, so he continued.

"You have all been issued new uniforms, and you'll be reissued your rifles. Go to the armory to take it and go take your orders. Sapper Hoagland, you come find me immediately afterwards."

"Yes, sir," the reply was more enthusiastic now, and the soldiers quickly left.

Johnny stared at the tunnel's dark ceiling. His jacket felt hot, and he used his sleeve to swipe some of the sweat gathering on his brow before removing it. The tunnel was low and crammed. The little corner they were sitting in was a dead-end that did not allow any air to flow. It was a forward tunnel that was designated as a listening post, so it hadn't been expanded.

After Johnny put his jacket next to him, he felt a little less like he was suffocating, but it was still incredibly hot. The soldier manning the listening instrument next to him was also in his undershirt, the jacket on the ground near his leg. They had both their attention to their environment, not relaxing, and their increased focus made the space even hotter, or at least that was how it felt to Johnny.

The corporal sitting by the entrance of the short tunnel was in a much better state, as he had access to at least some airflow. The soldiers besides Johnny were both British, and after what they had been told, Johnny had an eye on each. The corporal was in charge of them and would be the one to run off to report if they heard anything.

The light coming from the electrical lanterns allowed Johnny to read well enough. He was holding the latest letter he had received from Christina, reading it for the second time. He felt a nudge then from Private Bickle, who had been manning the instruments. Johnny looked up. The private gestured with his head to the instruments for Johnny to come listen. Johnny approached quickly and put the earphone in his own ears.

The scratching of shovels against dirt.

He gave a thumbs down to the British soldiers to let them know he had heard something, Pvt. Bickle hurried to the corporal, Cpl. Philips if Johnny recalled correctly. He spoke to him quickly and the officer left to find the sergeant.

Johnny focused on the sounds. It was so eerie, hearing the sounds of shovels digging through ground without having any visual confirmation. The sound was clear and unmistakable, the metal scraping against the soil and the rocks. It was also coming closer.

A big vibration shot through the ground, shaking the tunnel. Then, a wave of dust came into their nook, from the direction the corporal had gone. Johnny grabbed his rifle. The light of the electrical lanterns flickered, going out for a few moments before coming back in. Then, it faded completely. Johnny, with his free hand, patted the ground, looking for the backup light.

When he found the candle lantern, he lit it with a match with shaking hands. It was one thing to have your light go out in a mine, and a different one altogether to lose your light when you're taking part in aggressive tunneling operations. He lit the candle lantern quickly and moved it around. Pvt. Bickle was next to him, looking around with the same urgency Johnny felt.

"Know what happened?" Johnny muttered, as low as he could.

"No, mate," the British solder replied. "A collapse?"

Shouts came from the tunnels then, and Johnny heard calls for the rescue team. The two soldiers were holding onto their rifles, their knuckles white pointing at the tunnel's entrance, prepared for anything that might come their way. The lantern's weak light couldn't penetrate the dust cloud in front of them, so they just waited. Johnny felt that was the worst part. At least there were no gunshots.

Cpl. Philips appeared through the cloud, a kerosene lantern burning in his hand. It was much stronger and illuminated the whole tunnel.

"What happened, sir?" Pvt. Bickle said quickly.

"Germans blew up a mineshaft running parallel to ours," he replied, looking around their own dead-end little shaft. "What did you hear, exactly?"

"Digging, sir. Shovels," Johnny replied.

"Listen again," the officer ordered, and Johnny let his rifle down and grabbed the listening instrument with both hands. He tuned out the rescue team's voices that could be heard through the tunnel system and focused on the instrument's earpiece.

"Nothing, sir," he said after a minute that felt like an eternity. He turned to the corporal just as Sgt. Hudson appeared in the tunnel's entrance.

"Report," the sergeant said quickly.

"We heard digging noises, sir," Cpl. Philips said, "of shovels, approximately five minutes before the other tunnel collapsed—or, was blown up, rather."

"Sir, move, please," a soldier called to the sergeant, and Johnny realized the rescue team was carrying some people on stretchers. Their way was blocked by Sgt. Hudson, who immediately stepped deeper in their tunnel, letting the soldiers run by him.

"Continue listening," Sgt. Hudson told Johnny and Pvt. Bickle, and left as soon as the rescue team had gone away. The sapper and the private returned to their post, adrenaline still pumping through their veins. They could hear the heavy steps of their fellow soldiers through the instrument and tried their best to focus.

The shift lasted for several more tense hours. Finally, Johnny saw two British soldiers and an Australian sapper who had been with him in the hospital, Sapper Fysh, coming to greet them. He and Fysh exchanged a hearty salute, and the British soldiers greeted each other with similar warmth. Johnny quickly said his goodbyes to the officers and Pvt. Bickle and left to wash up. The dust from the collapse had coated everything and he was looking forward to that moment for quite a while.

Johnny hurried to the area designated for washing. The tunnels were much more alive with activity than usual, with medics and doctors rushing about, officers carrying orders, and soldiers carrying injured or dead fellow soldiers on stretchers. He saw that it was mostly the British doing the carrying, while the medics and doctors were of the Australian corps. When he finally arrived at the washing area, his mood was sour. He undressed and washed up quickly, then went over his clothes and cleaned them as well as he could, considering he was still in a tunnel underground.

After he put on his pants and shirt, he realized he had forgotten his jacket at the listening post. He didn't want to disrupt the other team's work, and he knew that he would be punished if they made a mistake because of his interruption, so he decided to take the jacket back the next time he had a shift there. It would be eight hours from now, so he returned to his sleeping area, put on his spare jacket and tried to rest.

His rest was interrupted often from the noise of the rescue crew helping the injured, and when it was time to go back to the listening post, he was feeling tired. When he arrived, he saw the jacket exactly where he had left it, but there was a growing dread in the pit of his stomach. He took it, checked if anyone was looking his way, and then went over the inside, his hands quickly finding the secret pocket he had sewn there himself. He had been using it to store some money, and as he dug his fingers in, he realized that all the money was gone.

Keeping his face impassive, he pulled out Christina's letter. He didn't want to show the thief he had realized he had been robbed, so he would keep his normal routine and get caught in one of the traps the others had set. Johnny read through the letter twice and decided to write her back. Since he had his pen back with the rest of his kit, he pulled out a crumpled piece of paper and his pencil, scribbling down a few words.

Footsteps came from the tunnels, and Lt. Hungerford appeared in the entrance. He greeted the soldier with Johnny, but when he turned to Johnny, his face was hard. "Sapper Hoagland, what do you think you're doing?"

"Sir, I'm writing to my wife back home. We've been——" he started, but the redness on the lieutenant's face cut him short. The man's eyes grew wide and Johnny could swear his lips pulled back, like a dog that was about to bite someone.

"Sapper Hoagland," the lieutenant started in a loud voice, and then went down in volume instantly to an enraged whisper, "do I need to remind you that several men died because the Germans found where we had been digging?" he started, and Johnny sat back straighter, realizing the depths of his mistake.

"If you weren't writing to your lovely wife, and were more interested in listening for German activity, perhaps we would be able to blow up the Germans, and not the other way around. I can have you charged with dereliction of duty, sapper," Lt. Hungerford said, his eyes shining like a mad man's eyes.

"You are right, sir," Johnny said quickly, packing away his pen and paper. He hurried to the instruments, even though it was not his turn, and put the second pair of earpieces to his own ears, focusing intensely. The lieutenant stared at the sapper's back, still enraged. If he had to tell his own Australian troops to not waste time while listening for enemy activity, he didn't want to even begin imagining how the British troops were doing. He turned to the corporal that was overseeing Johnny and the other soldier.

The corporal immediately paled. He knew exactly what was coming for him, as he had been responsible for those two soldiers.

"Sir—" the corporal started, but Lt. Hungerford interrupted him with a gesture.

"Use your manpower better," he told him, his eyes drilling holes in the man's skull. He took a few steps towards him. "I just ask for six hours of focus." He threw glances at the two soldiers, who despite having their backs to him, Lt. Hungerford was sure they were listening. "Six hours of focus that stand between us and sabotage by the enemy. Relax afterwards. While you're in the listening post, listen for the Germans." He paused and looked first at the soldiers and then at the corporal.

"Is that clear?"

"Yes sir," echoed the soldiers. The corporal lagged half a second behind, but he added his own voice to the choir. Lt. Hungerford stared at them hard, then retreated, his loud steps echoing through the tunnels.

Johnny's attention turned back to the instruments. He would write to Christina later, he decided, to avoid drawing the officers' ire. There were still soldiers going towards the collapsed mine, probably on their way to repair it. They made a bit of noise that distracted him, but when they left, he returned his complete attention to the instruments.

"Major Moore, sir," Lt. Hungerford saluted as he entered the major's office. The major looked up from what he was doing.

"Lieutenant, enter. I was waiting for your report," the man said.

"Yes, sir. As you know, it's not good," he paused. "Six men were killed in the blast, sir, and three men were injured."

The Major pushed back against his chair, resting his head on the top. "The Third Platoon has not had good luck," he muttered.

"No, sir. First the diseases, now this," he let his voice fade. He didn't want to tempt fate and say that it would soon change, and, besides, he didn't fell optimistic that it would.

"Write to the family of the soldiers that died," the major said after a few moments. "To those that are Australian, at least. I'll inform the British officers about their own losses, as soon as I receive the information myself so that they can send telegrams to their families."

"I will, sir," Hungerford said.

"Just remember, mention nothing about the way they died. Spies are reading the newspapers back home, trying to figure out what we're up to."

"I will reveal nothing about our tunneling activities, sir," the man assured his superior. He paused.

"Is there anything else, lieutenant?" the major asked.

"Yes, sir."

"More bad luck?" The major seemed tired, his eyes dreading the reply.

"I'm afraid so, sir. There's been a thief among our men. It began when the British arrived, but I am not accusing anyone without proof. Me and a few trustworthy men are working on discovering the culprit right now."

"That's good. We've had some bad luck, but the platoon is in good hands," he said, to which the lieutenant nodded, accepting the compliment to himself and to his sergeants. "How soon will you have the platoon up to its full productivity?"

"I will try to have it fully functional in less than a week. My objective is two to four days, sir. But we've lost men," he added, his voice regretful.

"I know, lieutenant. I will have more experienced men sent to you as soon as I can. There's a shortage of experienced tunnelers everywhere." He paused and pulled out a piece of paper. "In fact, I'll write to the headquarters myself, to request more miners from Australia. Though, I don't know how long the 175th company will stay here," he added thoughtfully, preparing the draft in his mind and wetting his pen again. This statement, however, caught Lt. Hungerford by surprise.

"What do you mean, sir?" he asked. Weren't they tasked with digging out the Vimy sector? Were they going to be reassigned just because of their bad luck?

"The Canadians will be taking over," Major Moore replied. "They'll be relieving us at some point in late October, according to the plan at least. There will be a transitionary period, though, so I don't know when we'll finally be leaving."

"And where will we be going, if I may?" asked Lt. Hungerford.

"I don't know," the major said truthfully. "All I know is that the

175th is behind as it is, and that we need to get our job done before the Canadians arrive. Don't talk about this even to your sergeants, yet," he added hastily. "This is war. Things can change at any moment, and the Canadians might take even up to November to arrive. Until we receive clear orders, you need to focus on the task at hand. Catch the Germans with their pants down."

"Yes, sir."

"They know we're here. Don't allow more tunnels to be discovered," the major reminded him.

"I won't, sir. Permission to be dismissed, sir. I need to write the letters to the families of the deceased," he said, his voice taking on an edge of sorrow.

"Dismissed, lieutenant," Major Moore said, and the man saluted and left. The look on his eyes was the look of a man stressed to his limits, the major saw, and he wouldn't want to be in his position. He had pressure from above, just like Moore had, and he had to deal with so many from below issues regarding the soldiers. Writing letters to the deceased was never fun.

"Cpl. Taylor, sir," Johnny called at the man. He was holding his jacket in his arm, wearing his spare one, having just finished his shift at the listening post. The corporal looked up from the orders he was reading and focused on the man.

"Sapper Hoagland, I'm listening."

"Sir, can I talk to you?" he paused, then looked around. "Somewhere away?" Realizing that the sapper probably wanted to talk about the thief, Taylor stood.

"Follow me," he said and quickly navigated the tunnels towards the makeshift lavatory they had created. Most soldiers avoided it unless they needed it, so there was no one around to overhear them. "What happened?" he asked.

"The thief stole from me, sir," Johnny answered in a low voice.

"What did he take?"

"Money. See, here," Johnny extended his arm where he was holding his jacket. He opened it and showed him a point on the inner lining. Cpl. Taylor didn't see anything where the man was pointing.

"What am I looking for?"

"Look closer," Johnny encouraged. The corporal shot him a curious look, then focused on the jacket. He took it in his hands and examined it closely. Then, he realized what Hoagland wanted him to find.

"That's where he took your money from?" Cpl. Taylor asked, surprised. He had barely seen the pocket, and he had been actually looking for something there, prodded by Johnny.

"Yes. I stitched the secret pocket there myself. He must have examined the jacket closely," he said, getting the offered jacket back.

"How come the thief had your jacket?"

"I forgot it at the listening post during my last shift, sir," Johnny said. "The thief is probably one of those who relieved me."

"That's good information," Cpl. Taylor said. "Do you remember who it was?"

Johnny shook his head. "I don't know the two British soldiers. I knew the other one though, it was Sapper Fysh. He might know who the British were, or they might be mentioned in some paperwork somewhere," Johnny suggested.

"Yes, they're definitely mentioned somewhere for having served in that shift. I'll pass it up the line to Sgt. Hudson, and he'll take care of it."

"Thank you, sir," Johnny said, relieved.

"How much was taken?" Cpl. Taylor asked, as they started making their way back.

"Most of my wages, sir. I've been keeping them so I can send them to my family soon," Johnny said.

"A good man," the corporal muttered, patted Johnny's shoulder, and retreated in his office. Johnny saluted and left, hoping to catch the thief himself. He'd love to break all ten of his fingers.

CHAPTER TWENTY-ONE

Steps on the paved path to the front door brought Christina's thoughts out of the dark corner they had been dwelling in and focused on the present. The steps were quick, running even. Could it be...? She left the kitchen and hurried towards the front door.

The door opened and Richard entered. Her face instantly fell when she saw his look. Richard saw Christina's disappointment and realized that there was no news here either. Christina had to ask, though.

"Any news?"

"No," he sighed. They had the same look on their face. The look of disappointment, of wanting answers. Richard wanted confirmation about the lack of news, so he asked, as well.

"Mark hasn't come this way either?"

"No." Two days. It's been two days since they lost the game of the year in Bendigo.

"Nobody has seen him," Richard said. He took a couple of steps in the house and looked around. "Where's mum?"

"She went to the church," Christina said. "She wanted to ask for help to look for Mark." The poor woman was going crazy with worry. Christina was worried about the boy as well as his mother. It couldn't be good for her. She had barely gotten back to a state where she could function after the death of her husband and Johnny enlisting, and now her youngest boy was also gone.

No, not gone, Christina told herself. *Just lost for a little bit. Probably out exploring, as boys do*, she thought, trying to calm herself down. But she couldn't shake the feeling of dread that had settled in her stomach.

"Good idea," Richard said. "You should stay here, though," he added, eyeing her. He knew that she was eager to help, but in her state it wouldn't be prudent. "In case he comes back," he added.

"Alright," the woman muttered. She was about to return to the kitchen, when she hesitated. "Have you eaten anything?"

"No," Richard said.

"Let me make you a sandwich before you go to the mine," she said.

"Make a couple more for uncle Jimmy and Jessie, please. They're searching Jimmy's mine right now."

The road was dark, as it was just after six, and the rain wasn't making things easier for Richard. But he knew the way to his uncle's mine, and he was sure he could navigate it even by the starlight. He had spent almost all the time after the match looking for his brother, but he had promised his uncle that he would go help Jessie in the evening.

It was raining hard as he entered the mine's area. He briefly wondered if Jessie had returned home for the day but saw a kerosene lantern hanging by the entrance, meaning that the man was waiting for him inside. Richard approached the mine's entrance.

"Hey, Jessie! You there?" he shouted.

"Richard?" Jessie's voice came from deeper in. Richard entered and started going deeper in.

"Yes, it's me," he called.

"Come down, hurry," Jessie shouted. "I need help." Richard's heart started beating even faster and he hurried deeper in the mine. There was some water going in, and he was instantly worried about the man. He followed the paths to the new tunnels and found Jessie, knee-deep in water, his one hand tinkering with the pump.

"What's wrong?" Richard asked. He remembered Jessie telling him that he knew how to work the pump one-handed.

"Something's stuck," Jessie said. "I need better light. I can't see what's going on." He was breathing hard and as Richard came closer, he realized the man was drenched to the bone.

"Right away," Richard said. There were makeshift candle lanterns on the wooden beams, which they had made themselves. He took one of the matches deposited there and lit it, then lit the candle. He did the same with the other lanterns around the area, giving sufficient light so that the two men could examine the machine more easily.

With the better light, Jessie started digging around inside the pump.

"Where is uncle Jimmy?" Richard asked.

"He's out there," Jessie said, gesturing with his head. "He's looking for Mark on his own." He returned his focus on the machine. "He wanted me to fix the pump, and he knew you'd be coming as you promised. He said you'd check with Christina for news. Do you have any?" he asked, not raising his eyes. He didn't want to see the look on the young man's face.

"No," Richard muttered, "no news. Mum went into town to gather people to start a search."

Jessie took a deep breath then looked up. "Don't worry, Richard," he said. "Mark has got nothing to be ashamed about. It was a great game, you all played like professionals. And you lost by a tiny margin, twenty-four runs is nothing. He has no reason to run away or to hide from anybody. He'll be back," he said. He returned his attention to the pump as he continued speaking. "Besides, he paid the bet off, fair and square. And I saw no one teasing or threatening him after the match was over. Did you?"

"No," Richard said. "Everyone treated him well. He played better than I did." He paused for a long moment, before focusing on the pump. "I don't know what to think, either. I just have that feeling that something happened to him."

With three hands on it, the pump was fixed relatively quickly, though they did have to disassemble parts of it, and then reassemble them. They worked in perfect sync, having been working together for so long. When the pump was running again, it started quickly removing the runoff from the tunnel they had blasted out a few days ago. Jessie and Richard were both drenched by that point, but at least the tunnels weren't flooded. They entered it with their candle lanterns, examining the walls carefully.

This was a new branch, following a quartz vein. Jimmy had done most of the planning, gathering leads from the surface and the other tunnels, and had blasted the branch out just before the match. They had been eager to see if they had found a good vein, before Mark disappeared. They were glad to see that they had followed the quartz vein successfully, though it was hard to see if it was a gold-bearing one.

"I see you got the pump working," Jimmy's voice came from behind them.

"Yes, Richard was a huge help," Jessie said, returning to the main tunnel.

"Good," Jimmy said. Richard realized the man was also drenched, even more wet than Richard and Jessie were, water dripping from his jacket.

"Anything out of the ordinary?" Richard asked.

Jimmy shook his head. "Nothing. Besides, there's no reason for Mark to be in the back areas of the mine."

"You searched them though, right?"

"Yes. I walked them twice," Jimmy said.

"But the weather might be hiding something, or you might have missed a nook," Richard said, and Jimmy saw desperation in the young man's face. His own face softened a little.

"I might have," he said, even though he didn't believe it.

"Can I have a look?" Richard asked. Both older men saw that Richard was simply anxious for something to do, a way to help find his brother, so Jimmy didn't hesitate.

"Yes, you can," he said.

"Thanks," Richard said, and started towards the surface, though he hesitated. "I brought some food for you two," he said then, and went to his things. He removed the sandwich and a container of coffee that Christina had prepared for him and had even packed in a leather satchel to avoid getting the food wet. He offered the items to the two men, who eagerly took them. As Jimmy took the container, he realized it had kept the coffee hot, and smiled ear to ear.

"That's a gift from God," Jimmy muttered.

"From Christina, actually," Richard said, though he was in no mood to smile or laugh at his own joke. "I'll be going, then."

"I'll check the other claim," Jimmy said.

"Do you want me to come with you?" Richard asked eagerly.

"It's best we split up," the man said. "That way, we cover more ground."

"Right." Richard put on his jacket, took his things, and said a quick goodbye before leaving.

"Do you mind continuing here for a few hours?" Jimmy asked Jessie, who nodded.

"That's my job," Jessie said. "I'll get on it after I eat this delicious treat."

"Good. Take care, mate. Try not to drown," Jimmy said and left after Richard.

"Here, Father," Christina offered a cup of hot coffee to the priest. The Hoagland house was full of the congregation, and Christina was glad she had two more women helping her. One was back in the kitchen making more sandwiches for them to take out, and the other was refilling empty cups with the coffee pot.

"Thank you, dear," the man said, smiling. "Is Mrs. Hoagland ready? I think it's time to go."

"Yes, sir, she'll be down in a moment," Christina said. Cathy had come home with the group and wanted to change into something that would allow her to brave the weather.

As Cathy left her room, she felt she was in a nightmare that wouldn't end. First, Mick died suddenly, working in his own mine, away from any other danger. Then, Johnny left for the war, abandoning them, even abandoning his own wife and child. And now, Mark had vanished suddeny. She started going down the stairs, but paused at the landing, staring at the pictures on the wall. There was Johnny, holding onto Mick's hand. She started going down. There was Richard, dressed formally. Mark, with his dog. The whole family together, laughing. There was a picture of their extended family, Mick's father and mother, and her own parents.

She wanted to break down and cry, but she didn't allow herself the luxury. Mark could be out there, waiting for her, all alone. He could be in the forest, lost, cold, feeling as much despair as she was feeling. She couldn't stand the thought of him feeling abandoned. When she arrived at the ground floor, she was surprised by how many people had gathered at her request in the end. Her boys were well-know in the town, and they had helped many with their troubles, and Mark's recent game was going to be discussed for years to come, she was sure. Her steps slowed down, and she hesitated by the entrance.

Just when Christina had finished serving coffee to the preacher, she raised her eyes towards the stairs, hoping to see Cathy. The woman was there, frozen by the staircase's first step. Christina thought she was probably surprised by the amount of people gathered, as she was surprised herself. It was good to see the Hoaglands were well-loved. She grabbed the preacher's attention politely then led him towards Cathy.

"Hello Mrs. Hoagland," the preacher said, and the woman greeted him back.

"Thank you for coming, Father." The act of speaking brought her back to the real world, and she focused on the task at hand. "Do you know how many people we have?" she asked, then scanned the room with her eyes.

If the preacher replied, she didn't catch it. While her eyes ran over the crowd, tying to count them, they found a few bottles of wine to be served to the gathered congregation, to help fight the cold. She instantly remembered the sweet taste of wine, and the numbness she had used to dispel the thoughts of her dead husband. She wanted it on that moment, she longed for it. If only she could lose herself in it… Maybe next time she opened her eyes, Mark would be back, and this nightmare would be over.

"Mrs. Hoagland?" the preacher said, bringing her back again. "I'm sorry, maybe you didn't hear me over the noise. Do you have a moment for a couple of questions I had?"

The urgency to find her son returned. There was no way she would numb herself with wine again and lose another loved one.

"I do. Do you have a plan?"

"Yes, I was thinking of starting at the fields, and work our way through the bush, going deeper in," he said.

"That's a good plan," Cathy said, her mind empty. It took all of her will to focus away from the wine.

"Do you think Mark might have a horse?"

"No, our horse is at Jimmy's right now. Jimmy's using the old wagon," she replied, instinctively glossing over the fact that the wagon and the horse both belonged to her late husband.

"That mean's he's on foot. He couldn't have covered much distance."

"No, he's just a boy," Cathy replied, her voice dangerously close to breaking. Her eyes returned to the wine.

"We will be going then, ma'am," the preacher said, and turned towards the rest of the men that were gathered.

Christina had realized the struggle the woman was going through. She had seen the looks of longing she had given the wine bottles, as if they were her salvation. And she knew that if the woman was left alone, she would seek her comfort there immediately.

"Cathy," Christina said in a low voice, taking a step towards her.

"Maybe it would be best if you took a kerosene lantern and went with them? You're dressed to go."

"I am," Cathy muttered, but looked at the wine bottles again.

"And you don't want to fall in *that* hole again," she told her, and lightly gestured towards the bottles with her head.

"You are right, Christina," Cathy sighed. "I don't. Not really."

"Good," Christina said. "That's a might force of will you got there," she added for encouragement, and grabbed a nearby lantern from a table with several more. "Here."

Christina saw the group leave through the narrow door, one by one, until she was left alone in the house. It felt strange, the sudden change between a full house and an empty one. Even the women had left, either to join the men or to return to their own homes. They had all gave her curt goodbyes as they passed, and Cathy had been at the lead, half from the urgency to find her son, and half to flee the wine bottles.

She looked up the stairs and decided to go to her room. As she walked up, she paused at a step and unhung a picture from the wall. It was Johnny, looking a little younger than she recalled, and he was well-dressed. He was alone in the picture, staring ahead. The picture was dusty, so she cleaned it quickly and hanged it back on the wall.

It was time to tell him, she decided. She hurried to her room and opened her drawer, retrieving her pen and paper. She would tell him that she was pregnant. It was important for him to know. Maybe it would make him come home quicker.

By the time Jimmy had arrived at the claim his brother used to work, he was drenched again. It was after eight in the evening and it had been dark for hours. He was truly doubtful the boy was here, but he would check it thoroughly, just as he had checked his own claim. It was important to make sure the boy was nowhere around, before they dismissed it as a possibility, and focused elsewhere.

As Jimmy turned to the mine's surface, he saw a figure moving in an area a little way ahead, behind the mine site, on a little plateau that rose behind it. Could it be Mark? He hurried after it, a mix of excitement and dread building up inside him.

The figure was holding a lantern, he realized after a few steps. And this part of the mine had nothing in it, wasn't used by them, not even for storage. His steps slowed down, and he carefully approached the mine's entrance. The wood planks had been pried open. Someone had tried to gain access to the mine's main shaft.

Jimmy cursed himself for not taking his gun. The figure he had seen was probably the claim jumper too. He decided against going inside the mine, and left the area, following the figure he had seen. He entered the bush, the rain hitting his hat and jacket making loud noises, but also hitting the trees and the ground around him, masking his own noise.

He could easily see the light through the trees, despite the rain, and he followed it, staying as close to the trees and the ground as he could. The water running down the edge of his hat was getting in his eyes, so he hid under the protection of the trees as much as he could. He neared the edge of the bush, and he saw the bearer of the light stop.

There were two men under a small natural formation of the cliffs, hiding from the rain. He could hear their voices, they weren't even trying to hide themselves. Probably thought that no one in their right mind would be out during such a thunderstorm. Jimmy wiped the water from his eyes and squinted, to see the two claim jumpers as clearly as he could.

One of them was slim, and had a hard face, while the other was significantly fatter. He had a huge gut and Jimmy realized the entrance of the mine couldn't fit him. Could it be that the boards were pried open by someone else and not these two?

His mind went to Mark. Maybe it was him who went inside the mine, and not the claim jumpers. That sounded worse to Jimmy, though he couldn't pinpoint the reason. Something told him that it was a horrible idea. He felt a strong urgency to check the mine. After one last look at the thieves, he left the way he had come.

The opening was too small for an adult. However, he couldn't understand why Mark would want to get in the mine. He pushed himself through and entered. The rain was still making noise as it met the ground outside, but inside the mine it was significantly more silent. The sudden change was jarring to Jimmy's already tired mind.

It was too dark for Jimmy to see, but he didn't want to risk lighting a candle this close to the door. He extended his hands and took a few steps deeper in the mine before lighting one of the candle lanterns hanging from the beams with practiced motions. The walls and ground were damp from the moisture, but he was glad to see that no runoff had reached the inside. This claim felt better built than his own, sometimes. Or maybe it was that he worked his own more, so there were more makeshift additions.

Using the light from the lantern, he walked carefully around the mine, looking for signs. Who had opened the door, and why? How long ago did it happen? Couldn't be more than a couple of days, as they had been working here on the day before the match. Was there a chance the jumpers knew their schedule?

The mine was smaller than the one he worked with Jessie, but it had many exploratory shafts that Mick had dug out, looking for quartz or gold. Some of them were vertical, with wooden ladders laying against the drop. As he looked around, he saw something at the bottom of one. It was a short drop, barely eight feet in depth. He climbed the ladder down and knelt next to the little bundle. He pushed against it and it felt too soft. Was it a bundle of clothes? His mind felt slow.

With a little shove, Jimmy turned the bundle around. Mark's lifeless eyes stared at him. There was blood on the boy's face, still a little wet from the moisture of the air, and there was blood on his clothes. There was a little puddle on the ground, too, making the dirt sticky.

Jimmy couldn't breathe. Why had Mark come here? And why did he fall so badly that he broke his head? The shaft was short, if Jimmy had felt surer of his footing, he wouldn't even have used the ladder to get down.

A wave of nausea overcame him, and he added his stomach's contents to the brown puddle Mark's blood had made. His mind felt numb, but the whole world had crushed around him. He loved the little boy, he had grown to love him and his brother like the children he never had after Mick had died.

He realized his brother and his nephew had both died in the same mine. He tried to understand that but failed. How could that be? Was the mine cursed or was someone playing a horrible prank at him?

No, the boy was truly dead. No prank. Jimmy didn't know how

long he stared at the empty eyes, but at some point, there was only an all-devouring sense of loss, and a need to do something. All he wanted to do was turn back time, catch Mark before he fell, before he even left the match. But he couldn't, so he would do the next best thing.

CHAPTER TWENTY-TWO

The house was dark and empty. Jimmy's wife was with Cathy, probably, helping with the search. Without pausing anywhere, Jimmy, water dripping from his jacket, his boots covered in mud, walked in his bedroom. Next to the bed was his rifle, which he took. He pulled the drawer open and shoved his hand in the box of bullets, pulling a good handful and putting it in his pocket. He did the same with his other pocket. Then, he loaded the gun.

He had no memory of the way to the house, and next thing he recalled was having already arrived back at the mine. It had to be way after ten in the night when he stalked through the woods, towards the spot he last saw the two men. He remained hidden in the edge of the bush, watching them carefully. Two, just like before. They were sitting with their back on the cliff, a small fire burning in front of them.

The rain's sounds didn't cover the noise of Jimmy's gun completely. Jimmy saw the second man, the fatter one, touch his face. It was wet with something thicker than water. The man turned his head to look at his companion but saw only a headless body. Jimmy's rifle was strong and used special bullets which he had to order specifically for it every time.

The man had no time to scream, as a shot opened a gaping hole on his chest.

The screaming coming from Cathy's mouth was incoherent, filling everyone with dread. Christina stared at Jimmy wide-eyed, unable to comprehend.

"How?" Christina asked, though Jimmy had already answered the question so many times.

"I don't know," he said once again. He was looking at the ground, his eyes red, so numb he could as well be dead.

Cathy paused screaming, her voice hoarse, out of breath. Then, a moment later, she started again. The preacher looked at the woman with pity, and he approached Christina.

"I have something to help her sleep," he muttered. "If you give me a few minutes, I'll bring some for her. It's a pill the doctor gave me, when I had trouble sleeping when…" he let his voice fade, and Christina couldn't bring herself to ask what had happened. "I'll be going now."

"Thank you, Father," Christina replied, her attention slowly returning to the present and to the issues at hand. She turned to the rest of the people. "Thank you, everyone, for your help," she told them. "As Mark's been found…" she paused, swallowed against the lump in her throat, then continued, "you can all go to your homes."

As they passed her by, each muttered something, ranging from simple "my condolences," to the typical "let me know if you need something, eh?" She barely acknowledged them, as she scanned the room. After a moment, it was just Jimmy, Richard, Cathy, and herself. Cathy was crying loudly, Richard was staring at the ground, standing in the living room as he had been when he heard the news, while Jimmy had the same emptiness in his eyes as the boy, sitting next to Cathy.

The preacher came soon and gave her a tiny paper bag with a few pills inside, gave them his blessing, and left. Christina went to the kitchen to get a glass of water and returned to Cathy.

"Here, take this, it'll help you sleep," she told the grieving woman.

"I don't want this," Cathy screamed, then bolted off her chair and went straight for the bottle of wine. She gulped down a few good mouthfuls before she vomited the contents of her stomach on the floor, the bottle falling from her shaking hands. Cathy brought her a towel, helped the woman up, and offered her the pills again. This time she took them, and Christina led her to her room. She was asleep in seconds.

But when she woke later in the night, her loud cries woke Christina, who had just fallen asleep after cleaning the living room. Christina heard her stumbling to the living room. She left her own bed and went to see what the woman was doing. She had already drunk a good amount of another wine bottle before Christina caught up with her. This time, she couldn't convince her to stop and gave up after a few feeble attempts. She had half a mind to drink herself to sleep, too.

The next time Christina woke up, it was from a loud crash. It came from Cathy's room, and she ran to her, just as Richard did. Only the adrenaline coursing through her body kept her eyes open. She was incredibly tired, and her mind was sluggish.

Richard threw the door to his mother's room open. Then, Christina saw him staring inside, unmoving. She pushed past him and entered the small room, to find a sight so unsettling she wished she was drunk. There was a thick rope noose hanging from the ceiling beams, an overturned chair, and Cathy, lying on the floor, crying loudly. Christina counted three empty wine bottles thrown about.

Following Jimmy's directions, Cathy was put in an asylum for observation, hoping that the alienists there would at least keep her from harming herself, if not help her get her mind back.

The whole world around Richard had been destroyed utterly. Mark was gone, cricket had no point, his mother tried to kill herself and even though she failed was in the end removed from his life forcibly, and if he went further back, even his father was dead and his brother gone to war. After seeing the nook his mother had so meticulously prepared despite the alcohol in her, he couldn't rest. His house felt alien and foreign. It was too dark and filled with nightmares.

As he walked with haunted thoughts through the town's streets, he heard a loud voice and followed it to its source. It was a recruitment officer. The moment he saw the man, Richard realized exactly what his brother had felt, and why he had done what he had done. And why he had to do the same if he wanted to keep his sanity.

"This says you're looking for tunnelers," he said when he was in front of the booth. "I'm Richard Hoagland, and I have experience as a gold miner. I can fix machinery, I know how to use tools."

Christina was patting the dog, staring at the slab of marble. *Mark Hoagland*, it was saying, *is buried here.* She couldn't bring herself to count the dates. He was too young, barely having tasted life. The dog, she knew, was called Bosco, and she was one of Mark's best friends. She was sniffing at the freshly filled grave, as if she could feel her owner was buried there.

"Thank you for arranging the funeral, Mr. Hoagland," Christina told Jimmy. The man did most of the things, even paying for everything, and making sure the boy was buried near his father. The few people who had come had left beautiful flowers for the boy, but Christina averted her eyes. She couldn't stay there any longer.

"He was my nephew," Jimmy said as an explanation. "And there was no one else. With Richard gone off to find Johnny, it's just you and Cathy."

"I need to write to Johnny," Christina muttered. She had still that letter about her being pregnant, not having had the time to send it. "I'll see you later," she told Jimmy and turned away. She gave her goodbyes and received the condolences of those present, parents and kids from Mark's school as well as teachers and friends of the family she knew, and hurried home.

The Hoagland house was empty and dark. It felt just like her head—numb, barely living, dead silent. When she opened the drawer to get out her drafted letter, she read a few words, then tore it to shreds. The letter was hopeful, even optimistic, but there was no hope in her anymore. She took a fresh piece of paper and her pen and started writing.

She gave as many details about Mark's death as she knew, explained Cathy's state clearly, told him that Richard had also joined the army, and then wrote about herself and her pregnancy. It was a hard letter, and she couldn't begin to imagine how Johnny would feel when he received and read it, but it had to be written and shared.

After putting it in an envelope, she immediately went to the post office to mail it off. If she put it off for later, she would rewrite it, hide things to soften the blow, or even outright lie. And she shouldn't. The way to the post office felt lonely and cold, and she walked with her head down. The transaction was quick and then she was on her way back.

When she entered the Hoagland house again, the place she had been calling "home" for so long, it felt even emptier than before.

Bosco ran to her, wagging her tail, and Christina pet the dog's head absentmindedly, thinking somber thoughts.

The house was too big for a single person, and the reason it felt so empty was that it used to house four people. Each person had left a mark in her, and the house now felt foreign and strange without them. She couldn't keep living here by herself.

On the other hand, though, she didn't want to go to her father's farm. She liked the freedom she had tasted while living with the Hoaglands, despite the difficulties it presented, and she was now a married woman. She had to live with her husband, not with her parents. But her husband was in another continent.

She needed to discuss things with Jimmy Hoagland. She didn't know who this house belonged to, and even though she had gained some knowledge regarding how living here functioned, there were things that Cathy did that she didn't know. And Christina didn't know, in the end, what would happen to the house. Mark was dead, Richard and Johnny gone, and only Cathy would live here if she left the asylum. When she would, she corrected herself.

But even thinking of tracking down Jimmy filled her with dread. Right now, the only thing she wanted to do, was feed herself and the poor dogs, and rest. She didn't believe that anyone would come barging in this very day, demanding payments or her leaving the house. She sighed, stood, and went into the kitchen.

CHAPTER TWENTY-THREE

The sky was overcast as Jimmy arrived at a seemingly unremarkable part of the claim's area. If the observer examined the area carefully, they'd realize that parts of the ground were freshly dug. Then, they'd see the two freshly planted gum trees, and think nothing of it. Or at least that's how Jimmy hoped it would go. Only an incredibly careful observer would realize that the part of the ground that was freshly dug was much larger than would be required for a tree to be planted.

Only Jimmy knew that the reason the two patches of ground were dug was to bury the corpses of the two claim jumpers. And he was determined to keep it that way. Satisfied that nothing had disturbed the burial place, he returned to the claim's main area to take a metal bucket, a hard brush, and the special heavy-duty soap he had bought earlier. He filled the bucket with water and mixed some soap in, and then went to the place he had killed the two men.

The rain had cleaned the gore well enough, as did the animals of the forest, but there were parts that still showed that something nefarious had taken place here. There was nothing moved or disturbed in any way since the last time he checked, he was glad to see that, so he drenched the brush with soapy water and started working.

Repeated movements like brushing brought Jimmy into a kind of trance, where he worked automatically, his mind wandering. There was something in his thoughts, bothering him. Four people had died in this mine, he had realized, in less than a year. This kind of thing leaves an imprint on a place, changes it, affects it deeper than the eye could detect.

And he had to count the people whose lives were affected by

those deaths. Cathy was in an asylum, with little hope of overcoming the trauma of losing both her husband and one of her sons. Johnny and Richard had left indirectly because of it. As his mind turned to Johnny, he wondered how his life was, if it was any better than the one his family led here, or if it was worse. He really hoped it was better, but war is not an easy thing to fight in. He knew that Jessie still had nightmares about his experience and that it had marked him forever, not only by taking his arm, but also mentally.

The bucket's water was red now. Maybe that was the true color of the mine's energy, the red of dried blood. Johnny and Richard at least escaped it. They would have died here too, Jimmy believed. He would have to write to them, to see how they were. He wanted to do it soon.

The hours passed and he changed the bucket's water three times. He took care to empty it in different spots, avoiding the little creek, to avoid detection. He even dug shallow holes for the bloody water to drain into, then filled them with soil again, to hide the red markings. Thankfully, the rain had done much of the work, so he only needed to finish up some details, like splatters on the wall, some gore embedded between small indents in the rock, and parts of the ground that had been colored red.

There was still light in the sky when he arrived back at his own claim. Jessie, without Richard, returned to his old methods. Jimmy saw he was bringing up the ore in buckets, one by one, after having blown up the spots they had marked. The man had created a system that he could follow, even with one arm. Jimmy was always impressed by Jessie's determination and spirit.

"Hey, mate," Jimmy said, waving at the man.

Jessie was raising up a bucket to the lip of the crusher, then using his stub to empty the bucket into it. He had no free hand to return the greeting, so he grunted. Jimmy helped him with the rest of the buckets before they let the machine do its work, and they retreated to the claim's firepit, where Jessie had been making some tea.

"How are things going?" Jimmy asked.

"Slow. It takes too much time to bring the ore up, and to work the crusher," Jessie said bitterly. "I wish Richard were here to help me. And to help me fix the problems that are sure to happen. I can't fix the machine with one arm," he added.

Jimmy nodded, not saying anything. He understood completely. He was about to pour some tea for them when Jessie stopped him.

"I have some beer," he said only, and Jimmy gladly accepted the offered drink.

"I will have a talk with Mr. Ansari," Jimmy said after a while. "I'll see if Faiz-ul would work here."

"And what about the other claim?" Jessie asked.

Jimmy was silent for a bit, then looked at Jessie in the eye. "I think the mine is cursed," he said. He paused and waited for Jessie's reaction, but the man only nodded. "It has seen so much death. I don't want to work it."

"Then sell it," Jessie suggested.

"I have considered it," Jimmy said. "But others may die there if I do. Something is going on there, I can almost feel it now. We need to do something." Jimmy paused speaking for a moment before returning to their previous subject of discussion. "But I'll have Faiz-ul here, if I can."

"That would be a great help," Jessie said gratefully. "I need all the help you can find me. And Faiz-ul is an able young man."

"Even if his father doesn't allow him to come, it doesn't hurt to ask," Jimmy said thoughtfully. They didn't speak for a long moment more, before Jessie broke the silence.

"You are serious about the mine being cursed, right?" he asked.

"Yes. It has destroyed so many lives," Jimmy replied.

"Then, I have an idea. We could bless the area somehow, dispel the curse. It could be aboriginal ground, you know, taken away from the Aborigines."

"That's a good idea," Jimmy said appreciatively. "I don't know the history of the mine, to be honest. Only that it used to belong to my father." He nodded to himself. "I'll research deeper into the subject," he added, encouraged by Jessie not dismissing him as a lunatic. "I'll find out what the problem could be."

"Good thinking. If you need my help, let me know."

"I will." Jimmy looked towards the crusher, which had just finished processing the rocks and was idling. "Have there been any more malfunctions in the machinery around the mine?"

"No, thankfully," said Jessie. "But there will be, for sure. With Richard gone to the war, I'm missing two arms!"

Jimmy pulled at his beard, thoughtful. "I wonder if Richard and Johnny will meet up over there, and what could happen if they do."

"Probably Johnny will get angry at his brother," Jessie said. "At least judging from what I've heard from the boys, Johnny seemed like a guy protective of his family." He paused, thought some more, and continued. "Has anyone written to him about Mark yet?"

"Christina did," Jimmy said. "She told me earlier, when she asked me about the house. She also wrote to him that she's pregnant."

"Damn," Jessie swore. "That's going to be a hell of a letter."

"It will. Even one of these things changes a man. Imagine going through both."

"You don't know what the bloody hell you're talking about," a shout came from the tunnels of the Vimy Sector.

"Do you really think you're going to get out of this—where do you think you're going?" another shout came, followed by sounds of struggle. Sgt. Hudson heard all this and hurried towards the source of the disturbance.

He arrived at a crossing of tunnels, seeing a British soldier and an Australian officer. He knew the officer, he was Cpl. Mandrake, but he didn't know the soldier's name.

"What's happening here?" he asked. The soldier was trying to escape the officer's grip, but when they saw the sergeant, they both stopped their struggling.

"We have our thief," Cpl. Mandrake said, gesturing at the soldier. Hudson realized the accused soldier had a bloody nose and a black eye, though he didn't know if that had been caused now, or even earlier.

"Who is this?" the sergeant asked.

"This is British Private Ronald Lloyd," the corporal said, his voice accusing. "This is the thief."

Sgt. Hudson stared at the accused soldier for a long moment. "You need to get cleaned up." He turned to Cpl. Mandrake. "Go get two soldiers right away." The corporal saluted and left, and Hudson remained alone with the private.

"What have you done, soldier?" he asked him.

Lloyd shook his head, looking at the ground. "I did nothing, sir."

"So, you won't happen to have any property that doesn't belong to you?" he said.

"No, sir."

"Look at me when I'm speaking to you, private," Sgt. Hudson shouted, and the man lifted his face, his eyes hard.

"No, sir," he repeated. "I am not a thief." There was hate in the man's eyes, though Sgt. Hudson was far softer than he needed to be. He briefly considered breaking his arm for his tone, then punching him until he blacked out, and forcing a confession out of him when he came to. Thieving soldiers weren't loved, here or anywhere else.

"Then, if we search your bunk space or your kit, we won't find anything not assigned to you by the quartermaster?"

"No, sir."

"Say so right now, because there's going to be a search anyways. Of everyone," he added, "and the surrounding area, too."

As he spoke, he examined the man's face carefully. When he said the last five words, he saw the man's eyebrows twitch slightly.

"And the surrounding area, mate," he added. The look on the man's face turned to a more composed mask, but he had caught the nervousness. "Come."

He had the soldier walk ahead as they went into his office, and had him sit down in the corner, in a small sandbag chair. Sgt. Hudson himself stood in the entrance, waiting.

"Sir," Cpl. Mandrake called, and Hudson turned to see him with the two soldiers he had requested.

"Stand next to him," the sergeant ordered, and the two of them hurried to take their place on the accused soldier's left and right.

"Keep an eye on him. Don't let him move, not even to take a shit."

"I'll get things started," Sgt. Hudson told the corporal. "You go and find Lt. Hungerford. He's in the forward part of the tunnels."

The corporal saluted and left quickly. He went to the less trafficked part of the complex, where the sappers were expanding the tunnels that would one day progress into the German-held areas. He found the lieutenant overseeing a few sappers in a freshly dug tunnel.

"We will put the supports here," he saw him speak to another sergeant, Sgt. Morrison, "and here. We need your men to put the support structures right away."

Sgt. Morison turned to a couple of sappers that Cpl. Mandrake knew. "Sapper Hoagland, Sapper Tilley, go fetch the timbers. They're stockpiled right at the entrance of the new tunnels."

"Right away sir," Hoagland said as he put on a pair of heavy gloves, an action Tilley mimicked, then walked out towards the entrance Cpl. Mandrake had just passed through. The corporal stepped aside to let them pass and then walked towards the lieutenant.

"Sir?" the corporal asked, catching the lieutenant's attention.

"Come here, soldier. Don't shout too much in these tunnels," Lt. Hungerford said, and gestured to the corporal to approach.

"Sgt. Hudson requests your presence immediately, sir," the corporal said in a low voice when he was near enough.

"What for?" the lieutenant asked, curious.

"We've caught the thieving rat, sir."

Lt. Hungerford's eyebrows shot up and he smiled tightly. "Let's go, then." He turned towards Sgt. Morrison. "Carry on the work. I'll be back in two hours to see the supports."

"Yes, sir," Sgt. Morrison replied, then saw the two sappers coming towards him, carrying a couple of pieces of timber each. "Sappers, put the timber here," he gestured.

When the two officers left the activity-filled newly dug tunnels, Lt. Hungerford turned to Cpl. Mandrake.

"Who's the rat, then? And how was he caught?"

"It's the British Private Ronald Llyod, sir," he replied, "and here's how we trapped him."

End of Book One

REVIEW REQUEST

If you enjoyed this first story please consider putting up some feedback for it so we can make the second one even better than the first! Find any mistakes? You can really help us out by letting us know about them. Share with potential readers what you liked about this book. The more reviews we obtain the broader the reach we'll have in the future. Thank you in advance for your participation and continuing support! To examine other books that I've written or produced please visit www.whiskey-jackpeters.com. Have yourselves an awesome day!